Joseph W. Bebo
Hudson, MA, 01749
Email: joewbebobooks@gmail.com
Editor: James Oliveri
Cover Design: Elyse Zielinski
Proof Reader: Paul Kelloway

Library of Congress Cataloging in – Publication Data
Joseph W. Bebo
Sometimes Deadly /Joseph Bebo – First Edition

ISBN: 978-1-7339308-6-4
Fiction, Crime Drama

*This book is dedicated to my karate instructor, Larry Rae, wherever he may be. He not only taught me the how to fight, but how to avoid a fight. Everything I learned about the martial arts, I learned from him.*

# Prologue

Ibn al-Jathrine folded his arms and looked at the three young men kneeling in front of him, with an expression both fatherly and predatory. It was amazing what you could do with minds so pure and malleable. Give him enough naïve nineteen-year-olds like this and he could conquer the world.

Some may laugh at his dreams, to conquer the world, without a country, without an army, without even a place to call his own. Those are the dreams of a madman, are they not? But stranger things have happened in the world of men, far far stranger things.

Al-Jathrine missed his home almost as much as he loathed the place he found himself now. It was a cold, barren, brown land where one could not see beyond the next band of grey mountains or treeless hills. Oh, how he longed to see the limitless sky-filled horizons of his desert home. There the eye could roam free forever amidst the ever-changing landscape.

He looked again at the three youths in front of him. They stared back at him with awed expectancy. They had heard of him from their family and friends, in hushed tones of respect. Not a little of it was mingled with fear. They had heard of his wisdom and his piety, his learning and his immense power, power which he wielded more like a feather than a sword, so subtly was it exerted. Their families expected such great things from them, but that was nothing to what Ibn al-Jathrine expected of them.

"The world is full of sin, my sons," he said, finally, after peering at each one attentively for some time. "This life is full of misery and woe. But Allah has granted us a chance of a much better life if we can but live up to our destiny. You have all experienced hardship. You have seen your homes destroyed by foreign invaders, your families murdered before your eyes. You know the pain and sufferings of this earth. It is time you hear of the rewards for God's faithful, for those who have the courage and faith to do their duty, no matter how terrible that may seem. Now is the time for you to hear the will of Allah!"

# Chapter 1

Four men surrounded me. I turned slowly, facing each in turn, waiting for the attack to come. The one facing me charged in with a knife. I blocked it with a reverse-crescent kick, knocking the knife out of his hand. Following up with another crescent kick to the side of his head, I leaped in the air spinning my body 360 degrees to deliver a flying-crescent to his chin. He flew backward and lay prone on the floor. At that moment the second attacker came in with a club. Without stopping, I spun again and delivered a wheel kick to his temple. Another wheel kick and flying-crescent stopped the third man, who came in with a crowbar. Both went down. I stomped the closest one's skull with my heel. Suddenly, the fourth man seized me around the neck from behind. Using his forward momentum, I grabbed his arms, and dipping suddenly, threw him over my shoulder. He landed on the floor in front of me. I nailed him between the eyes with a board-breaking two-knuckle punch, kiaing loudly and stamping the floor. The punch was pulled a fraction of an inch from his head, as had been all the strikes. The four attackers, two of whom were my black belts, stood and bowed to the spectators, who clapped in appreciation. Thus ended the demonstration, but my evening was just beginning. It would be one I remembered for a very long time.

The night my life began to unravel was like any other. I had just managed to begin putting it back together. Little did I know that was about as good as it was going to get. I was playing a little trio gig, with Denise and Paul, at a new gourmet restaurant and club that had just opened up in town. It wasn't much, but it helped pay the rent when I wasn't spying on cheating spouses.

The 'burgh' had recently been shocked by the brutal murder of the area's teenage beauty queen, the one that was supposed to go all the way. She went all the way all right, all the way to the city morgue. They found her on the beach spread-eagled and naked in the sand. She had been stabbed multiple times with a large-bladed knife. The thought of it, after the events of ten years ago, made me shudder. It was deja vu all over again, as Yogi used to say.

After my lethal run in with those errant Russian moles back in '89, the ones who almost dropped the big one on the nation's capital, I couldn't wait to get back and take up where I left off with Suzy. You probably haven't heard about that fiasco, about the B-52 crashing into the Potomac carrying enough nuclear bombs to level a dozen Washington, DCs. If the authorities have their way you never will. Who knows, the story may still get out, someday. Then you'll know the truth, not that it will do me any good.

As soon as I got back to town, I asked Suzy to marry me. Much to my surprise she said yes. Much to my further amazement, when she wanted to start a family, I continued with the affirmatives. Now my Dad is a granddad, much to his delight.

Suzy somehow managed to keep Mazerka's Insurance Agency going in spite of the official inquiry into his death. She even turned her love of travel into a moneymaking concern, and opened up a travel agency as well. She runs it out of a small office right next to Mazerka's, in the same building. She can not only sell you a trip, but the travel insurance to go along with it. Not a bad racket. It has managed to keep our burgeoning family in milk and diapers. In a small town like this, with no airport and more people going than coming, well, it's been an uphill battle with my investigating business.

I help where I can, gigging with the band on weekends, teaching martial arts a few nights a week. Without the cash flow from Suzy's agency, however, it would be hard to make ends meet.

When I got back from my enforced stay in that Maryland hospital, I started my own private investigating agency. Suzy didn't really have any need for an insurance investigator at the time, even if she could have afforded me. A few people who knew the story spread the word around town of my small role in the affair. I had something of a reputation as someone who could find things out and get things done. I knew I could parlay that into something I would enjoy doing, and make some cash in the process. What I ended up doing was watch sleazy husbands cheat on their lonely wives, while horny housewives cuckolded their clueless Dagwoods. Not quite what I had in mind, but then again I'm not sure what I had in mind. My life was on autopilot, just going where the wind blew, which was nowhere.

The night was slow as usual. I wondered how long the gig would last. Given the money Kali, the owner, was paying us, and the meager crowds we were pulling in, I didn't think we'd be working there long. But then again my cup is always half empty. Kali didn't seem to mind. He was as gay as a holiday banner, but he played John Coltrane as background music during the breaks and paid the three of us top dollar to play anything we wanted. As long as the bar was packed with his friends he was content.

The three of us were sitting in the dining room, next to the bandstand, surveying the empty chairs and tables. It was after ten and the kitchen was closed. Most of the diners had left. Few stayed for more than a song or two after their meals before they were on their way. Most of the regulars were in the bar, where the bandstand should have been, but Kali had other ideas. As a matter of fact, he had a million ideas and seeming unlimited funds to go with them. It was little wonder he didn't care if he had customers or not.

"We're really packing them in tonight," I said, in my usual cynical way. "How does this guy stay in business?"

"He's got a lot of friends," said Denise, the piano player. "What are you complaining about, Jay? It's a great gig."

"Yeah, but how long can it last?"

"The bar's always busy," said Paul, her husband and the bass player, trying to be optimistic as usual. With his constant smile Paul was the everlasting optimist, unlike me with my storm cloud disposition. We were exact opposites, right down to his receding light-blond hairline and gray-blue eyes. "The Sunday sessions bring in a good crowd."

"Yeah, a good crowd of yahoos. Not one of them spends a dime," I said. "I've been here since seven, and there's been hardly anyone in the restaurant. I told you a high-priced gourmet place like this wouldn't do well in a lowbrow town like this."

"Why do you have to be so negative all the time?" asked Denise, for probably the millionth time since I'd known her.

"Since when is telling it like it is being negative? I'm honest, that's all."

"Yeah, an honest pain in the butt," said Paul. "Don't complain. We get to play anything we want."

"Great, we sit here all night playing Bill Evans tunes at fifteen bucks a drink, while the hillbilly joint down the street is packing them in at two bucks a shot."

"You want to play hillbilly music, Jay?" asked Denise.

"No, I just hate playing to an empty room."

"Well, at least you've got a gig, so stop complaining."

"I know I shouldn't complain. It would just be a lot more fun if we had an audience. Maybe we should liven it up, get a sax player or guitar and do some Latin or soul tunes."

"We're playing what Kali wants, jazz," replied Denise.

"How's the karate school going?" asked Paul. He had always wanted to study, but never followed through.

"OK, it's breaking even. I got a few new students, a real gung-ho bunch, three young guys who just moved down from Montreal. They're from Lebanon originally, I think. They're loaded, paying top dollar for lessons, twice a week. They want to progress as fast as possible. Now if the band can just keep working, I'll finally be able to get ahead. I can take over a little more of the expenses. Suzy won't have to work so hard."

"And you won't have to do housework and babysit Little Bud. That'll be nice," said Paul.

"Bite me, maggot," I responded, stung by his joke. "If you got off your ass and worked out a little like you always whine you're going to do, you wouldn't be such a sorry specimen of manhood."

"Speaking of manhood," he shot, "whose wife are you spying on this weekend?"

"Screw you, Paul. That's not funny. I'm just trying to make a living and take care of my family.

"You should have done what your dad told you to do and taken your uncle's job at the Holiday Inn," Paul countered.

"What, and be a glorified security guard? I'd rather be a candy-ass music teacher like you. Although I have to admit, seeing all the sleazy stuff doesn't do a lot for my faith in the human race, if you know what I mean"

"That must explain your lousy disposition," said Denise.

"You don't know the half of it," I replied.

"Speaking of the lowness of the human race, do they have any leads on the Patterson murder?" asked Paul, sipping the last of his gin and tonic.

The murder of the local beauty queen was all people were talking about.

"I don't know," I said, not wanting to get into it.

"Didn't you see the body?" asked Denise.

I was immediately sorry I had ever mentioned it to them, and was instantly transported back to that morning by the lake. Normally, Jerry would never have called me into a case like this, let alone let me onto the crime scene. There was something about the murder, however, something unsettlingly familiar, which prompted him to break longstanding departmental protocol. I wish I had never seen it. It was something I had seen before — *images of another young girl cut up and naked flooded my mind.* I shuddered involuntarily coming back to the present.

"Yeah," I said finally. "But I don't want to talk about it. It was pretty awful. Anyway, it has nothing to do with me. It's strictly police business and Jerry doesn't talk shop with me. You know as much as I do from reading the paper."

"I hope to God it's not starting again," said Denise, voicing everyone's feelings.

"I wouldn't worry about that," I told her. "I can assure you he's dead. I made sure of it that night out on the landing."

They both looked at me as if I was some kind of freaking Frankenstein. Who could blame them, after what I'd done. As much as it haunts me, I did what I had to do or I wouldn't be here telling this story.

I wondered. Could Denise's fears be warranted? However much I didn't want to admit it, the same thought had crossed my mind. Could it be happening again?

"If you say so, Jay," said Denise, in a tone that indicated she still wasn't convinced. "It's just all so terrible. Why do people have to do this kind of thing?"

"Don't know. Human nature, I guess."

"What he did to her isn't human," she said.

"What makes you think it's a man?" said Paul, trying to bait his wife. "Maybe it was some jealous female. You know how they can be."

"Don't be stupid, Paul. A woman would never do that, not like that, not with a knife."

"Yeah," I agreed. "Chicks are more apt to poison you or kill you in your sleep. I'd be careful if I were you, Paul."

"You're both such chauvinists. Jay, why don't you roll behind the drums so we can do another set."

I went back to my drums, but didn't feel much like playing.

After the gig, we went to the all night diner and ordered breakfast. It was the tradition on a Saturday night, and none of us had to get up in the morning. I called Suzy to let her know, leaving a message, even though she knew where I'd be. She was probably still awake, but not interested in picking up the phone. I invited her down to join us, so she wouldn't feel left out. She wasn't happy about me coming home late, probably afraid I'd be drinking. I wasn't. That would come later.

We sat in a booth and talked over our pancakes, and steaks, and eggs. When Betty, the waitress, brought our orders she told us the news.

"Did you hear about the murders out on McKenna's farm?" she asked, handing me my pancakes.

"No, what murders?" I responded.

"Out on Bob Moffit Road?"

"No. What happened?"

"They found old man McKenna and his wife dead this afternoon. Police say it was a murder-suicide. He shot his wife then himself with a shotgun. Pretty near blew both their heads off, from what they say. You might have gone to school with one of the kids, Jay, he's around your age."

"Oh, yes," I said startled. "McKenna, Bobby McKenna, I was just talking to him a few days ago. Now I could imagine him blowing his brains out. What a depressing character. He was going on and on about how the government is making it harder for the small farmer, trying to drive them all out of business, stifling agricultural research to keep the fat cats in Washington rich, while they tax the honest worker to death. Said he was doing a lot of research out at his place, growing a bunch of new kinds of fruit trees, I guess. He's more than likely growing pot."

Paul laughed.

"As a matter of fact," I went on. "He mentioned his father was against his research. Bobby said all his old man was interested in was making money. If it didn't make a profit, his dad wasn't interested. Then I made the mistake of asking how his wife was. I guess they're not getting along too well. Sounds like she left him and took the kid. Boy, did I get an earful. Jeez, after five minutes of talking to him, I was ready to put a shotgun to my own head."

"The paper didn't say much. I was wondering if you'd heard anything," Betty asked me. "I used to be friends with Bobby's older sister."

"No, this is the first I've heard about it. I guess Bobby will be able to grow all the experimental trees he wants now. I know the place you're talking about. That's quite a spread. They have those four big silos out by the highway. Must be tons of grain in those things. I wonder if they were sick or something, the old couple, I mean."

"I don't know. I guess you just never know when people are about to crack."

10

"You can say that again," I answered as she moved away to gossip and serve another customer.

My pancakes were cold. I left them uneaten on the plate as I sat and digested Betty's news. Another murder? How come I was always hearing about homicides from waitresses after a gig? What was going on? Except for Jack Bailey, who shot his wife in the sack with the real estate salesman back in '94, there hadn't been a homicide in town since the series of grisly murders that I got involved in. They led me to a terrorist plot to bomb Washington, DC. It happened ten years ago. If you don't believe it, don't feel bad, most people don't. That doesn't stop me from reliving it every night. Now three murders, or call it two murders and a suicide, in under four days. Things were picking up.

I couldn't help wonder if they could somehow all be related, or even more disconcerting, if they could be connected to the past. The whole idea was just too far-fetched to be entertained. That was over. It had ended on a beach that damp drizzly night when I took the life of the maniac who had been killing young women, and anyone else he happened to come across, around town. I saw him kill Dick Mazerka, my boss, down on St. Petersburg beach. He sliced his throat right in front of me. I had been hogtied in his boat, for Christ's sake! He tried slashing my head open with a machete. He hadn't counted on me being such a fast, sneaky, little bastard, nor the samurai sword I had in the back of my car. No, he was dead. I know a dead person when I see one. I know a mortal wound when I make one. There was enough of his blood and innards on that beach to soak a bullring. He was dead. He had to be.

I've been telling myself this ever since that night, every time I wake up in a cold sweat thinking of him coming up behind me with his lousy Bowie knife, like he did that night on the beach in St. Petersburg. He couldn't be back. It had to be someone else. Though the resemblance of that girl on the beach to the one I had led to her death like a mouse to a trap was just too much of a coincidence to be ignored. It wouldn't have been so bad if his body had been recovered from the landing where I left him, but it never was. Someone had taken it, perhaps his father, on his mission to bomb the capital.

Later that night, after coming home to a quiet house and being too hepped up with grisly thoughts to sleep, I sat and watched late-night TV.

I couldn't help thinking how my old schoolmate must be feeling. To have your father take up with your old girlfriend, like my dad and

11

Mary did, is bad enough. But to have him blow your mother's and his heads off with the family shotgun, well, that's just plain traumatic. I made a note to look Bobby up at the first opportunity and offer my condolences, and perhaps my services. Maybe there was something I could do to help. Better yet, maybe there was a job in it for me.

I sipped from a half empty bottle of bourbon left over from a New Year's Eve bash as I pondered events. That was my last mistake of the evening.

# Chapter 2

I woke up on the couch six hours later, with a terrible headache and a mouth that tasted like a chicken had nested in it. Suzy was already up and had breakfast cooking. The smell of the food almost made me nauseous, but the thought of fresh coffee and a shower finally got me moving.

"Have a rough night last night?" she asked as I sat at the table and scanned the Sunday papers for news of the McKenna murder.

"No," I lied. "Got in late and didn't want to disturb you, so I slept on the couch." She didn't seem interested in my explanation and went into the next room to play with Little Bud.

There was little of interest in the morning rag except for a notice of the McKenna funeral and burial, which was to take place later in the week. There was no wake due to the state of the bodies, which were apparently cremated. I resisted the urge to call Bobby McKenna so soon after the tragedy, but looked up his phone number, which was in the book. He lived at the farm with the parents. He must be busy cleaning up the mess in the kitchen.

It was a beautiful spring morning. Neither of us had to work. It was a day we should have enjoyed as a family, but that was the furthest thing from my mind. I was too busy thinking about the past. When Suzy asked me if I'd like to take a drive in the country and have a picnic, I mumbled a half-hearted yes. It was more from the lack of a good objection than a desire to actually go. We drove out to the Head, a fat finger of land protruding into the lake to form a large bay, with the town on the opposite shore. We stopped by the side of the road at a small stretch of stony beach. Little Bud got out and waddled among the rocks and boulders, chasing seagulls and throwing stones, while his mother watched close by. I leaned against the hood of the car and looked out at the lake and the not too distant opposite shore.

I should have been content, happy to be with my little family, but I was in a grand funk. I felt depressed and empty, as if I was missing something, the whole world passing me by. I was bored and unhappy and I didn't even know why. All I knew was that for some reason, when I should have been at my happiest, my heart felt like it weighed a ton, like I had just lost my best friend. What was wrong with me? Why couldn't I be happy?

Suzy instinctively stayed away from me. We hardly talked, even when we stopped for ice cream on the way home. She concentrated her baby talk on the other baby in the car, while I stewed in silence. Finally, back at the house, while Bud was taking his nap, she asked me.

"What's the matter with you today?" she said. "You seem preoccupied."

"Oh, nothing, just thinking about a case. Well, not exactly a case as much as the possibility of a case. There was a suspicious murder-suicide out on the Bob Moffit Road the other day. The whole thing's kind of a mystery. They might need some help."

"I doubt anyone's going to hire a private detective for that. It sounds like a police matter."

"I know, but I went to school with Bobby McKenna. He might want more information about it than he'll get from the police."

"Oh Jay, what do you want to get involved in that for?" she asked, not for the first time. "You haven't been the same since you saw that poor girl on the beach. Why'd they have to drag you into that? What does all this have to do with you?"

"It's my job. It's what I do."

Although she had agreed to it at the time, Suzy had never been that keen on the private-eye business. Once she saw just how sleazy it really was and how little reliable money it pulled in she had second thoughts entirely.

I studied criminal law in Boston. I was on my way to a master's degree and a job with the FBI before my crummy half-life came tumbling down around me. Like everything in the life of the man-with-a-thousand-excuses it didn't quite work out the way I had planned. I got kicked out of school and busted for possession of narcotics. By the time the system was through with me, so was the FBI. To make a long story short, I ended up back at this end-of-the-road town investigating insurance scams for a friend of my dad's.

"It's not a job," she reminded me. "It's something you do as a hobby. Job's pay a salary! What you do is follow people around and spy on them. No one needs a big time private investigator around here but you. There's a thousand other things you could do."

"Yeah, like what? I'm doing what I know how to do and I'm good at it too."

We had gone down this road a thousand times before and that road wasn't getting any less bumpy over the years.

She said something about me cooking supper that evening, and dashed off to see her mother, sweeping up the kid in one arm on the way out the door. Like they didn't see enough of each other every day of the week, they had to spend Sunday together too? It made me think of my father.

Good old Dad. Don't know where I'd be without him. He helped me get my broken life back together and only threw it in my face occasionally. To my absolute mortification my father remarried. That's bad enough, but he married my old girlfriend, Mary, the town mortician. At least she's retired from that profession. Now she lives off my old man. I try not to dwell on it and avoid the two of them as much as possible. As a matter of fact, it seemed I was avoiding just about everything lately.

I wasn't thrilled when Suzy told me she was pregnant, but I wasn't that disappointed either. I guess you could say I didn't know what to think. I was in denial. I thought I could continue to live my life as usual, that somehow Suzy and the baby would take care of themselves. I thought that having a kid would be fun. But it hasn't been that way. It hasn't been fun at all. Maybe it would be different if I could pay the bills and Suzy didn't have to work so hard, but the way it was, she was the real breadwinner of the family. I got to stay home and babysit. That's not quite the way I envisioned things.

Maybe with this latest homicide I'd get some much needed detective work. Things would finally take off for me. My dreams would come true. Boy, I really was starting to sound like a ghoul.

I drank a few beers and watched a baseball game. I had a good buzz on by the time Suzy came home around six. The first words out of her mouth were why I hadn't gotten dinner ready. I answered with a dumb stare. She ended up cooking, but didn't have much to say to me after that. She went to bed soon after her favorite TV show, saying she had a busy day and had to get up early the next morning. She would take Buddy to daycare if I could pick him up. It was agreed. I followed two hours later, the half bottle of bourbon now empty.

Suzy was already gone by the time I woke up. It was my day to do the chores, laundry and shopping. I knew I should have bought a new washer and dryer when I had the chance, instead of relying on my dad's antiquated appliances. Now I had to spend days sitting in a Laundromat. Later in the afternoon, before picking Bud up at daycare, I stopped by the office to see if I had any calls.

Suzy let me use the back office at the agency, the same one I used when I worked for Mazerka. I don't advertise and I don't have a cell phone. My chief form of inducement is a small ad in the yellow pages and an answering machine, which I check once or twice a day. My case drawer comprised half a filing cabinet and I didn't have a computer – Suzy had three in the travel agency next door.

It was early afternoon, the sun finally coming out after a damp start. Figures it would stop raining as soon as I finished all my errands.

I walked into the insurance agency. Suzy still had Mazerka's sign up. Why mess with name recognition. He may have been a creep, but he and his father had run the business for forty-five years, until his rather abrupt departure from this planet. Everyone in town knew the name.

Alice, another friend of Suzy's, who managed the office when the boss was booking travelers next door, looked up from her paperwork and smiled.

I said hi, and walked rapidly to the cramped tiny office space I shared with a filing cabinet, my metal desk, and a seen-it's-best-days swivel chair that no longer swiveled. Much to my surprise, I had a message.

I sat down, grabbed a notepad and pen, and hit the 'Play' button.

"Hi, Mister Lawless. You don't know me. My name is Sheila Patterson. I'm Becky Patterson's sister, the girl that was murdered. I want to find out who did it. The police don't seem to have any leads. I was hoping you might be able to help. I got your name from the phone book. The chief of police said you were a very good investigator. I'd like to meet with you as soon as possible. I'm willing to pay whatever is required to see my sister's killer brought to justice. Please call ..."

I was still digesting the message and missed the rest of her words. I had to play it two more times to get the phone number. Something about her voice intrigued me. Maybe it was that soft vulnerable quality I was always a sucker for. Maybe it was the prospect of thirty bucks an hour. I had trouble focusing on the details. Here I was being drawn into something I wanted no part of, but I knew there was no way I was going to say no.

Without further delay I called the number, an exchange I recognized but couldn't quite place. After a couple of rings, a small, hardly audible female voice answered, full of grief.

"Hello, Patterson residence, who is this, please?"

"Hi, this is Jay Lawless calling Sheila Patterson. I'm returning her call."

"Just a moment."

Before long another soft female voice answered, the same one that was on the message.

"Hello, this is Sheila."

"Hi, this is Jay Lawless returning your call. How can I help you?"

"I was hoping you could find out who killed my sister."

"Well, I'm sure the police are doing all they can. They've got the 'Staties' helping. I'm not sure there's much more I could do."

There was a pause on the other end of the line. She was probably wondering about my hesitation. I hadn't entirely lost my distaste for the whole grisly affair. It reminded me too much of something from my past that I was trying desperately to forget.

"The Chief of Police told me you were very good. You might be able to help. He said they had wanted you to work on it with them, but couldn't afford you. I can pay you whatever you want, Mister Lawless."

This last statement piqued my interest. Still, I resisted. I don't know, maybe I was playing hard to get.

"It's not that. Like I told them, I'm not sure what more I can do that they can't. I don't have half the resources they do."

"He told me that a few years ago there was a killer in town, a real bad one, and that you tracked him down and killed him, and stopped the killings. Is that true?"

This time it was my turn to hesitate.

"Jerry LaGrande told you that?"

"Yes, and I want you to do it to Becky's killer. I want you to find him and kill him."

I sat for a long time after the conversation ended staring at the wall, wondering what I was getting myself into. Of course, the one word that would have caused most people to hang up the phone caused me to tell her I'd take the case. If she was that desperate, maybe there was something I could do to help. She didn't seem to have a problem with my thirty dollars an hour fee plus expenses. I should have asked for more. We made arrangements to meet the following day.

It's amazing how a simple phone call can change your life. Here I was depressed and worried one minute, the next, I felt on the top of the world. The part of me that wanted no part of the grisly murder, too reminiscent of murders past, was quickly fading, giving in to the voice of greed and avarice. This was the type of case that could buy us a new washer and dryer.

I rushed over to tell Suzy the good news. She wasn't exactly happy to hear I had taken the job, but didn't complain when I asked if she wanted to go out to her favorite restaurant for dinner, my treat. Her disappointment gave way to pleasure, at least for the time being. Things were looking up, or so it seemed.

# Chapter 3

I picked Bud up later that day at the daycare center, and played with him until Suzy's mom stopped by. She watched him until six, when Suzy came home. When I say play with him, I mean mostly watched as he looked at his favorite book or his favorite cartoon show, or played with his favorite toys. Daddy is pretty much ignored. Daddy doesn't know how to relate to four-year-olds, who barely know how to speak the language let alone understand simple concepts. Like, "No, don't stick the screw driver in daddy's drumheads." "Yes, go to the bathroom in the little round porcelain bowl, not your pants."

Maybe I'm getting a little ahead of things, but I thought fatherhood was playing catch and roughhousing. Little Bud doesn't seem to like any of those things. He's not even interested in doing karate kicks. I mean, what four-year-old doesn't want to do karate kicks?

When I came back to town after my harrowing encounter with the two errant Russian agents and their demented accomplice, the first thing I did was open a karate school. It was something I had always wanted to do. With Suzy's help, I rented a few spare rooms over a body shop at the edge of town and put up a sign – 'School of Self-Defense: Kung-Fu, Karate, Tai-Chi, and Aikido'. It was a long way from the days when I taught a few guys in my old man's basement, two of whom had stayed with me and were now black belts.

With my reputation and experience business was soon thriving. Stories of my real life exploits didn't hurt, nor did the fact that I taught self-defense to the local police and military establishments. Everything was going great until some mega-chain karate school opened up a branch right dab in the middle of town. I call it the MacDonald's of self-defense. The damned place takes up the whole corner of Main and Hilleary streets. It's replete with wall-to-wall mirrors – which cost a fortune – and carpets – an unnecessary luxury in my opinion. Nevertheless, they had ten students to every one of mine, and ended up taking most of mine as well, although a few die-hards stayed with me. After that, I could barely afford the rent on my tiny dojo. At least I had a place to work out and a few hard bodies to bang on. That would have been enough in the old days, when I didn't have a family to support.

Then, about three months before the Patterson girl's murder, these three guys showed up out of the blue wanting to study karate. They signed up on the spot. They said they wanted to make black belt as quickly as possible. I told them it wasn't that easy, but if they stuck to it, they would be amazed at what they could accomplish.

They were young and in good shape, and eager to learn the secrets of the martial arts. They said they were from Lebanon. They had grown up watching Bruce Lee, but had never had the chance to study in their homeland. They watched kung fu movies and practiced on each other, however. They had all gone to college in Montreal, and were now taking courses at the local college in town before looking for good paying jobs in the city – New York City. The three of them were from rich families, and threw cash around like there was no tomorrow. The extra hundred and sixty dollars a week came in handy even if it didn't pay the rent. After their arrival, things started to improve around the dojo. I picked up a few more students, mostly females. Even the travel agency business – which Suzy was trying to jump start at the time - started to pick up.

As it turned out, not only were my new students eager to learn self-defense, they were even keener to travel. They flew back and forth to Canada and the Middle East, it seemed, almost every other week. When they weren't flying to these places, they were taking vacations to Mexico, the Caribbean, and Europe. It must be nice to be wealthy. At least they were spreading some of that wealth around.

Monday nights I gave private lessons. In the past, I just sat around the dojo waiting for customers. Now I was pretty much busy in the evenings from 7:30 to 10:00 teaching. Monday was my best night. I had the Brody boys from 7:30 to 8:00. Then Doctor Mills from the college, followed by Stephanie at 8:30, who at blue belt was my most advanced female student. Praveen and Mustafa, two of my new students, took up the last hour with their privates. If this kept up, I'd have to expand my hours.

Mustafa, the biggest of the three and in my estimate the least intelligent, showed up alone for his nine o'clock. About six feet two, two hundred pounds, with a trimmed beard and broad shoulders, he looked like a born athlete. He was early so I had him punch for Stephanie.

The single-punch technique teaches combinations of counterattacks against someone coming at you with a punch, club, or knife. They range from simple block and counter and submission holds

20

to complex hand strikes and kicks that usually end with the opponent being taken off their feet. The idea is that no matter what position you find yourself in relation to your attacker, you have something effective to do to defend yourself. The moves become second nature. The main thing is not remembering the specific techniques and combinations, but learning to react in any situation, without thinking. The main thing is to react! Two of the worst things you can do in my dojo are to not kiai when struck in the midsection, and to freeze when someone punches at you (unless I tell you to).

The various lessons went well. Several of them dropped off checks that night. Stephanie was delighted to have someone tall to punch for her, instead of a shrimp like me, not to mention a young, good-looking, exotic, rich mid easterner. I took the occasion to teach Mustafa how to fall.

"Slap your palm and forearm to absorb the force," I told him. "Kiai, expel your breath in a loud yell. Like this." I demonstrated, "To keep the wind from getting knocked out of you."

I gave Mustafa his lesson after Stephanie left. To reward him for punching, I gave him a couple more advanced techniques. His partner, Praveen, who usually worked with him, wasn't there that night, so Mustafa asked if I would punch for him. There is a certain dojo etiquette, unwritten rules of conduct that when violated can lead to pain. Discipline is important to maintain, otherwise, students - and teacher - could get hurt. When your sensei tells you to move, you move. When they say, stop, you stop. Your life could depend on it.

In Len's school, where I studied, black belts did not punch for white belts. Never! They hadn't earned that right. The same holds true in my school. Another unwritten rule is to never ask a black belt what degree he is, unless you want them to demonstrate it on you. It's enough that they have attained the rank. It's presumptuous and shows disrespect, which can be dangerous.

In any case, degrees don't matter on the street. Some martial artists, who have been out of it and haven't practiced in years, will tell you they are fifth degree black belts. Everyone seems to be fifth degree for some reason. I should mention that if you tell someone you are a black belt on the street, you'll liable to get your head handed to you on a platter. That's another good reason not to announce your rank. Let your hands and feet do your talking.

"Have you ever seen me punch for a white belt in my school?" I asked him, becoming serious.

"No," he answered nervously.

"You want *me* to punch for you?" I asked. I looked at him like I would like nothing better than to punch him. "Would you?" I said louder.

"No, Sensei, sorry," he said quickly.

"We'll do the techniques in the air. You can practice on Praveen at home. Now, with me, step in with the left..."

We did them together, while I explained each move.

After bowing Mustafa out and taking his check, I closed down the dojo, changing out of my gi. Then I locked the door and left for the night. It was late, after ten.

My car was parked behind the body shop. It was dark and off the street. I reached in my pocket for my keys to unlock the door. Without warning, someone grabbed me from behind. They locked my neck in the crook of their arm and squeezed tight. This wasn't a gag. I clamped my chin down and drew my Adam's apple in at the same time, before they got a good hold. Whoever it was pulled my head back as he choked me. At the same time, someone rushed at me with his fist raise. The pressure on my neck almost made me lose consciousness. I only had a few moments before I'd black out.

I nailed the man in front of me with a thrust kick, knocking him off his feet. At the same time, I grabbed the groin of the man choking me - it was the only thing within reach - and twisted violently. I'm constantly squeezing tennis balls and bottles as I walk around the dojo, working on my grip. A good Kenpo man can remove your testicles through a thick pair of jeans. This guy was wearing sweat pants. He screamed and let go of my neck in an instant. As he did, I spun around with a right hook, hitting him square on the jaw. There was a loud crack. He went down like a dead weight and didn't move.

Before I could see who my attacker was, I was grabbed from behind in a bear hug and lifted off my feet, my arms pinned to my sides. As I was seized, I kicked the inside of his knee with the heel of my foot to loosen his grip. Quickly stepping behind his right foot with my left, I spread my arms apart and swung my left elbow back, striking him in the throat. The move forced him backward over my extended leg. He let go and fell on his back. I followed up with a fist between the eyes. He, too, did not get up.

It all happened so fast that the second assailant, the one who had rushed me earlier, had no time to react after getting to his feet. He stood about four feet away from me, hesitating, and looked at his companions. I could just make out who it was in the darkness. He looked familiar, and took off running when I made a move toward him. At the same time, the other two came to and wobbled off together as fast as they could.

I could have caught them easily, but I've learned never to chase after someone you just had a fight with. They may have friends nearby. I got into my car and drove away. I didn't go to the police station. I didn't want the cops to get to them before I did.

I knew who it was, and could guess why they attacked me, but I couldn't believe it. How could they be so stupid?

There's nothing like beating up three guys and not breaking a sweat to help your self-confidence. By the time I got home I felt on top of the world. It actually felt good to nail someone with a hard two-knuckle punch after pulling punches for so long, especially after they tried to choke you. I'd need some confidence for what I had in mind.

I got home a little after ten-thirty. Suzy was sitting up watching TV. We still lived in the second floor, two-bedroom apartment she had before we were married. It was starting to get crowded. That was another reason I wanted my school and business to work, so we could get a little place of our own.

"I passed your mom on the way in," I said, as I walked in the door. "What's she still doing here? It's after ten-thirty."

"I had to work late at the agency tonight. I just got home."

"What, this late on a Monday night?" I asked. "What was so important you had to work all night for?"

"Alitalia went on strike and stranded all my customers. I've been on the phone all day dealing with stupid Italians and irate clients."

"Now just a minute," I said, laughing. "Just 'cause you married half of one doesn't mean you can call us stupid. I resemble that remark."

She didn't laugh. I guess her problems with Alitalia were no laughing matter.

"What happened to your shirt, Jay? You look like you had a fight or something."

I looked down at my chest. The pocket of my shirt was torn, probably by the guy who tried to choke me."

"Oh, nothing. Had a small problem leaving the dojo. Three guys attacked me."

"What? Someone attacked you?"

23

"Yeah, as I was getting in the car, behind the dojo. One guy grabbed me by the neck from behind. Another one tried to put me in a bear hug. It was over in seconds, with both of them on the ground and another guy running away."

"Who was it? Do you know? Why?"

"Oh, I know, all right. I recognized one of them as they were running off."

"Who was it?"

"One of the black belts at the other karate school in town."

"What? What would they do that for?"

"I don't know. Maybe they want to put me out of business."

"That's ridiculous. Are you going to call the cops?"

"Why bring them into this?"

"You were assaulted!"

"I'm the one who did the assaulting."

"They attacked you. Who knows what they might do next time. You have to go to the police and press charges."

"It's my word against theirs. There's no evidence. No, I have a much better idea."

"What are you going to do, Jay?" she asked with a nervous tone.

"Don't worry. They were trying to put me out of business. Maybe I'll pay them a visit and put them out of business."

"Jay, don't do anything crazy. I don't know why you have to teach karate at that stupid school in the first place."

"Hey, it's not like I'm out drinking with the boys or anything. I'm trying to help people and earn some money. I know how hard you work and how stressful it is. I'm only trying to keep up my end of the bargain. We need the extra money from the school. You'll thank me in the end. Now we'll be able to get that house you've been looking at."

"Yeah, right. What you pull in with that school isn't worth all the time you spend there. You can't depend on it. Students come and go. Now look at all the trouble it's causing. Why don't you sell the school to them?"

"What, after what they tried? No way. They want competition, I'm going to give them competition and then some. Look, you've got the agencies. I've got the dojo. It's finally starting to turn a profit. I wouldn't underestimate the potential if I were you."

"Oh, Jay, it's just not worth it."

"It's what I do. You knew that from the start. Don't tell me to change now. And don't tell me to bend over and take it in the ass from those mother-f'ers. Things are finally taking off at the school with my new students. I'll take care of this other thing, don't worry."

Suzy went to bed angry a little after that, even though I promised to consider calling the police in the morning. I did, I considered it stupid. I was too wound up from my encounter behind the dojo and my spat with Suzy to go to sleep. Instead, I stayed up and watched some sci-fi movie on the late show, nursing a Crown Royal and contemplating my visit to the McDonald's fast food school of self-defense.

# Chapter 4

The next day I had an appointment in the afternoon to see the Patterson girl. She said her name was Sheila. Nice sounding name. Nice sounding voice, too, now that I think of it. I didn't bother telling Suzy about the meeting or the case. I didn't want to rock the boat until I knew more about what, if anything, I'd be doing.

Suzy didn't say much and soon left for work after I told her I'd talk to Jerry down at the station. I didn't tell her what we'd talk about. I certainly didn't plan to talk about my altercation of the previous night.

I tried to relax and do some chores, but I was a seething bundle of anxious anticipation as I waited for Suzy's mom to come take Bud for the day. After she came at ten, I drove by the other dojo, but the place was still closed. Cruising around for an hour, I went by several times, but there was no activity. Around eleven I stopped at a small park in the center of town and did some kata. I had on a loose pair of pants, and took off my t-shirt so it wouldn't get all sweaty. As I worked out, I saw a couple kids walk by carrying their gis. After cooling off a bit, I put on my t-shirt and followed them.

When I walked in, around noon, there was a class going on. The students were standing in rows doing basics, following the instructor's commands. It was a good size group class, around twenty students of all ages. I was happy if half that number showed up for my groups. The instructor was the third man I had faced the previous night, a tall kid around twenty, with long black hair. I walked up to him and faced him with my back to the class, inches away from him. Although he was taller than me, I shoved my face into his.

"I'm here to take up where we left off last night," I growled. "Where are your friends, tough guy?"

I could hear people gasp behind me.

"Take that belt off!" I ordered. "You don't deserve to wear it. You're a disgrace to the rank."

He went to assume a defensive stance, bringing his hands up, but I was already too close for him to do anything.

I hit him on the side of the head with my palm, and again with the other hand, so fast he never saw them coming. Right, left, right, left, like lightning, I backed him into the wall. He hit it hard, almost shattering the large mirror there. Someone yelled out in alarm. One of the women screamed. People were fleeing the dojo, running out the front door.

At that, the head instructor came busting into the room. He had five red stripes on his black belt. Yeah, you guessed it, another one of those fifth degrees.

"What's going on here?" he bellowed.

I turned and faced him. I knew him enough to say hi on the street. A heavy-set guy with a beard, he looked more dangerous than he really was. We had talked a few times. He was a blowhard. I was looking forward to showing him up in front of his students.

"I'll tell you what's going on. This bozo and two of his friends tried to beat me up last night."

"That's a lie," said the guy from the previous night, gaining his courage now that his sensei was there.

"Oh, yeah, where are your friends? I bet one of them has a broken jaw."

I turned to the head master.

"I'll wager you have two people who needed medical attention last night. Ask them how they got beat up."

"You just can't come in here like this," the head honcho said. "Who the hell do you think you are? Get out of here or I'll call the cops."

"You do that," I replied. "I'd like to see how you explain your students' behavior to them. Maybe they'd like to hear what kind of place you're running."

"Get out of here!" he yelled, taking a step toward me.

"Did you send them?" I asked him, moving toward him. We were now about four feet from each other. I stood leaning forward as if there were three guys trying to hold me back. Instead of denying it, he started to walk toward his weapons wall, where assorted oriental instruments of war were hanging.

"You're going for a weapon?" I asked with disbelief. "Why, you sniveling coward."

He reached for the nun-chucks hanging on the wall. I leaped across the intervening space with a flying front-ball kick, knocking him back against the glass. As I landed, I grabbed his arm and the nun-chucks. He pushed against me to drive me back. I pivoted suddenly, and using his momentum, flipped him over my shoulder. He landed on the floor between my legs, the nun-chucks in my hand. I stood over

27

him, threateningly. The other black belt was nowhere to be seen. He must have left the building.

"Tell your underlings that if I see them again, they better have guns, because I'll rip their fucking eyes out. I'll be looking for them. They better make themselves scarce and leave town. If I see them here I'll take this place apart and them along with it. I'm holding you personally responsible if anything funny happens. If it does I'll fucking make you regret you were ever born."

"You can't threaten me like that. I'm going to call the police," he said as he slowly got to his feet. He didn't make any move to come at me. I still had the nun-chucks in my hand, with one of the sticks under my armpit ready to strike.

"Go ahead, call them. Tell them that Jay Lawless just threatened you. They'll tell you I mean what I say."

Then I moved close to him. He almost cringed, but otherwise stood still. I whispered to him harshly. I could hardly believe what I was saying. It was like I was in a movie. It hardly seemed real, but I wanted to end this thing here and now. I wanted him to think a dozen times over before he fucked with me again.

"I've killed three people, with my bare hands. Understand? I'd be very careful if I were you. I don't want any trouble, but don't provoke me. I'll be very sorry if I have to hurt you or any of your people, but that won't be much help to you or them."

I looked at him hard.

"Understand?" I whispered into his ear.

He tried to avoid my gaze.

"Look at me!" I yelled hitting him in the back of the head with my opened hand. I was smaller than he was, but much faster and just as strong. I doubted he did many pushups during the day.

He came at me with a series of karate punches and kicks. I blocked these easily as I backed away from him, circling, but I never countered. I stopped him in the middle of the room with some hard, powerful blocks, and held up my finger. "Do you understand?"

He was about to say something, but thought better of it and nodded his head in assent. I left him standing there, his gi open and his t-shirt hanging out. A few other students, those who hadn't fled, stood at a distance watching with their mouths open.

"Remember what you saw here," I told them. "How I subdued your instructor after he tried to attack me with a pair of nun-chucks. His attack was unprovoked, but I took them away from him without hurting him. Remember that when this sniveling coward calls the police. If you want to learn how to fight like that, come to my dojo." I handed out a few cards. The students looked more impressed than scared. I hoped my precipitant actions had gained me some students and not a rap sheet.

I went home to change, expecting a cop at my door any second. None appeared. Maybe they wouldn't call the cops. I'd have to keep my eyes open in case they tried to retaliate. That would have been a big mistake on their part. Hopefully, they had learned their lesson, but I was ready for anything.

It was almost time for my appointment with the sister of the murdered girl. I hopped in my second-hand Toyota and headed west out of town. I was still surprised at how much this end of the 'burgh' had been built up over the past few years. There were acre upon acre of restaurants and motel chains, gas stations and shopping malls. I had to drive a good ten minutes to get past all the congestion and lights and reach the country. There, farm houses and orchards took over for the concrete and steel, and soon after that, lush wooded hillsides. The land started to rise as I got nearer the mountains, the last peaks of the long Adirondack chain. They marched up from the south to end just short of the Canadian border. Driving up this road on a clean spring morning brought back memories that were less than bright. I tried to dispel them but could not, so I focused on the present case and that day on the beach when Jerry called me from the scene of the crime.

"The knife marks are the same, eh?" he had said, under his breath as I approached the white sheet spread out on the sand. The form of a slender young female was obviously visible beneath. The sheet was stained with red blotches. It was a sheet I didn't want him to remove, but he did anyway. I looked, trying not to let myself realize this had not long ago been a vibrant young person, full of life and promise. I tried to focus on the plain objective facts, the forensic evidence that held the answer to this poor girl's death. But it was hard, especially when I saw her tan-line and toenail polish. It spoke loudly of a young life shorn short. The senseless tragedy of the thing, the wrecked lives left in its wake, just wouldn't leave me. On top of it all she was stunningly beautiful, one of the most beautiful dead women I had ever seen.

"I see what you mean," I answered after I had studied the grisly work of death and mutilation. "Looks like she's been stabbed a dozen times. I admit it looks similar to the one back then, but it could be anyone, Jerry. Any fool with a knife could have done this. Do you have the murder weapon?"

"No, but we're looking," he had said, replacing the sheet much to my relief. I had seen more than enough.

"Well, you should have the victim's wounds compared to the ones from ten years ago. Looks like they could have been made with a large butcher knife or something. Should be easy enough for the coroner to determine. It can't be the same weapon, though. You guys have that down at the station, right?"

Jerry hadn't answered right away. When he did, it wasn't exactly the answer I was expecting.

"Well, that's the funny thing, Jay. A few days ago the thing went missing."

"What do you mean it went missing? The bowie knife you found in the girl on the base is gone? You've had that at the station ever since the murders ten years ago. When did this happen? How do you know?"

"I was checking over the evidence bin, you know going through stuff to archive things we didn't need anymore. I was looking specifically for the knife. I was thinking of asking you if you wanted it. Ah, it seems to have disappeared. Not exactly sure when, but Ted remembered seeing it not too long ago, so it had to be fairly recently. Didn't think much of it until now, figured someone at the station grabbed it as a souvenir or something. Now with this murder, well, I'm starting to wonder if it's somehow connected."

"Well, you're going to have to have the coroner compare the wounds," I suggested. "Even if it is the same weapon, which would be pretty strange, it can't be the same person. Maybe there's a copycat killer out there, someone who knows about the previous murders. Could someone have seen the morgue shots?"

"I don't know, but I'll check it out," he said, making a note on his pad.

"Whoever it is has flipped their lid," I told him. "It could be just a coincidence. More than likely it has nothing to do with the past, just another senseless act of a sick individual, maybe a jilted suitor, who knows. That's what they pay you guys the big bucks for."

I had left the crime scene with a sinking feeling that had nothing to do with viewing the dead, mutilated, and naked body of a beautiful young pageant queen. Now here I was going to see her sister.

Driving back up the road west out of town toward the mountains did nothing to dispel the gloomy thoughts. Much of what took place those many years before had happened in this same vicinity.

A short distance before the town of Dannemora, before the red brick walls of the state hospital for the criminally insane, I turned left down a small country lane. The road descended and curved into a wide flat area interspersed with farm houses and fields. I spotted the dwelling I was looking for across from a rundown filling station and restaurant. The house was narrow, with white shingles and a corrugated metal roof. A dilapidated garage stood next to the house, separated from it by a narrow dirt drive. I turned into the driveway and parked the car. A large oak tree cast spotted blotches of sunlight onto my car's hood. A wide bush next to the house was covered with Lilacs. Their scent filled the air.

Going up a short flight of steps, I entered a screened-in porch full of old furniture and dust, and knocked on the door. Someone answered after the second knock. It was Sheila Patterson.

"Hello, Mister Lawless?" she said. "I've been expecting you."

I glanced at my watch. I was exactly five minutes late, which is on time in my book.

"Hello, Miss Patterson. Please, just call me Jay. I'm very sorry about your sister. Is there somewhere we can talk?"

"Yes, there's a small restaurant across the street. It's usually not too crowded this time of day. Perhaps we could have a cup of coffee."

"Sounds good to me."

"Let me get my purse and I'll be right with you."

I waited by the car and gave the place the once over. Not well kept by the looks of it, kind of run down. It gave me the impression of being owned by someone who had just about given up on life, even before their daughter had been killed. But then who was I to judge? What did I know about these people? Absolutely nothing! All that would have to change if I took the case. And there was every reason to suspect I would. Thirty dollars an hour was nothing to scoff at. As a matter of fact, by my reckoning I had already made my first thirty bucks just sitting there.

Sheila came out a short time later. She was dressed in tan shorts that went down to her knees and a light, white sleeveless blouse. Her hair was long and light-brown, full and curling at the ends. She was at least an inch taller than me, slim and athletic, a regular pink-cheeked country beauty. She had on wide-rimmed glasses that made her large, blue, unsmiling eyes seem bigger.

We crossed the quiet country road to the parking lot of a small restaurant. The sign above the door said 'Tina's Diner'. It was only eleven, but it was already hot as we walked in. The place was empty, not a good sign for a country diner at eleven in the morning. It meant either that no one went out to breakfast around here or the establishment wasn't that good. By the looks of it, with its shabby interior and the dirt-spattered counter top, I assumed the latter. At least we would have some privacy. We took a booth by the window, as far as we could get from the counter and the only other patron in the room.

We were there a good twelve minutes before the bored teenaged waitress put down her book and sauntered over to take our orders. As we waited, we got the preliminaries out of the way.

"Like I told you over the phone, Miss Patterson, I'm not sure I can do much more than the police. I'd certainly have to report anything I found to them first. If I do take the case, it'll cost you thirty dollars an hour plus expenses. The clock starts an hour ago when I left my house. There are no guarantees and no refunds."

She looked out the window, her expression a thousand miles away, not seeming to hear a word I said. I took out the standard contract I used in these types of cases, a couple pages of legalese that covered my ass in just about every conceivable way my conniving shyster lawyer brother, Tony, could contrive.

"Do you know what it's like to lose your sister to a maniac?" she asked. "To see your parents' lives destroyed right before your eyes? To see such a wonderful life, so full of promise, struck down in its prime, when she had so much to live for? Do you know what it's like to want revenge so bad it consumes your every thought, your every breath?"

She said these words in a rush, her eyes burning into mine. I sensed the distress and anguish behind them, the unspeakable pain. I felt a compelling urge to help her. Some human sentiment I haven't been able to totally repress, bubbled up from my being as the tears bubbled up in her eyes.

"Yes," I said, looking back at her, holding her gaze with mine and not blinking. "Ten years ago. My brother was killed, much like your sister. Murdered, and there was nothing I could do about it. I know what it's like to lose someone, Miss Patterson…Sheila. And yes, I know what it's like to want revenge, but it's not as simple as that. You have to think of the consequences. What I can do is help you fill in the gaps, maybe bring some closure to all this. Maybe I can turn up some leads that will help the police, help prevent this type of thing from happening again. I really would like to help you. I think I can help you," I said finally, with conviction.

"I think you can, too, Mister Lawless, or I wouldn't have called you. Where do I sign?"

It was then that the lazy waitress came over and we ordered coffee. I'm sure she thought the walk across the dirty linoleum floor had hardly been worth her while. She returned a short time later and poured some lukewarm brew into our half-cleaned cups.

After she signed the contract, I started to gather as much background information as I could.

"Tell me about your sister," I asked.

"What do you know?"

"Just what I read in the papers. Her name was Becky Jo. She was a beauty queen of some type. She was eighteen years old and had recently graduated from the local high-school."

"She wasn't just a beauty queen. She was on her way to becoming Miss New York State. She had a good shot of becoming Miss America. No one from this area had ever gone this far before. Her potential was incredible, modeling contracts, magazine covers, you name it, she was doing it."

"Did she have any enemies, a jealous competitor that wanted her out of the way?" I said, asking the obvious questions.

"Yeah, plenty, I suppose, but no one who would do something like this. No, the worst thing you can expect from that bunch is a scandal or malicious gossip. It doesn't take much to ruin a career in the beauty pageant business. Just a reputation for flirtatious behavior will make you enemies on the judges' panel. No, it's not a competitor, but I know who might have hated her enough to do this to her. That bastard."

"What, she had a stalker?"

"Yeah, that miserable little rat bastard has been stalking her since she was a kid."

"Who are you talking about? Have you told the police?"

"Sure I have. They took it all down, but they haven't done a thing."

"OK, slow down. Suppose you tell me about him, from the beginning."

"His name is William Riley, we call him Billy. He used to be my boyfriend before I went away to college. Then he latched on to my kid sister and started to pester her. At first she liked it. She had a crush on him since she was a kid, always tagging along on our dates. Becky Jo was only two years younger than me, although it seemed a lot when we were kids. She felt flattered.

"Anyway, when I left, Billy kept coming around, and after awhile, even though he was four years older than she was and out of high school, they sort of dated for awhile. That is until she started taking her pageants a little more seriously. Then when she went big-time and was traveling all around the state and country, she dumped him. Not hard or anything, that wasn't Becky's way. She was always so kind and gentle, even with a big old horse or cow.

"No, she tried to let him down gently, but that only made it worse, I guess. From what my folks tell me there were some pretty bad scenes, yelling and swearing. He even punched a hole in our wall once. Dad made him pay for it. He apologized and didn't come around any more, but I'm sure he brooded about it. I know Billy, and he's not the kind to let something like that go without doing something."

"Like murdering your sister with a knife? I don't want to upset you, Miss Patterson, but what happened to your sister was more than just a lover's spat. Whoever did this had a terrible, malicious rage in him. He didn't want to just kill your sister, he wanted to torture her."

I was sorry I said it as soon as the words came out. Something about the murder scene and my past experiences made me doubt it was a jealous next door neighbor that had known her and her family all their lives. That is unless there was something especially wrong with the guy.

"I'll check Mister Riley out," I said, making a few notes in my pad. Sheila helpfully supplied his phone number and address, which I also wrote down. "What'd the police say when you told them this?"

"That they'd look into it."

We exchanged glances. I had a sudden urge to smoke, but had never taken up the habit. Some prop to give me time to think of another pertinent question, while I puffed and looked professional. Instead, I searched my empty brain for the obvious follow-up, feeling awkward and stupid, and coming up empty.

"What about you?" I asked finally, for lack of a better line of inquiry. "Do you live around here? Do you know what your sister was doing the day of her murder?"

"No, I live in New York. I went to college there and stayed afterward. There's not much call for advertising executives in this neck of the woods. I haven't been back here in five or six years, since I was out of high school. I told her to leave this place as soon as she could. She never listened to me. She was into the beauty pageant glitter by then, and didn't want to go to college, too much hard work. Now look what happened to her, she's…"

Her voice faltered as she realized what she was saying.

"It's all so terrible," she continued. "Please help me find who did this."

"I'm as much in the dark as you are, but there are ways to light up the tunnel. I'll talk with the coroner and the police. I'll ask around, find out what I can about her movements the day of the murder. I'll talk to William Riley and anyone else even vaguely involved with her. If any one so much as looked at your sister the wrong way, we'll find out about it. The cops will do what they can, but they really rely on the Staties to do the heavy lifting and, well, frankly, the State Police are more concerned with counterterrorism and drug interdiction. They have their hands full.

"I doubt very much anyone's doing any investigating around here. The city boys won't come out this far, they don't have any jurisdiction. Even though they rely on the Staties, the town cops resent needing their help. To make matters worse, because of professional jealousy they don't share information. So the State investigators probably don't even know about your old boyfriend, Billy. I'll be able to slip between the cracks and find out things the police would take months to uncover, if they found it at all."

My talk was braver than my walk, but part of the job is making the client feel good, give them some hope to fight the gnawing feeling of helplessness they feel at night when they wake up thinking of their loved one's last moments on earth.

"I'll submit a running summary and status report to you every week, listing the hours I spent and what I was doing, a complete accounting. You have the right to review it and question any of the activity if you like, but if you fail to pay, the investigation's over. You will not get any more information. If you prefer, you can also pay a lump sum, rather than by the hour. It may turn out cheaper in the long run, depending on how much work I have to do. A murder case like this can run into the thousands in a few weeks."

"The money doesn't matter. What's ever easier for you."

"Well, the accounting is a whole lot easier with a lump sum."

"How much then to investigate my sister's murder? Give me a number."

I thought a little, jotting down some numbers on a napkin.

"Thirty dollars per hour times, say for four weeks, twenty to forty hours a week, that's, hmm...Let's make it an even $3800. That will cover the duration of the case, however long it takes, and all my expenses. You have the option of pulling the plug at any time."

She agreed without hesitation, pulling a checkbook out of her purse. So much for the business end of the transaction, now I actually had to do some work. The money would make a significant difference to my measly bank account, maybe even enable us to get that house we've been talking about. All I had to do was find her sister's murderer.

On the way back to the 'burgh', I tried to collect my thoughts, organize my activities, who I would talk to, what information I needed to gather. My first stop would be Jerry, my friend, the chief of police. I could swing by his house some evening when I knew he'd be home and bring a few bottles of his favorite brew. He would be able to fill me in on all forensic findings. After all, he's the one who dragged me down to see the corpse in the first place. Now I could help him as he asked and get paid for it. I'd also have to figure out how to talk to Sheila's number one suspect, William Riley. He sounded like quite a winner, but hardly someone who would have done such a thing. That is unless he had a background of mental illness, which would be easy enough to find out. I'd also have to check out the area, talk to the victim's friends and acquaintances about her activities leading up to the time of her death. It was something the police, even in their ineptitude, were sure to already have done.

All in all, none of this was something I was looking forward to. I mean who wants to talk to a private dick. It looked like I would be earning my $3800 fee. I was starting to regret I hadn't asked for more. Then again, a case like this could make my reputation and put my little detective business on the map. It was a fantasy I had indulged in once before. It had only gotten me into trouble. I guess some of us never learn.

# Chapter 5

I got back to town around five, and stopped by the office to check my messages before heading home. I planned to call Jerry from there, but already had a message from him waiting for me. He wanted me to phone him as soon as I got it. I clicked the call-back button on the machine and waited for him to pick up.

I had known Jerry since we were kids. We grew up together and had been next door neighbors. He started on the force right out of high school and worked his way to chief of police. He had been a big help ten years before when his boss, the old chief, Eddie McNeil, tried to pin the whole damn series of grizzly murders on me. If it hadn't been for Jerry and a few other friends, I'm not sure what would have happened to me.

Now that he's the chief, however, I'm sorry to say Jerry has turned into something of a stiff. Must be the pressure of the job or something, but he's not the happy-go-lucky guy he used to be. Dealing with the underside of human nature every day probably hasn't helped his disposition any. He sure has had a rag up his anus lately. Maybe it's the case. The murder of a promising young beauty queen on your watch is liable to spoil anyone's day.

He answered after the fourth ring.

"Hi, Chief, it's your old pal, Jay."

"Lawless, where the hell have you been? We've been looking all over for you."

"I was out doing an interview for a new case I'm working on. Why? What's up?"

"What's up is I want you to come down to the station. Now! I have a good mind to send a squad car to get you after what you pulled this morning. What's got into you, Jay?"

"What, you mean that little thing at the McDonald's School of hamburger?"

"This isn't a joking matter. They want to press charges. Assault, threats, damages. I should have you arrested on sight."

"You want to hear my side of the story before you throw the book at me, right?"

"Yes, so get your ass down here, pronto."

"Yes, sir, Chief, I'll be there before you can wipe your ass with flypaper."

I hung up and got back into my car.

I wasn't too concerned as I drove to the station. Even though Jerry had turned into a stiff, he was still a fair one. After he heard what had really happened, he would probably slap my wrists, but he wouldn't arrest me. He needed me.

When I walked into the station every cop in the place eyed me. Some of them looked at me curiously, some laughed. A few glared at me like they wanted me to make their day. I kept my head down and made my way to Jerry's office, where I sat down across from his desk.

He glanced up at me as he signed some papers, but otherwise ignored me. When he finished, he looked at me like I was a truant kid.

"Well?" he said.

"When I was leaving the dojo last night, around ten, I was attacked by three punks. One tried to strangle me, another grabbed me from behind. They weren't fooling around. The grip the guy had on my neck would have choked out most people. I took care of them, no problem. As a matter of fact, I may have broken one of their jaws. There was a third person, standing ready to attack me, but he smartly backed off and ran after he saw what happened to the first two. I recognized him from the karate school here in town. He's one of the instructors. When I went in this morning to check it out, he was there teaching a class. The guy mugging people at night teaches karate to kids in the day. Isn't that nice? I confronted him and told him to take his belt off.'

"In front of his class?" Jerry exclaimed.

"Yeah, I told him he didn't deserve it. I asked him why they attacked me. He didn't answer, but went to slug me."

"He says you attacked him?"

"Does he have any bruises?" I asked. "Are there any marks or contusions?"

"No," Jerry admitted.

"Then I didn't attack him. If I did, there would have been physical evidence, some damage."

"I know you can inflict damage without leaving marks."

"How do you know that?" I asked.

"Because you told me so. I know you like a book, Lawless."

"Well, then you know I wouldn't attack someone like that unless I was attacked. When he made a fist and raised his arms to hit me, I forced him back into the wall with a few slaps. If I wanted to hurt him, he would have been on the floor bleeding. I wanted answers, that's all. There were witnesses. What did *they* say?"

"Everyone had a different version of what happened. I guess it was pretty traumatic for some of them, seeing their karate instructor get beat up. It happened so fast many of them aren't sure what happened, but the kid didn't appear to be hurt, just angry. Why didn't you come in after you were attacked and sign a complaint? We could have picked them up and held them in custody. Now you're the one that's going to be held in custody."

"Come on, Jerry. For what?"

"For trespassing and assault. That kid you roughed up isn't the one pressing charges. It's the guy that owns the school, the head guru there."

"He came out and started yelling at me, trying to intimidate me with his five stripes. He tried to throw me out."

"Can you blame him, coming in like that in the middle of his class?"

"I wanted to demonstrate to his students what kind of people they really are, a bunch of thugs."

"You're the thug if you think you can take the law into your own hands."

"I know, Jerry. You're right. I'm sorry for causing you trouble. God knows you have enough to worry about with the real criminals, especially this murder business. I only want to help, not make things worse. I didn't come to you because it was just my word against theirs. You wouldn't have been able to hold them."

"If they had the injuries you said they did, we could have. That would have been all I needed."

"I know, Jerry, but they could say I attacked them first, or that they got them somewhere else. A good lawyer would have had them out before you finished signing the arrest warrant. And anyway, you have enough to worry about, like I said."

"Well, what do you want me to do about this? It's not going away."

"You could find out why those guys attacked me. Did the owner, what's his name? "

"Omar Johnson."

"Yeah, that's him. Did he tell you that I hit him?"

"Yes, he said that you kicked him and knocked him down, and then threatened him with those nun-chucker sticks."

"Well, that's close but not quite accurate. I asked him if he had anything to do with me being attacked. Instead of answering me, he grabbed the nun-chucks off the wall. Those things are lethal."

"Yes, I know. I would have shot him."

"Exactly. I didn't kick him, but I covered the ground between us in a flying leap. The kick only made him back up. It never landed. I was too far away, but it gave me a chance to grab his arm, the one with the weapon. Then he tried to push me down, but I flipped him."

"Yeah, I know. You're a sneaky little bastard with those flips of yours."

"I didn't lay a finger on him."

"I know, there were no marks."

"What do the witnesses say?"

"Like with the other guy. They all saw something different. Some say you flew through the air like Bruce Lee, with a flying side kick. They all say you flipped the guy. One witness said you hit the master so fast that you couldn't see your hands. You could only hear the punches land. You must have put on quite an exhibition."

"I'm a legend in my own time."

"You'll be doing time if you're not careful, Jay. There are a hundred ways you could have handled that better than you did."

"Yeah, what, other than coming to you?"

He couldn't answer, only look at me and shake his head.

"Are you going to arrest me?" I asked.

"I don't see I have any choice."

"I'm working on the Patterson case. Her sister, Sheila, hired me. I started today. She gave me some leads. I'm working on the murder, just like you wanted."

He continued to stare at me and shake his head.

Thankfully, he decided not to arrest me, but he made me sweat, which was probably his intention in the first place. He didn't seem especially happy to hear I was working on the Patterson case, in spite of his previous request. I repeated what Sheila had told me about William Riley. He said the state police were conducting the interviews. He hadn't heard the name and wrote it down. He made me promise to show him anything else I found. He also asked an interesting question.

"Do you think this attack on you has anything to do with the murder?"

"What, the karate school? I don't know. The thought never occurred to me."

"Well, you know, knives and swords and things."

"There certainly are those types of things on his wall, mine, too, for that matter, but I doubt they've been used for anything like that. The attack on me probably had something to do with competition. We've been taking a few of their students. After today, we'll be taking more."

"You just stay away from them."

"I will, but now you've got me thinking. If I find any connection between anyone there and the Patterson girl, you'll be the first to know."

"Good. Stay out of trouble."

It was almost six-thirty. I was late for dinner and hadn't called Suzy to inform her. Her mom usually left at six. I prayed there wasn't a disaster waiting for me at home.

On the way to the apartment, I stopped at a combination filling station, convenience store across from the old base. I needed to get gas and call Suzy to let her know where I was. The wire fence is gone and the officers' homes have been turned into townhouses, but there's still an old B-48 sitting in a field to remind people what had once been there.

As I went in to pay for the gas, I noticed Bobby McKenna, the son of the man who had killed himself and his wife with a shotgun a couple of days earlier. He sat at one of the booths in the combination convenience store/ice cream parlor. He was unmistakable with his shoulder-length, unkempt hair and rimless, thick glasses. Dressed in his habitual blue-jeans and work shirt, he looked startled to see me, as if I had caught him masturbating, although all he was doing was sitting there minding his own business.

He had been staring out the window absentmindedly, lost in thought. Who could blame him for his reaction on seeing me after what had happened. That's probably the way he reacted to anyone he knew, poor guy. I went over to offer my condolences. I should have paid my bill and ignored him.

"Hi Bob, sorry to hear about your mom and dad. If there's anything we can do."

I didn't finish. He looked at me as if I hadn't spoken, right through me, as if I wasn't there.

"Are you OK, Bobby?" I asked, concerned at his expression. Finally, he spoke.

"No need to be sorry. The Goddamn fool put himself and my ma out of their misery. What's to be sorry about?"

His words stunned me. My concern rose to alarm. I looked around. Other than the kid at the counter, the place was empty. I sat down opposite him.

"Look Bobby, I know it must be hard to take. I lost my mom when I was young, so I know how it feels. Can I do anything to help? You want to take a walk and talk about it. It might be good to talk with someone."

He looked at me and then at the door, as if he was waiting for someone. Then he looked back at me with an expression I couldn't quiet interpret, but which again seemed out of place with his present situation. It wasn't sadness or even anger, but a look of scorn, as if the idea of me being of any help was somehow an insult.

"If I need your help I'll ask for it. You always were a busybody. Why don't you mind your own business, Lawless."

"OK, Bobby, I know you're upset, but there's no need to be rude. Suit yourself."

I stood up to leave.

"Wait, Jay," he said. "I'm sorry. I'm upset. I can't stand the way everyone's looking at me, like they expect me to be in mourning or something. I wish everyone would just mind their own business and leave me alone."

"Look, Bob, it might help if you knew more about what happened. Maybe if we understood it better, it wouldn't be so bad."

"What do you know about it? Please, Jay, I appreciate your wanting to help, but I'm fine. You may not understand, but it's probably the best thing for everyone."

I wanted to ask him what he meant, ask him if his parents were sick or in some kind of trouble, but thought better of it. After all, I wasn't a psychiatrist. This guy needed more help than I could offer. So I decided to leave well enough alone.

He hardly acknowledged me as I said bye and left. He was looking out the window anxiously again, like he was waiting for someone. As I drove off, I thought I saw one of my new students pull up, but I was moving away with traffic so I couldn't be sure. I waved anyway. Whoever it was didn't wave back.

# Chapter 6

That night I took Suzy and Bud out for Michigan hotdogs. It was the least I could do after coming home late. I couldn't help feel a little disconcerted after my talk with Bobby McKenna. He had always been a little taciturn, but I'd never seen him like that. It was out of character, though I really didn't know him that well. I hadn't talked to him in years. I guess bitterness and resentment can really change a person, or was it something else.

The following morning I decided to stop by and see my cousin Pat. She knew Bobby's older sister. Perhaps she might know what happened to the old man to make him shoot himself and his wife. It wasn't really my business, but Bobby had made me curious. Maybe he needed help.

Pat lived in an assisted-living apartment on the south end of town, not far from where the base used to be. You'd think someone in a wheelchair, with muscular-dystrophy, would be slowed down a little, but not Pat. She's a social worker with a full caseload of battered women, welfare mothers, troubled teens, and drug addicts, which our small town seems to have more than its share of. Pat knew the street, the seamy underbelly of our little town, better than any cop or detective. She would know what the people there were saying.

I swung the car around and headed toward her place. It was the middle of a Tuesday morning, but I found her home. She buzzed me up. I took the lift to the second floor. She was waiting at the entrance of her apartment across from the elevator when the doors slid open.

"Well, Mister Lawless, to what do I owe this pleasant surprise?"

"Nothing, just thought I'd stop by and see how my favorite cous' is doing."

"I'm fine, Jay. How's Suzy and Bud?"

"They're doing great. Suzy's been busy with the agency. Business is booming."

"Glad to hear it. What have you been up to?"

"Not much."

Pat was too young to know much about what happened in town a decade before. She didn't know anything about the murders or the terrorist plot but secondhand gossip. She certainly didn't know about my part in the affair. What she didn't know wouldn't hurt her.

I mentioned that I had bumped into Bobby McKenna, the son of the dead husband and wife.

"Talk about your sour characters, but who can blame him," I observed.

"The whole thing is odd," she agreed.

As I had hoped, Pat was able to fill in a lot of information.

"McKenna had one of the biggest farms in the area," she informed me, "mostly corn and livestock. The place is worth a lot of money. Bobby and his sister stand to inherit the whole farm."

"Nice, he'll be able to plant his experimental trees."

"What?" she said.

"Oh, nothing. Bobby wanted to plant more experimental trees and things. I guess now he can plant all the exotic weeds he wants. Who knows, maybe he'll start a marijuana farm."

"It's not very funny, Jay. How can you joke after what happened to those poor people?"

"What do you mean? It was a murder-suicide wasn't it?"

"I'm not sure," she replied. "From what I can make out the old man had no reason to kill himself. He was healthy as an ox. So was his wife. They were real religious, too, went to church every Sunday. His farm was doing well. They had everything to live for. They didn't fight. He was the most considerate polite man I ever knew. No, it just doesn't make sense."

"You sound like you knew them personally."

"No, I'd see them in church and at the mall occasionally, that's all. Never spoke other than to say hi, but I watched them. I know human nature."

"So do I, and anything is possible. People don't follow rules. They're not always rational. They're liable to do anything. Who knows what goes on behind closed doors. You should know that. Look at the characters you have to deal with."

"They're just people like you and me. A lot of people aren't as fortunate as you."

"Hey, I make my own luck. I don't need handouts. I'm not relying on the government to take care of me. I don't break the law and make excuses for things. If everyone took care of themselves, instead of wanting someone to take care of them and complaining, the world would be much better off."

"Jay, if everyone lived like that the world would be a jungle."

"It is!"

I still needed to talk to Jerry. I wanted to find out how much they knew, to help me get up to speed on the case. I hadn't had a chance to pick his brain the previous night. I knew he had the day off, so I decided to visit him after dinner.

I grabbed a bite to eat at the 'Spoon'. I had group classes that night and a test afterward. Just in case there was any trouble with the other school, I made sure both my black belts would be there. It promised to be a busy night.

Jerry and his wife were just finishing up supper themselves. Their two boys no longer lived at home. The oldest was married with a kid of his own. The younger brother was going to college in Albany.

"How's Jeffery doing in college?" I asked.

"Good. It's his last year." said Jerry, smiling and guiding me down to the basement den. "So, you've decided to get involved in the case after all. I thought you weren't interested."

"I'm interested in making a living. Who knows, maybe I can help. Stranger things have happened."

"Well, that's why I asked you down to the crime scene in the first place. It looked familiar. Like that case we were involved in a few years ago."

"We've been through all that, Jer. This girl's murder has nothing to do with that. It's just another sad case of some jealous lover or a jilted fan, or a sick opportunist with a knife. Unfortunately, this kind of thing happens every day."

"Not on my watch it doesn't," he shot back.

"Has anyone talked to the boyfriend yet, William Riley?"

"You mean the boy next door who couldn't take no for an answer? The Staties talked to him yesterday. They filled me in this morning. He has an alibi. He was home with his parents and sister at the time of the murder. It looks pretty tight."

"Well, I'd like to talk to him just the same."

"I'm not sure that's such a good idea," Jerry said.

"Why not?"

"Remember what happened last time. Everyone you interviewed turned up dead."

"That's because we had a maniacal killer in town."

"What makes you think we don't have one now?"

I couldn't answer his question. Instead, I asked one of my own.

"What's the coroner say?"

"The wounds were deep, inflicted to cause maximum pain and prolong death. She was tortured. It took her awhile to die. There was a lot of blood loss, but little blood at the scene."

He paused and stared at the floor, obviously remembering the grisly sight.

"We still haven't found her clothes," he continued. "She was apparently killed and brought to the beach."

"They don't think she was killed at the beach?"

"No, forensics seems to think she was attacked somewhere else and then left in the dunes. She was killed some time in the early morning hours. She was last seen at a friend's house, where she was staying for the night. She was sleeping on the couch next to a sliding door that leads out to the front lawn. The yard borders the highway. When her friends came down the next morning, she was gone, but her clothing and purse were still there. There was no blood found at the house."

"So you think someone abducted her from the house, and then killed her?" I inquired.

"It makes sense. She was probably lying on the couch in her skimpy PJ's. Someone could have spotted her through the sliding glass door, grabbed her, stuffed her in a car, then killed her. It could be anybody."

"Or it could be the boy next door," I replied. "My client said he used to go with her. Then when she went to college he started dating the younger sister, Becky Jo. She liked it at first, but after she started doing well in the pageants, she wanted to move on. Apparently he resented her success and started to stalk her."

"Yes, her parents told the State Police the same thing. Riley's got a good alibi, like I said."

I asked him a few more questions about the case, but he didn't have much to add. I told him I'd keep him posted and left to get ready for my class.

Tuesday and Thursday nights we held group classes. While private lessons allowed an individual to advance faster through the ranks, learning more techniques quicker, the group classes were where you put it all together. You got a chance to work with a lot of different people, of all sizes. This is very important when preparing to face some unknown assailant on the street.

Tonight I made sure both my black belts were there. These guys have stuck with me through the years, thick and thin, and are my pride and joy. I'd put them up against any martial artist their weight class and rank, bar none. They would help with the test and be a big deterrent in case there was any trouble with Omar and his henchmen.

Group classes are half the price of privates, so many students only signed up for those. Even so, those who could afford it, like my three new students from Montreal, often opted for private lessons as well.

This evening was special. Tonight we were having a test. There's always electricity in the air the night of a test, especially a first test. This is usually the hardest, the one you always remember, because you have no idea of what to expect. That's the whole idea. You won't know what to expect on the street either, unless you've been there before. The test is to get you ready for that moment, to push you beyond your comfort limit.

I've had twelve, fifteen students go up for an orange belt test, the first rank, and have only two or three come back. That's how hard we ran them. Anyone can learn the moves proficiently enough to execute them in a calm safe environment. Can you do it when you're choked full of adrenaline, when it's pounding through your temples so you can't think straight? That's the question.

I ran the first class through some light stretching and basics, my three new students among them. Even though some were being tested later on, I ran the class as hard as usual, though I didn't let any of those being tested spar. I had the students go through the gauntlet. This is where the attackers lined up in two lines facing each other, like Daniel Boone's angry Indians. The student has to move through the gauntlet, defending against each attacker in turn, who can throw any strike they want. After this exercise, I paired them off and let them practice their single punch techniques, focusing their counters on weak areas of the body with speed and precision. When the class was finished, I bowed them out and told those waiting to be tested to stay warm and stretched out.

You could tell nerves were at a fever pitch. Much of testing is kept secret. The students are admonished not to talk about them, although that's next to impossible. A kind of myth builds up around them, clouded by rumor and innuendo, but little hard fact. It doesn't help that a lot of it is made up on the spot, so that no two tests are the same. This is especially true when you have sadistic and imaginative people like me and my black belts dishing out the punishment. The whole idea is to make the students think on their feet, in the midst of chaos and fear, when they think the sky's falling down around their ears. In fact, they are in a safe controlled environment. I call it controlled violence.

There were nine people going up for their orange belts – a couple teenagers, a retired teacher from the college, a lawyer, a carpenter, a female pastor, and my three mid easterners.

I ran them through ten minutes of brutally fast basics, yelling at them to punch harder and kick higher. I had them do 400 punches up and down the body. They all had looks of intense concentration on their faces. Everyone was beginning to droop with the frantic pace. I had them drop for twenty pushups. Then I had them do more basics. Finally, I let them rest standing in their horse-stances, but not for long. As they stood there trying to get their wind back, we walked among them, hitting them in the midsection and sweeping them off their feet.

One of the most important, and thus the first things we try to instill in our students, is a loud kiai. This is the karate yell you are probably familiar with. Not only does this have the effect of startling your opponent, it adds adrenalin to your system. This adds power to your strike. It also forces air down your windpipe, which can prove very beneficial when you're struck in the solar-plexus. Since we're struck there all the time, one of the first things we have to do is build some sort of defense for such an event, and thus the kiai.

My students are taught to kiai as loud as possible, as if their lives depended on it, when even the slightest move is made to strike their midsection. This is so it becomes second nature to them. This is one of the things we stress in their first test. We do this, of course, by hitting them.

We only hit them with one third power, just enough to keep them honest. Everyone did exactly as they'd been taught, except for my three Mid Eastern students. Not one of them kiai'd. They stood there like bull-headed jackasses! I couldn't believe it, after how much I had stressed it in their classes. I had actually warned them that if they did nothing else in a test, if they kiai'd, they'd be OK, they'd pass. I was livid.

I went through them again, applying slightly more power to the strikes, yelling as I did for them to kiai. Only Ali, the youngest of the three, muttered a grudging muffled grunt. There was not so much as a peep from the other two when I struck them. I had seen this before. It was a kind of perverse macho pride. They stood there and took it, looking straight ahead as if saying, 'See, I'm tough. I don't need to kiai.' It was time for a lesson.

I looked at my black belts. They looked back with a knowing expression. It was like the kind you might see from witnesses when someone's about to step off a curb into an on-rushing bus, a desire to help the victim, but knowing that anything they might do would only endanger them.

"Kiai when I tell you to kiai!" I yelled. "What's wrong with you?"

The other students looked on as if they were about to witness a murder. A couple of them were actually shaking. My black belts eyed them with hostile intent.

I stood in front of my two recalcitrant students. Facing Mustafa, the biggest of them, I hit him with a three-quarter power round-house kick, driving the ball of my foot deep into his solar plexus. The nerve there spasmed, sending fluid up the esophagus and forcing the air out of his lungs. He grunted and doubled-over with the wind knocked out of him. Lying on the floor, he tried in vain to suck air back in. The class looked straight ahead with stern faces, breathing evenly.

"See what happens when you don't kiai," I said. "And that wasn't even full-power."

Ali, was next in the line. I hit him with a little less force. Much to my relief he actually kiai'd, although it was just a stifled snort. It was almost as if he didn't want to show any weakness in front of his friends. I hit him again harder. He yelled a little louder.

"Louder!" I screamed and hit him a third time, with more force. Each time I punched him, he kiai'd a bit louder. I was starting to get through to him.

The last of the group was Praveen, the spokesman for the three. He was the leader of the pack, and refused to kiai when I nailed him with a ridge-hand. Beardless and slightly smaller than Mustafa, he glared back at me in defiance. I hadn't hit him that hard, wanting to give him the benefit of the doubt. I had hoped that he would do as instructed and we could get the test back on track. Apparently, he still hadn't learned.

Things suddenly got very still. His friend, Mustafa, was being administered to and soon had his air back. All thoughts of lucrative customers had vanished. All I could see were two stubborn students who had refused to follow my instructions in the dojo during a test, something akin to mutiny on a ship. Praveen had already seen what happened when you neglected to kiai when hit in the solar plexus.

Mustafa was bigger and stronger than he was. I could have knocked the wind out of the stubborn white belt easily, but it would have served no real purpose. The demonstration had already been performed. No sense repeating it.

I calmly asked the class to kneel in meditation, while I had Mustafa and Praveen stand in front of me and bowed them out. Then I informed them that they would not be allowed to continue training in my school.

"You both have failed the test," I said.

They looked at me in surprise and started to object. My two black belts had come over to stand on each side of me, both with angry looks on their faces. They were just as pissed-off as I was and would have liked nothing better than to spar with the two offending students.

I made Mustafa and Praveen sit in the corner until the test was finished, and wouldn't let them leave, despite their threats to sue me for assault and kidnapping. We lock all the doors prior to a test so there are no interruptions. I wasn't going to delay the test any longer just to let them out.

They had to sit and watch the rest of the class get their belts and diplomas, but there was nothing they could do with three black belts in the room. Finally, the test finished and I unlocked the doors so they could run home. Ali, who had gotten his belt, left with them, but said nothing. I doubted he would be back.

All in all, it had been a less then successful evening. Not only did I probably lose my three best paying customers, I'd probably be sued in the process.

Suzy was up when I came home, but not in the mood to hear my tirade. She went to bed early and told me I'd have to take care of Bud the next day, her mother had a doctor's appointment.

# Chapter 7

The following day I was feeling a little sheepish after the test of the night before. The last thing I had wanted to do was kill my cash cow, but it looked like I had smashed my gravy-train in a fit of anger and pride. Rules were rules, and the rules of the dojo were supreme. Without complete obedience and discipline it's just not possible to teach the art of self-defense in a proper manner, at least not the way I've been taught. It's critical that we instill this in the student from the earliest lessons. Their ability to keep still when told, and to move when instructed could be the difference between a serious injury and a good lesson. If I'm demonstrating a technique, slashing full power hand-swords at your Adam's apple, and you move without being told, you could move right into the blow you're trying to avoid but don't see coming. When I've got two two-hundred pounders going at each other without pads or gloves and I yell, "Up!'", they need to stop moving like automatons with the cord pulled. If they don't, someone is liable to get hurt. No, when I tell a student in a test to kiai, they'd better do it at the top of their lungs or there will be fucking hell to pay.

I told myself that as I stared hard at my reflection in the mirror. Wiping the last bit of shaving cream from my face as if it were blood, I snapped a punch at the mirror, pulling it just short of the glass. I got by before these prima-donnas showed up. I'd get by after they'd gone. Let them try to get their money back for those lessons they won't get. I had more important things to do, like ring up some prime $30.00 an hour fees.

After taking care of Little Bud for a few hours in the morning, until Suzy's mom came back from her appointment, I decided to spend the day tracking down leads that Sheila Patterson had given me the day before. I'd start off with the boyfriend, since I was just about in the right frame of mind. I jumped into my second-hand Corolla and headed west up into the mountains, along that fateful highway that had held so much terror and death ten years before. Now I was following another trail of destruction, the murder of a young beauty queen.

It sickened me, but then a lot sickened me these days. It seemed things got more corrupt and hate-filled with every headline on the evening news. Husbands killing wives, boys raping girls, lowlife predators stalking kids on every street corner, while politicians robbed us blind behind our backs, spouting promises and smiling in our faces.

The whole stinking mess made me sick. Maybe it was this job. Yeah, I was definitely in the right mood to talk to a suspect. Or was I? I remembered what happened last time I ran up this road to interview someone and eased my foot off the pedal, sliding back down within the speed limit.

Pulling off the highway into a roadside diner, I stopped to mull things over and have a cup of java. I sat at the counter with a few trucker types in work clothes and jeans, and ordered the combo plate, with bacon, eggs, and pancakes, something I seldom do. As I sat there waiting for my order to arrive, sipping my coffee, I considered my next move. Perhaps it would be better if I followed a few of the other leads first. I could talk to some of the murdered girl's friends and get an idea of her movements and contacts on the night of the murder. I figured I should probably gather up some more background info before I moved on to confront the boyfriend.

I went over my notes and jotted down some addresses and phone numbers from a page I ripped out of a phone book, to make them available as I drove around town. When the waitress came with my food, I asked her a few questions.

She didn't know the murdered girl, who had been several years older than her and had gone to another high school, but she did know the people she was staying with when she disappeared.

"I know Leslie Haywood," she told me. "She's my age. The Patterson girl was a friend of her older sister. I guess she was staying overnight. Isn't it awful, something like that happening right here in our own backyard?" She paused but didn't wait for me to respond. "Her father's an ex-professor at the college in the city. They have a house right on the highway."

I thanked her and paid my tab. Then I headed out to interview the Haywoods, the last people to see Becky Jo alive, except, that is, for the murderer.

Following the waitress's directions, I drove up the highway another few miles to a neighborhood of spacious, modern-style homes that bordered the highway just before the town itself. The Haywood place was a low ranch-style house, with blue-gray shingles and full-length, plate-glass windows. Lush bushes and tall pines dotted the yard.

There was a late model station wagon in the driveway, built more for safety and comfort than drivability. I rang the bell. After several minutes an older man with a day's growth of gray stubble answered the door and peered at me through watery eyes.

"Mister Haywood, my name is Jay Lawless. I've been hired by the family of the murdered girl, Becky Jo Patterson, to help investigate her death. I was wondering if I could ask you a few quick questions."

"I've already told the police everything I know. The girl was a friend of my eldest daughter, Joan. She was spending the night. She stayed here a lot when she was in town. They were good friends. My daughter's devastated, as you can well imagine, but there's nothing more I can tell you that I haven't told the state police."

"Yes, I know, Mister Haywood. I've seen the police reports, but well, there're a few things I've noticed that may help find the killer. He's still out there. You have daughters. You know how important it is we don't leave one stone unturned."

"I know, that's why I've sent my wife and daughters away to visit their grandparents up in Malone. It's not safe around here with that maniac on the loose."

"Why didn't you go with them? I know I wouldn't want to be separated from my family at a time like this."

"I would, but I have some business to attend to first. Anyway, the police said they might want to talk to me again. I guess I just want to see justice done. Becky wasn't just a beautiful girl. She was a beautiful person, with a lifetime of happiness and promise ahead of her. It's just too damn close, know what I mean? If something like that happened to one of my girls I don't know what I'd do."

He clenched his fist and tightened his jaw. Ex-college teacher or not, I wouldn't want to have this old dude after me. I told him I knew what he meant, that's why I was here asking questions. He seemed to warm up to me, and volunteered some more information, stuff he hadn't thought to tell the cops. He also let me snoop around the premises.

There was still yellow tape outside the sliding glass door where Becky Jo was assumed to have been taken from. It led to a room with a flagstone floor, furnished with wicker-chairs and thick cushioned couches. The Patterson girl had been sleeping in one of them the night of her abduction and murder.

The door gave out onto the front of the house and was flanked by a wide stone chimney. Several trees separated the house from the two-lane highway.

The police assumed someone driving by saw the sleeping beauty queen and abducted her. But from where I stood, by the side of the road, looking at the house in broad daylight, it was difficult to see how someone driving by would have seen her. Even if it were dark outside and the lights were on inside, their view would have been blocked by the trees. No, whoever it was must have been snooping around to begin with, maybe someone who knew the girls were having a slumber party. Perhaps it was someone who made a habit of peeping into bedroom windows. Maybe this time he spotted something he couldn't resist. The opportunity presented itself and the sicko reacted, on impulse, on the spur of the moment. From the road, someone snooping around the front of the house would have been hidden by the trees. It was a perfect spot to stop and peep. It was just another random, meaningless crime of passion. Then there was the boyfriend.

After investigating the property a bit more I decided to ask the professor a few more questions.

"Did you see anyone suspicious that night, someone hanging around? Were there any phone calls, anything at all out of the ordinary?"

"No, the police asked me the same thing. It was just another night. The girls were having a party for Becky. They hadn't seen her in awhile. She'd been out of town, I think. She was just here for a few days between competitions. They were all excited because she was a finalist."

"Do you know if Becky's boyfriend came by or called? Did they talk about him? His name's William Riley. They call him Billy."

"No, don't know anything about that. Like I said, she hadn't been in town for some time. I don't think she was dating any boys from here. My girl Joan said she had a new boyfriend, a rich guy from the city. I think they said his name was Larry. I can call them up and ask if you like."

"Yeah, that would be a big help. Every bit of information, no matter how small, may help."

I gave him my number and told him to call me if he had any more information. I mentioned that I'd really like to talk to his daughter if possible, and asked for the names of the other girls at the party. He said he'd ask her and her friends, but he really didn't want her to get involved. I told him I understood, but she was the last person to see the dead girl alive and it was important I speak with her. He seemed reluctant to have me talk to her or her friends. I didn't push it. There were other ways to get the information.

I stopped at the Patterson residence a short time later. Sheila was there with her mom and dad, all three still in mourning. The parents reluctantly agreed to talk to me, but seemed put out that their only remaining daughter had hired a private detective. They said that Becky Jo had been doing a lot of traveling lately. She was home a few days before going back to Albany for the state finals. She had every reason to believe she would be the next Miss New York and on her way to the Miss America Pageant in Miami this year. Yes, the Riley boy had been around asking for Becky, but as far as they knew they hadn't gone out or met. They were aware that their daughter was seeing an older man, but they didn't know his name or address. They could think of no one who would want to harm their outgoing, popular daughter. She didn't have an enemy in the world.

She may not have had any enemies, but someone sure bore her a grudge to slice her up like that. They gave me the name and number of her agent in Albany and a few other friends and acquaintances that might have some information. I was thoroughly depressed by the time I left the place. Sheila escorted me to my car.

Their sense of loss was overwhelming. I had seen this before. Looking into that old man and woman's eyes as I asked them about their dead daughter was like staring into a pit. The hole her loss left in their once happy lives was as black as empty space. Their deep sorrow seemed to draw all light, everything around it, into itself. I could see the hopeless pain in every breath they took, every word they uttered. Worse was the fact that their remaining daughter, the one still alive, no longer seemed to matter, as if she too had died that night on that beach. I saw the resentment in her eyes when she looked at me.

"Have you talked to Billy yet?" she asked as I opened the car door to the chiming of my key alert.

"No, I'm on my way out there now. I talked to Mister Haywood and checked out the place. I agree with you. It seems unlikely somebody would have driven by and seen her sleeping there. It's much more probable that it was someone snooping around the house, maybe a peeping-tom. I'm not sure why the police would be following the drive-by theory. It seems kind of weak. I'll let you know if I find out anything."

She thanked me. We made arrangements to meet later in the week. I told her how much time I had spent so far, and that I'd probably need another twenty-four to forty-eight hours before I had anything definite to tell her. She said that would be fine, whatever it took. Money did not seem to be a concern.

I followed the directions out to the boyfriend's place. It was a trailer park on the other side of town, where he lived alone. I found the spot without too much difficulty and parked behind a red and white pick-up truck in front of the yard. It had a plow on the front even though it wouldn't snow again in these parts for another nine months. A rusted lawnmower sat on the corner of the lawn. A Pontiac Trans Am that looked like it was being restored rested on blocks and took up most of the driveway. A row of trees stood in the rear of the trailer, separating it from the property behind. A dog barked somewhere close by.

I had a bad feeling about this, which wasn't that surprising. I was about to ask some stranger if he had anything to do with his ex-girlfriend's murder. For thirty dollars an hour, I'd do just about anything.

I rapped on the door and waited. It was opened by a rather large-boned young man. His expression turned instantly sullen when he realized it was someone he didn't know, someone more than likely selling something. His manner became even more menacing when I explained my business.

"You a cop?" he asked.

"No, I'm a private investigator. I want to ask you some questions. The police consider you a leading suspect. I may be able to help you."

"The cops don't know shit. Why would you want to help me? Who hired you?"

"I can't say who hired me, but it's someone who wants to find the truth, just like you and me. They don't believe you did it."

"Who said I did it? Who told you that? Did that stupid bitch Sheila put you up to this?"

"I don't know what you're talking about, but you don't have to be rude. Don't you want to help find Becky Jo's murderer?"

"I don't care what happened to that bitch. She was whoring around with every Tom, Dick, and Harry, any rich cat who could help her career. She wasn't as sweet and innocent as everyone thinks. Some old guy was boinking her. I told the cops everything. Who told you they think it was me?"

"Well, you and her had some history, right? She tried to break up with you and you two got into a big fight."

"That was years ago. It's ancient history."

56

"Some people can hold a grudge for a long time."

"Fuck off," he said, shutting the door.

I hadn't come all this way to get a door slammed in my face.

"Wait!" I said, putting my foot in the door like an aggressive vacuum cleaner salesman. "I'm just telling you what the cops think. They'll lead you on, make you think they're on your side. Then when you least expect it, they'll show up at three in the morning and arrest you. I think they're wrong. This is the work of some out-of-towner, either someone driving by and seeing the girls, or someone from the city that followed her up here. No one from around here would do a thing like that."

"That's what I told them," he said, opening up the door and stepping out. "It's one of her big-time boyfriends. She got herself involved with some big city hoods and they bumped her off. Everyone knows how corrupt those beauty pageants are."

"I know, that's exactly what I was thinking," I said, trying not to crack a smile.

I let him talk for awhile, nodding in agreement as he railed against the 'man', 'suits', and 'big city know-it-alls', but didn't pick up anything useful.

"What do you do for a living?" I asked.

"More than you," he answered. By the look of his arms, he lifted and carried heavy objects.

"You dated the older sister, too, didn't you?"

"That fucking whore," he spat.

"Don't hold anything back now," I said, laughing, trying to lighten things up. "No wonder the cops suspect you, if you talk like that."

"I'll talk any goddamn way I want. I don't care what they think. I never did anything to Sheila. She's just jealous because I took up with her sister when she went away to college. Big deal. Like I said, it's ancient history."

"Did you call Becky Jo or see her when she came back to town?"

"I don't know. I guess, a couple of times. I mean, what the hell, I've known her since we were kids. There's no harm in trying to be friendly."

I asked him if he could give me some names of people who could vouch for his whereabouts on the night of the murder. He gave me the same names he gave the police. He seemed to have a pretty tight alibi, as Jerry had said, but I wasn't sure.

"I've talked to some people that said you were hassling Becky, following her around."

"That's a goddamned lie! Who told you that?"

"Oh, no one in particular, it just seems to be the general impression. And, well, you know how impressions are."

"Why don't you just get out of here, mister. I don't have to talk to you. Get out of here."

His demeanor changed suddenly. He looked down at me menacingly. His bravery increased as he estimated our relative body weights and sizes. He outweighed me by a hundred pounds. I almost laughed out loud. Instead, I smiled and tried to act suitably intimidated.

"Hey, calm down. I don't want any trouble," I said, holding my hands up and handing him my card. "I'm sorry to bother you, Mister Riley. If you think of anything that could help, please give me a call."

"I'll give you shit!" he yelled, tearing up the card. He followed me as I walked away, like one of those stupid dogs who seem to bark louder the farther away you get, gaining courage as you retreat. I almost wished he would have tried something, but he stopped at the edge of his lawn with his hands on his hips. He stared at me like a tackle at a guard as I got into my car and drove away.

I wanted him to think I was scared, and decided I'd keep an eye on him. Maybe I would even do a little moonlighting on the side for free, just for the sheer pleasure of finding some dirt on this frigging a-hole. Sheila was right. If he wasn't the killer, he sure was an antisocial degenerate. The more women he could be kept away from the better. But was he the killer? My instincts told me no, but my instincts had been wrong before.

# Chapter 8

Later that afternoon I made some calls from the office. I called Becky Jo's manager in Albany. She answered after the third ring. She was obviously upset at losing her number one client and a good friend. She agreed to talk to me when she learned I was working with the police to find Becky Jo's killer. She didn't believe anyone connected with the competitions could reasonably be suspected of doing such a thing. She knew quite a bit about the older man Becky was dating. She had been the one that introduced them.

The boyfriend, John Henry Sinclair, had been out of the country on a business trip when the murder occurred. He wasn't expected back until the next week, and had been informed of Becky Jo's death and the circumstances surrounding it. According to the murdered girl's agent, he was devastated, but apparently not enough to cut his trip short and come home. I got as much information about the boyfriend and his whereabouts as I could and thanked the woman for her help.

Nothing in the conversation about the boyfriend triggered any red flags or suspicions. Although at twenty years her senior he was hardly a boy. I made a note to call him on his return. At this point, anyone with the monogram 'boyfriend' was a suspect. As a matter of fact, the whole damn world was a suspect as far as I was concerned. I had to narrow things down. After all, it wasn't beyond the realm of possibility that someone driving by actually saw the girl sleeping by the window and decided to grab her. Weirder things have happened. But to have carried her off without making a sound, that was another matter. Maybe she had gone outside for something. Perhaps she decided to take a leak in the bushes. Then again, if she knew her killer she might have gone out to talk to him. Anything was possible at this point. My job was to reduce the forest of possibility to one or two good leads, then follow them like a rabid bloodhound.

I stopped by the agency to see Suzy. She was pounding on the keyboard and taking reservations on the phone.

"Hi, honey, how's it going?" I asked.

"If these people change their reservation one more time, I'm going to have a conniption."

"Don't do that," I teased. "I don't think there are any conniptions left. I just ate the last one."

"Very funny. What's up? You need something to do? Mom needs a hand with her lawn."

"Oh, I'll give her a call. I've actually been busy working on the Patterson case. I told you about it. I had to make a few calls. Don't worry. I'll take care of the phone bills this month. I had some interviews this morning too. Things are coming along."

She didn't seem particularly interested and went back to her work.

"Give mom a call, will you," she yelled over her shoulder.

"Sure," I said as I left the office, sorry I had popped my head in.

As I went out to my car I noticed a middle-aged woman walking aimlessly up and down the street past the agency. She seemed to be looking for something, or uncertain where she was. She was vaguely familiar. Something about the wire-rimmed glasses and small eyes reminded me of someone, although I couldn't quite place the face.

As she passed me a second time, I asked her if I could help. She looked at me for a second, as if recognizing me, and stopped.

"Are you Jay Lawless, the private detective?"

"Yes," I said, a bit surprised that it was me she had been looking for. "Can I help you?"

"I'm Grace McKenna, Bobby's sister. Pat, your cousin, told me I should talk to you. I remember you used to come to the house once in a while to play with my brother when you were kids."

"Oh, hi, Grace. I didn't recognize you. It's been a long time. How are you doing? I was sorry to hear about your mom and dad. I saw Bobby not too long ago. He seemed a bit upset. Is there anything I can do for you?"

She looked a little uncertain, as if she couldn't make up her mind what she wanted to say.

"Would you like to go some place to talk?" I asked, sensing she had something to get off her chest. Whatever it was, it would take some tact to elicit. My interest was percolating. "There's no room in my office. If you like, we can take a little walk down to the city park and talk there."

She hesitated for a moment, as if gauging the risk of being seen with me in public, and finally agreed. We strolled down two blocks to a small park in front of the town monument commemorating the explorer who had discovered the lake. Stopping at a café on the way, I bought her a latte. I had a hunch what she had to say would be worth the three bucks. After we were settled on a park bench overlooking the monument and the bay beyond, she told me her story.

"It's dreadful what happened to my parents," she began, full of emotion, the tears almost audible below the surface of her words. "Just horrible, but that's not the worst of it. My father never would have committed suicide like that, and for no reason." She stopped at a loss for words.

"Have you told the police this?" I asked.

"Yes, but they just think I'm a hysterical woman in denial. But I'm telling you, this just can't be. They were murdered."

"What makes you say that?" I said, with some concern. At that she was silent.

"I just know," she said quietly at last. "I know my father, that's all. And there is no way in the world he would have done that."

"Then who do you think did? Who would have a reason to kill two old people? Did they have any enemies?"

"Yes," she said emphatically.

"Who?"

"My brother."

"Bob?" What makes you think that? I mean, he's not the friendliest guy in the world and he says some pretty strange things, but to say he killed his own mother and father, in such a gruesome way, well, that's just a bit much."

"He hated them, especially my father. They were arguing and yelling all the time. I used to worry about my father's heart, he'd get so upset, but I never thought this would happen. I know it was him."

"Do you have any proof, anything at all to prove your suspicions?"

"No, that's why I've come to you. I want you to investigate my brother. I want you to find proof of what he did and expose him for what he is to the world. My parents left the farm to both of us, fifty-fifty, but Bobby's trying to contest the Will. Says I don't know nothing about farming and I don't deserve to have it, just because I didn't go to agricultural college like him. I grew up on that farm and worked on it all my life, until I was an adult and married on my own. I've been living there since my husband died. I've got nowhere else to go. Now he wants to buy me off with a pittance and kick me out. It just isn't fair."

I was momentarily taken aback. Events had taken a turn I wasn't quite prepared for. Another murder case? Double the fees! My mind worked feverously to determine if I had the bandwidth to take on a second homicide. My greed quickly taking over, I said yes before I finished my calculations. I should have done the math on paper, but I couldn't resist the promise of the added cash. She agreed to my terms and gave me more dope on her brother, who kept some strange hours and stranger company. It was enough to make me think he was up to something illicit, even if he hadn't killed his old man and mother.

"Well, Miss McKenna, if we can show that Bobby is any way involved in the death of your parents as you suspect, well then, I don't think you'll have anything to worry about with the inheritance."

Of course, it did cross my mind that Grace could have had ulterior motives for casting suspicion on her brother. This would be especially true if he was trying to cheat her out of her share of the inheritance. Who knows, maybe Grace was doing the cheating. Then again, my motto is whoever's paying the bill is the good guy. I mean, a man has to have some principles.

After taking Grace McKenna back to the office, where we signed the usual contracts, I stopped by my mother-in-law's to pick up Bud and mow the lawn. I enjoyed the physical activity, working out the cases in my mind as I pushed the mower back and forth across the lawn. Little Bud followed in my tracks with his wagon, picking up tufts of grass.

I had told the McKenna woman that I was already working on another case and that it would take priority. I planned to spend at least twenty hours on her job starting the following week. That would be enough to get some preliminary information to see if it was worth pursuing further. I planned to spend a couple of days on each case and see where things led from there. The bulk of that time I planned to do some old-fashioned shadowing and stakeouts. It was something I had become a bit of an expert at after all my spying on cheating husbands and housewives. All of this meant that I would more than likely not be able to keep up my teaching schedule at the dojo. That, however, didn't look like it would be a problem, since I had lost my three best-paying customers. I'd have to get my black belts to cover for me, maybe even pay them, although I hated to set that kind of precedent.

I hadn't heard a word about my altercation at Omar's dojo. I kept a watch on my school and home just in case, staking them out as if I was spying on myself. I didn't see any suspicious characters or assassins. Perhaps Jerry had gotten to them.

That night at the dojo, as anticipated, the three mid easterners came in. I expected them to cry about wanting their money back. Instead, they apologized for their conduct at the test and admitted they were wrong. They explained that it was a cultural thing, relating the Kiai to crying out in pain. This was anathema in their religion and culture. They were taught to be stoically silent in the face of adversity. They realized, however, that this was wrong and that my teaching was correct. To achieve what they sought, they must transcend their culture and go beyond their beliefs. Thanking me profusely for the abject lesson, they promised to work even harder to become worthy.

I was surprised, to say the least, and somewhat relieved there was still the possibility of not losing their considerable fees. Yet I hesitated. They had committed the ultimate dojo sin. They had disobeyed their sensei. I had told them they couldn't come back in front of the whole class. I might seem soft and wishy-washy if I gave in. Yet if I spun it the right way, it might be OK. Maybe they had learned a valuable lesson. They seemed sincere. I told them I'd think about it, but not to suit up. I wanted to talk to my black belts. It was no use saying yes if my partners didn't approve. The three of them would only get hurt. They said they understood and hoped I'd agree, because they thought I was the best teacher they'd ever seen. I had to agree.

I was overjoyed. That evening at dinner I told Suzy about the events of the day and how much I had earned. She wasn't impressed, and was critical of me for thinking of taking back my students after how much I had complained about them the night before.

"How are you going to work on two cases?" she asked reasonably. "You barely have enough time now. Who's going to take care of Bud while you're out playing detective?"

"I'm not playing. This isn't a game. People's lives depend on it. What are you complaining about? The extra cash is going to make a big difference. Anyway, your mom can take care of Bud."

"My mother is not a live in maid. Why are you taking those creeps back again, anyway? I thought you said they failed the test and quit. Now you're going to take them back! Make up your mind, will you."

"Oh, give me a break, for Christ's sake. They came in tonight and apologized. Since when did we stop giving out second chances around here?"

"You have commitments to me and Bud, what about that?"

"Now that things are going better on my end, I was hoping you could take more time off from the agencies. Take a few days off this summer, spend more time with the kid."

Those words resulted in a two hour argument that ruined both our nights and made it hard for me to get a restful sleep. It seemed the better things got in one area, the worse they got in another. It must have something to do with the second law of thermal dynamics and the increasing disorder of the universe. My entropic life seemed about ready to come apart at the seams.

# Interlude

'Jim' lived in the moment, totally within his five senses. There was no inner dialog to distract him or bring him out of the everlasting present. He lived like an animal in the forest by his instincts and primitive wits alone. He searched for moisture to wet his lips when he was parched with thirst. He hunted warm-blooded creatures when his belly ached and growled with hunger. He scavenged among the dirt for grubs and roots when no game was found. When he wasn't curled up in a ball in forgetful oblivion, he roamed the countryside ceaselessly. He didn't so much sleep as slip from one form of unconsciousness to another.

He had long ago forgotten how he had come to be here or who he once was, but he remembered sounds and smells and the pain he had endured. The pain seemed to go on forever, until it was the only thing he knew. Then there was nothing. Yet some inner portion of his mind still functioned, cut off from any link to his awareness. His senses still took in information. The brain stored what the eyes saw as he walked the streets at night. It digested what the ears heard from passing radios and people. The images and sounds came to his mind like messages from outer space. One minute they were there, the next gone.

He was a big man, though he weighed much less than in former times. He dressed in rags and pelts of fur. What he had lost in weight and body fat, he gained in sinew and wiry hard-muscle, built up from living in the wild. What he lacked in rational thought, he more than made up for in animal cunning.

He walked along the same route he had walked that night a week ago. He had been bidden, as if by some unseen hand, to leave the woods and head down the mountain to the city in the valley. He moved silently, unthinking, driven by some inner urge he didn't understand. He found himself standing outside a brick building. He didn't know what it was, but he knew there was something inside he had to retrieve. It was something that was part of him, like his arms and legs, but something even more important. Instinctively, he had kept to the shadows as he moved to the rear of the building. His spirit guide spoke to him, guiding him in a language no words could convey.

He had moved down the concrete steps leading to a rear doorway. He moved like a predator, his large size deceptive in the half light. Without hesitating, almost reflexively, he smashed the small window in the door with his elbow, and opened it from the inside. Somehow he had known where it would be, as if he'd seen it in a dream. It was a good thing for them that the night staff was on the upper floors listening to the radio and dispatch messages, or out on their appointed rounds. No one was in the storage area where they kept old evidence.

It hadn't taken him long to find it, the object of his search. The glittering hard blade shined in the gloom, almost as if it were calling to him. He knew it when it slipped into his hand, that old familiar grip. It quivered in the darkness, a long, shiny, sliver of steel. 'Jim' was back. Soon after that he had blood.

# Chapter 9

The next few days were rough, as I tried to figure out how to juggle the unexpected case load and my other obligations. I decided to reinstate my three errant Mid Eastern students, but held off telling them for a few days so I could concentrate on other things. Let them stew. It'd be good for them.

My mother-in-law, God bless her, was able to take up some of the slack with Little Bud. I still had him for a couple of days a week, however, and was trying to figure out just how to manage it. I spent my first paycheck on a new Canon SRL camera and telephoto lens. The old Polaroid I'd been using had seen better days. It may have been good enough for snapping a couple necking in the parking lot, but just didn't cut it in the high-level spying I'd be doing.

Although the Patterson murder was by far the more sensational case, I planned to spend a couple days focusing on the McKenna murder-suicide. The questionable deaths of my childhood friend's parents hit a little closer to home. I decided to pay the farm a visit. Killing two birds with a single rock, I took Bud with me. He would be a good cover. I could say he wanted to see the cows if someone asked what I was doing there taking pictures and asking questions.

I brought up the idea of a field trip at breakfast.

"Thought I'd take a little drive in the country, take some pictures. I want to break in my new camera. I thought Bud could come along."

Suzy thought that was a great idea, although she had a dozen warnings for me. Then she burdened me down with way too many baby things. I grabbed my camera and Little Bud and headed out the door.

"Let's go to the farm," I said as we drove out of town. "We can see the cows."

"I want to see the moo-moo cows," he said.

He had a thousand questions, two more for every one I answered. He'd ask the second one before the first was out of his mouth. I couldn't keep up with his curiosity. Today I was busy with my own thoughts, trying to plan my actions. I needed to develop contingency plans. I definitely didn't want to meet Bobby McKenna. The last thing I needed was a confrontation, especially with Bud along. I knew what a sour prick Bobby could be. He certainly wouldn't like learning I was working for his estranged sister, investigating him for the murder of their parents.

I decided to check the place out and take some pictures. I'd get the lay of the land and see what I could find out. As far as anyone was concerned, I was just a dad with his kid out enjoying the country, taking pictures of the animals. No harm with that, right?

I took the back roads west out of town to the old Bob Moffit Road. Although the area was built up with large malls and new development, it didn't take long to get past all the glitter. I soon found myself among broad fields of corn and knee-high grass. A few barns with silos dotted the flat landscape. Groups of shade trees clustered along the highway.

I pulled off the road at a small spot beside a wide-planked, white fence. It encircled a grassy meadow. There were horses in the field munching on the grass. Behind it, off the road, was a large red barn. Four tall, white-topped silos stood together behind it. Next to the barn was a white farmhouse.

I got out and snapped a few pictures, making sure to get a few good close-ups of the McKenna barn and house. I used my new camera with the telephoto lens. Bud pointed at the horses and asked questions. I muttered a few answers, while I used my high-powered lens as a telescope. Slowly driving around the property, I stopped and took snapshots from different vantage points. We went along the two highways that bordered the property for at least a mile in both directions.

Even though it was a fine spring morning, there didn't seem to be anyone about. It looked like a farm on a Sunday afternoon. I expected to see men working in the fields, or at least a cow. From the road, there didn't appear to be much happening.

"Where are all the cows?" asked Bud, peering out the opened window, echoing my own thoughts.

"They must be in the barn. Maybe they're on vacation."

"Do cows take vacations, Daddy?"

"No, but the farmer might. Let's go take a look."

I drove down a private dirt road leading between two fields of half grown corn. As I drove closer, I noticed the rundown appearance of the place. Old man McKenna used to keep it in tip-top shape. His yards and fields were manicured like golf greens. His corn stood straight and tidy. It had only been a couple of weeks, but already I could see the difference. The hay was almost waist high, and stood uncut. It should have been bundled in bales by this time. The fields were unplowed and unplanted. The buildings needed repair. The whole place looked like it was in mourning. It probably had something to do with the recent sudden demise of the farm's owner. There's nothing like a suicide-murder to take the wind out of your sails.

We turned a corner around the side of the barn and came to an open gravel area between the barn and the house, which had been hidden from the road. There was a wide lawn in front of the house. The lawn was torn up. There were a few workmen planting what looked like fruit trees. The trees were clustered together with little thought of appearance or symmetry. Certainly not the way farmer McKenna would have planted them. A red pickup was parked along the side of the yard. The men were digging more holes to put more saplings in. They looked up in surprise when we drove in. I stopped the car and got out.

"Morning," I said. "I'm a friend of Bob's. I thought I'd drop by, see how he's doing. I was hoping he might be in."

"Bob's not around," said one of the men, standing by the road with a shovel. He was dark and muscular and didn't seem at all happy to see us.

"Can I show my son around? He's never seen a farm up close before."

"No, you'd have to talk to the owner. Like I said, he's not around. This is private property. You'd better get out of here."

"OK, sure," I said, slightly offended by his manner and tone of voice. He gave me the impression he'd just as soon hit me with the shovel as talk to me. I got back in the car and left, but stopped just before we were out of view of the workmen to take a few pictures of them. I wanted them to see me. It may have been my imagination, and more than likely due to the recent tragedy, but something seemed out of place. I certainly didn't care much for Bobby's surly hired hands.

Maybe Grace McKenna was right and there had been foul play. I became more determined than ever to pursue the case and help her, see if I could find enough evidence to gain what was rightfully hers. I made a note to try and contact some of the men who had worked for Bobby's father. His sister was sure to know how to get in touch with them.

I spent the rest of the day with Bud, taking him on a drive up toward the mountains west of town. I was unable to find the Riley boy, but had a good day bonding in the country with my son. That night at dinner I was the hero of the day. Bud could talk of nothing except the farm and the town with the giant stone walls. Suzy was less than impressed.

"You took him on surveillance with you? Isn't that kind of dangerous?"

"No, don't be silly. We just went by the McKenna farm and snapped some pictures. We didn't even go in," I lied.

"Why'd you take him to the prison? Are you on another stakeout there too?"

I didn't honor that remark with a reply.

"I don't want you taking him with you on the job. It's bad enough you're involved in these things, but you are not to involve our son. OK?"

"Sure, no problem, but you're going to have to have your mom or someone take care of him. I'm going to be very busy for the next few weeks. These are the first big jobs I've gotten. They could establish me once and for all. Besides, the money is going to help a lot. You can cut back on the office hours and spend more time at home."

She just looked at me with what I interpreted as contempt and didn't answer. We had been all over this before, each night for the past week. It was becoming an old subject, so she changed it.

"Jerry LaGrande called today. There was another murder. They found two more bodies."

"What? Another murder? Who? Where?"

"I don't know. Jerry didn't say much, except for me to have you call him. He sounded pretty upset. I guess it was a couple kids necking down at the boat landing behind the old base."

The mention of the location gave me a sudden chill. I tried to ignore the rising panic and stay calm.

"I'll have to call him from the dojo," I said as I finished dinner and stood up.

"We have to talk, Jay," she insisted.

"Not now," I answered as I rushed out the door.

I had finally decided to reinstate the three errant students. I talked it over with my two black belts. Neither of them had an objection. I planned on telling them the following week. With their added fees, I would actually be pulling in more than Suzy for the first time since we were married, which did a lot for my self-esteem.

The class went well. We even got a few new students. No one was waiting to mug me when I got in my car.

70

I called Jerry from the school, but he wasn't in. I left a message saying I'd call him early the next day and went home.

The following morning I decided to take the camera and make another drive out to the Riley kid's place. I wanted to see what he did when he wasn't stalking ex-girlfriends. Before I left, I called Jerry from the phone in my office. He came on the line after being paged by one of his subordinates.

"Hey, Jay, where you been? I've been trying to get in touch with you. I told your wife it was important police business."

"Hi, Jer', I've been busy earning a living, which is more than I can say for you."

"Quit the bull, Jay, this is serious. Did she tell you there was another murder the night before last? Two kids necking down behind the bluffs. Real bad. Look's a lot like the Patterson girl's murder, same type of weapon, same pattern of wounds. I think we have a serial killer on our hands, and that's not the worst of it. They found them down at the boat landing."

"So, they were down on the beach behind the bluffs having sex. Kids neck down there all the time. It's just a coincidence."

"That's where you said you killed him."

"This has nothing to do with that, Jerry. Anyway, what do you expect me to do about it? I'm working my end for the Patterson girl's sister. I'll fill you in if and when I find something."

"I want you to come down and look at the crime scene photos, see if you can pick up anything."

"Jerry, that last one was bad enough. I'm still trying to get the sight of that poor girl out of my mind."

"Well, this is even worse. It looks like the same type of thing we were seeing back in '89."

"We've been over all that. It can't be. I'll stop by later this afternoon and see what I can do to help."

"Thanks, Jay. I appreciate it. I'll be waiting."

Another murder, this time a young couple having sex. It sure sounded like the killer of ten years ago, the one with the penchant for hacking up young people in the act. But it couldn't be. I had killed him. I was sure of it. Or was I? What had happened to his body?

I wanted to get an early start, but was already behind schedule. At this rate my quarry would be long gone by the time I got there. It was almost nine. Twenty-five minutes later I was parked unobtrusively across the street from Riley's trailer. His Trans Am was in the driveway and off the blocks, so I knew he was still at home. I waited almost an hour before he emerged unshaven and groggy-eyed. It must have been a wild night. He got in his car and drove off. I followed at a discreet distance. Even though it was a rural area there was enough traffic to give me cover.

He drove slowly into the hills, along country roads. We passed fields and woods. At one point, in a particular quiet spot across from a meadow, he stopped the car by the side of the road. I drove past, around the bend just out of sight, and stopped. Getting out, I took my camera and made my way back along the side of the highway, keeping to the trees and bushes. When I could see him clearly, I snapped a few shots of him sitting in the car. I couldn't tell what he was doing, but he had taken off his shirt.

He sat there for the longest time, unmoving. I wondered what he could be doing. He wasn't sleeping because I could see him move and turn about. He kept looking around as if making sure no one was watching him. I suspected he was up to something weird, but couldn't determine what. He sat in the car like that for over an hour without getting out. Finally, when a state police car drove past, he started up his car and pulled out onto the road. Making a U turn, he headed back in the opposite direction, toward town. All in all, his actions were very strange. Perhaps he had killed those people after all, and was sitting in his car masturbating while he re-enacted the murders. I was almost beginning to believe it.

Instead of going back home, he stopped at a small sporting-goods store on the edge of the city limits. Then he went across the street to a diner for lunch. I sat in my car and ate the ham and cheese sandwich Suzy had made for me. It reminded me of another time, ten years ago, when I sat here in my car watching somebody. I prayed this time things would turn out better.

I was wondering if there was something better I could be doing with my time than watch this pathetic loser, when he came out of the diner and got into his car. This time he drove south out of town, down toward the old sand pit. I followed. The 'sand pit' is an unused piece of land surrounded with high sand cliffs, where chunks have been gouged out by steam-shovels. The sand was once hauled away in the backs of huge trucks to be spread on roadways across the county. That had been years ago. Now the place was used by kids and locals as a shooting range and unofficial dump. It was littered with garbage, old washing machines, tires, junk cars, and large piles of sand. I parked my car a little distance up the road and circled back to the pit through the woods on foot, along a well-trodden path.

I heard the shots before I reached the sand cliffs. My young friend was target practicing. Great! Not only was he a freaking stalker, he was an armed and dangerous one. I crept a little closer to see what kind of shot he was.

He was standing with his legs apart, with the gun out straight in a classic side stance that he had probably seen on TV. The gun was big, probably a .357-Magnum, with what looked like a six-inch barrel. At least it would be hard for him to conceal.

As I watched and snapped pictures, he squeezed off another round. The sound echoed off the surrounding hills. The sand spit a few hundred yards away from where he was standing. The awesome power of the weapon was apparent even from this distance. Then without stopping, he fired off three more shots. This time, he twisted his body at the waist from left to right, as if he were shooting several adversaries hiding among the bushes at the base of the cliffs. His bullets ricocheted off rocks and boulders that were strewn about the ground. Not what I would call safe or approved target shooting.

Suddenly, I had a bad feeling about this guy. His potential as a threat became magnified tenfold. He wasn't that good of a shot, but with a gun that size, he didn't have to be. He certainly didn't seem to have any respect for the weapon. This guy could be trouble.

Standing there, unarmed, in the middle of the woods, watching the creep target practice was giving me the heebie-jeebies. I decided to head back to the car and check out his trailer. I'd have enough time to peer through a window or two and reconnoiter the place before he got back. Perhaps Billy boy had something to hide.

It only took me ten minutes to get there. I figured that gave me another twenty to snoop around. I wasn't worried about getting caught. I could always say I wanted to ask him a few more questions. What was he going to do, shoot me?

I parked my car on the street behind Riley's. Then I strode down the road to his rear neighbor's trailer. No one was about, so I quickly skirted across their lawn and slid through the trees and bushes separating the two properties. Facing the back of Riley's place, I crossed a narrow, overgrown lawn and went up a set of steps. They led to a small porch and the rear door.

I peered through the window into what appeared to be the kitchen area. Pots and pans hung from hooks over the stove. The sink was clear of dishes. Apparently Mr. Riley kept a tidy place. Remind me to give him the Good Housekeeping seal. I couldn't see much more from my vantage point, so I tried the door. It was locked.

Moving back down the stairs, I walked along the rear of the mobile home. There were no windows to speak of, just small ones too high for me to reach. I went to the front and cautiously peeked around the corner. No one was home yet. I walked nonchalantly up to a large front window, but it was too high for me to see through. So I went up the steps to the front porch to get a better vantage point. Still not able to see, I climbed over the porch railing. Holding on to it with my left hand, I leaned out as far as I could to peer in.

I could make out a couch along the far wall and a television next to it. A recliner faced the TV, with its back to the window I was looking through. I could see an ashtray and packs of cigarettes on a coffee table next to the chair. This room, too, except for the butts in the ashtray, appeared well kept. Then I noticed them, a set of four or five large-bladed hunting knives gleaming in a glass case against the wall. Just then his car drove up.

I swung down from the porch, and walked toward the car as he was getting out. He didn't waste any time on pleasantries, but then I didn't expect he would.

"I thought I told you to keep away from here. What are you doing? You're trespassing."

"Sorry, Mister Riley, I just wanted to follow up with a few quick questions to help clear your name. I'm on your side."

"Sure you are, you and all the other mother-fuckers in the world. You're just like a stinking cop only worse. Get out of here before I…"

"There's no need to threaten me, Mister Riley, I'm going. It only makes it look worse for you. I know you have an alibi, but the cops don't believe it. They think your old man and sister are lying for you."

"That's a fucking lie!" he yelled, "The cops just have it in for me, that's all. They're fucking liars."

"I know, Bobby, I agree with you. Those pricks will say and do anything to make themselves look good. They don't care how many innocent people they hurt. That's why I'm trying to help you."

"You ain't trying to help anybody but yourself. Get the fuck out of here!"

"OK, sorry to bother you. I can't make you talk to me, but if you..."

I never got the rest of the sentence out of my mouth. Obviously not thinking I was moving fast enough, he went to grab me. I don't know, maybe he was used to throwing his weight around and assaulting older, smaller people. Perhaps he was all pumped up after shooting his big gun. It could be that he was just a dumb shmuck who never had to control his impulses. A bully who always got away with things, but wouldn't you know it if the clown didn't actually try to grapple with me.

I slapped his large paws away. I kept slapping them as he tried again and again to take hold of me. My hands were a blur of speed. As I did this I moved forward, forcing him back against his car with well-aimed punches pulled inches from his nose He was leaning so far backward his head was nearly lying on the hood. It was all over in seconds.

"I'd advise you to be a little more polite in the future, Mister Riley. I only wanted to talk, ask you a few questions. I'm on your side."

Then I turned and walked away. He stood there with a surprised expression on his face. I guess he'd never been bitch-slapped before. As I walked back to the car, I had the sick feeling he was going to go for his gun. I ignored it and kept moving. I trusted that if he was crazy, he wasn't crazy enough to shoot me in public, in broad daylight. Still, I didn't linger.

I had broken my own rule. It was something I tell my students all the time, especially when they start to get good. Never show off your ability to an opponent. If you have to fight, make it for real, don't pull punches. You'll get your face smashed in. I certainly didn't want to hurt the guy. After all, he was just a kid, not more than early twenties, and it was his property. He had every right to throw me off it, even if he was being a bit hasty about it. I only wanted him to keep his hands off me, make him show some respect. I think he got the point, in spades. In any case, he could consider himself lucky I didn't clean his clock.

# Chapter 10

It was late by the time I got home. Suzy had already had dinner and cleared the table, even though it wasn't quite 6:30 yet.

"Where have you been?" she asked as soon as I was in the door.

"I told you, I had to do some work on the Patterson case today. I was on a stakeout. Why'd you eat already? It's not even six-thirty yet?"

"I have to go back and take care of mom tonight. I've been with her all day. She hurt her back at work and now she can barely walk. I'm taking the day off tomorrow to take her to the doctor's. You're going to have to take care of Bud."

"I have a lot to do myself tomorrow. Can't you take him with you?"

"If you think I'm going to wait hours in the emergency room with a four-year-old, you're crazy. Jay, we've been though this a thousand times. He's your child too. He's just as much your responsibility as mine. I need your help now more than ever, and you're not being very supportive."

"I'm sorry," I said for the second or third time that day. "You're right. What happened, did she hurt herself at work?"

"Yeah, some ass-hole in a suit bought some fertilizer and made her put it in his truck."

"What? Was he feeble or something?"

"No, he was a big guy, young. She said he had a foreign accent and looked like a rich Arab. The name on his credit card was Abdul Waheen. She said that he was very rude. He told mom he was the customer. If she couldn't do her job, he'd find someone who could and let her boss know the reason why. Some people are just so mean, to make an old lady lift those heavy bags. He had her put all four of them in his truck. It was all they had left in the store. Can you believe that?"

For some reason this news made me see red. I flew into a rage.

"What's wrong with people these days? That stinking piece of shit. I wish I was there. I'd teach that mother-f'er some manners. That son-of-a-bitch!" I yelled banging the table.

Of course, that only made things worse.

"Oh, Jay, why do you have to be so, so…?"

"So what, caring? I'm only mad because of what happened to your mother. Is she OK?"

"No, she has a bad back sprain. Hopefully, the doctor can give her some good pain pills. I have to take her in tomorrow for x-rays. You have to babysit after daycare."

"OK," I said as I took some still warm meatloaf out of the fridge and made myself supper. "Whatever you say."

Suzy went to bed soon after coming back from helping her mother. She wanted to get an early start. I stayed up and watched bad movies on the tube, thinking about the cases over a couple of brews. Had there been anything stronger in the house, I would have probably drunk that. Too lazy to take the trip to the package store, I made do with what I had.

I called Jerry around ten. He was home in bed with the wife watching the news.

"Any progress on the latest murders?" I asked after the obligatory small talk. He said he couldn't talk about it there with his wife and that he'd call me back from the downstairs phone. I told him Suzy was sleeping and I'd call him back in five minutes.

"So what have you got?" I asked when he answered the second time.

"Not much, Jay, but enough to make me wonder if it's all happening again."

"What? What are you talking about? What's happening again?"

"The murders! It looks like we have another serial killer on our hands. This last one, down behind the old base, was pretty bad. From what the coroner told me they were in the act when they were killed. Even worse, he said the blood had been, er, squeezed out of them, you know, after they were killed."

"Christ!"

"Yeah, sound familiar?"

"Not really."

"Aren't you forgetting that last murder, Tech Sergeant Joe Adams and the two women? That's just how we found them."

"Well, maybe it's just a coincidence, another sick fuck with the same sick ideas."

"That's not all. The wounds were practically identical. Shit, it was a carbon copy killing."

"Bull!" I said in denial. "No f'ing way!"

"F'ing way. I compared the crime scene photos. They were stabbed in virtually the same places, in the same manner. Look at the pictures if you don't believe me."

"No thanks, I've had enough bad dreams."

As we were talking his beeper went off.

"Sorry Jay, I'm being paged. Something must be up. I've got to go. I'll talk to you more tomorrow. Why don't you stop by the office? We can do lunch."

"OK, if you're buying. I don't have an expense account like you big-shot police executives."

"That's not what I hear, Mister Private Dick."

"Have 'dick', won't travel."

"See you later Paladick," he said and hung up.

Jerry's information did nothing to help my sleep. I lay in bed next to my snoring wife and tried to put things together. A mutilated couple at the boat landing was the carbon copy of a murder that took place ten years ago. It had been one in a string of homicides that involved me in a nightmare I'd just as soon forget. Then there was the slaying of a young beauty queen and the unexplained death of an old farmer and his wife. Were they connected? Could it really be happening again? I tried to dispel the thought and concentrate on the here and now, on hard reality, on something I could get my mind around instead of vague phantasms and fears.

Could this Riley kid be the murderer? He certainly had a nasty attitude, but being rude didn't make him a serial killer. Then again, anything was possible. Perhaps it was a copycat killing. Was it someone at the station, a sick cop? Riley had a knife collection. Had anyone checked it out, compared his knives with the wounds on the victims? I made a note to mention it when I met with Jerry. So what if he had knives, every half-baked Rambo wannabe had a knife. Was he capable of the grisly murders of three people, that was the question. I had trouble taking the punk seriously, that is until I remembered him clicking off rounds from his .357. At some point I drifted off, but didn't wake much refreshed from whatever sleep I got.

The next day was raw and windy. The rain held off until I left the house. Figures! I felt guilty about my lack of progress on the McKenna case, so decided to spend a few hours asking questions around town. I wanted to see if there were any financial or medical reasons the old man would want to do himself and his wife in. Their daughter certainly didn't think so.

My inquiries at the local banks and insurance agencies verified that McKenna had no financial worries. He seemed to be in good health and spirits. I called Grace McKenna to get the names and phone numbers of the people who worked for her father at the farm.

Suzy had taken Little Bud to daycare. I was to pick him up at 2:00. I checked my watch. That gave me two hours, plenty of time.

As I drove to the diner to meet Jerry for lunch, I listened to the news on the radio. There was nothing about the murders, just a story about the recent theft of 800 pounds of fertilizer from the local agricultural training center. There was also a report of a huge barn fire out on Beekertown Road. Must be the economy, I mused. When things get bad you see a lot of this type of thing, theft and insurance fraud. You can't be in my line of work for long without turning cynical. Problem was, I was a cynic long before I was in this line of work.

Jerry was sitting alone in a booth. I joined him.

"Take a look at these pictures," Jerry said as I sat down.

"Well, hello to you, too, sunshine." I could instantly see they were crime scene photos and was immediately sorry I had come. I knew lunch would be out of the question if I looked.

"Spare me the gruesome details," I said. "I don't need to see that."

"I thought you wanted to know the facts."

"Yeah, a picture's worth a thousand words," I remarked, picking up the photo to get a better look.

"Notice the knife wounds, identical. Kind of strange wouldn't you say?"

"Who else has access to those old crime scene photos, the earlier ones? Could someone have seen them and be copying the murders? You say the knife is missing. Maybe whoever took the knife saw the pictures, too, got turned-on, and wanted to try it himself."

"Hmm, I hadn't thought of that. Most of the guys at the station have access to the files. Anyone could have seen them."

"Has anyone taken a special interest in them or the case?"

"No, not that I know of, but I'll ask around. It's worth pursuing."

"I think that's a lot more likely than our butcher with the bowie knife returning from the grave."

"I guess you're right. At least I hope so. Hey, did you hear about the fire at old Fred Potter's farm last night. Entire barn burned down. Old Fred was killed in the fire."

"Yeah, it was on the news, out on Beekertown Road. But I didn't know the owner was killed. That's too bad."

"Yeah, he was a nice man. Had quite a spread. The barn was one of the biggest in the area, size of a small stadium, completely destroyed.

Fred apparently died trying to save some of his prize bulls. Body was so badly burned it was hardly identifiable."

"That's too bad. Do they know how it started?"

"No, but arson hasn't been ruled out."

"Hardly sounds like an insurance scam, with the guy running back in to get his bulls and all. I wonder how he was doing financially. I'm working for Bobby McKenna's sister, Grace. She doesn't think her father committed suicide. She thinks it might be murder. Kind of strange, all these old farmers dying off like this."

"That's what she told us when we talked to her, but she was pretty incoherent. We may have to interview her again, but her theory sounded crazy. I mean to kill your own parents like that."

"What, you've got a better theory? Have you checked out the old man's bank account, found whether he was in debt or not?"

"All these farmers are in debt. It's part of doing business. No, I don't think it was anything like that, probably just an unfortunate accident."

"Yeah, the guy was probably just cleaning his gun when it went off two times and blew both their heads off."

I mentioned the knives I had seen at Riley's place.

"I noticed them when I was asking him some questions yesterday. He was acting kind of strange, not that that means anything."

"I'll mention it to the state boys. They can check it out."

"Yeah, OK, sure. Between you guys and the Staties a fellow couldn't get arrested around here if he was the Son of Sam."

"Don't be like that, Jay," he said. "You know we're doing our best."

"Yeah, and you can use all the help you can get."

When I left Jerry the rain was coming down like lead pellets. I was soaked by the time I reached the car, having neglected in my rush out of the house that morning to bring a jacket or raincoat. It was just as well. The water helped wash away the dirty feeling I had from looking at those pictures. I hardly touched my burgers and fries, a rarity for me.

It was almost two by the time I left the diner. I rushed across town and picked up Bud at daycare. The rain hadn't let up all day. It was coming down as if it was angry, like it wanted to wash all us human scum into the lake.

Suzy wouldn't be home for a couple hours yet and I still had more to do. This was the time Suzy's mother would normally be taking care of Bud. I wondered if I could drop him off there for a couple hours. Then I thought better of it. After her lecture of the previous evening, I knew Suzy's mother was off limits until she got better. On a whim, I headed over to my cousin's place. She loved the kid. Maybe she would watch him for awhile. In my desperation for a babysitter, I didn't even consider the fact that she was in a wheelchair.

Pat was in when I rang the bell, and buzzed us up. She was pleasantly surprised to see Little Bud, as I seldom brought him to visit. I made it seem like that was the main purpose of the trip.

"Hey, Pat, guess who I brought."

"Hi Bud," she said, wheeling herself backward in her electric chair to let us in. "What do I owe this pleasure to?"

"I just picked Bud up from daycare, thought we'd drop by. Suzy's mother hurt her back at work and can't take care of him. Some creep made her load fertilizer into his truck."

"Oh, I'm sorry. People are so rude. Hi, Bud, want a cookie?"

"What do you say to your cousin Pat?"

"Yes, thank you," he managed while running to the kitchen to get his treat.

"Not working today?" I asked.

"No, I only work three days a week through the summer, and a couple evenings down at the clinic. You got me on my day off. How's the case coming?"

"Oh, it's going. Got another one. Been real busy. Hey, do you think you could watch Bud for a while," I asked, changing the topic unexpectedly and catching her off guard. "I've got to follow up a few leads and Suzy doesn't want me taking him on the job. Can you keep an eye on him? I'll be back by four."

"I don't know," she said, hesitantly. "I'm really not good with kids. I'm not sure I can handle him in the chair and all."

"What do you mean you're not good with kids? You're a social worker, aren't you? He's no trouble, really. He sits and watches TV all day. Just put one of your VCRs on and let the boob-tube babysit him. That's what my parents did."

"Yeah, and look how you turned out."

"Please, I promise I'll make it up to you."

I could tell she was nervous about watching him, but knew she would enjoy the company. She reluctantly agreed. I gave him last minute instructions, then left him eating cookies and playing with one of Pat's three cats. I kept my fingers crossed that everything would be OK.

I had talked to Grace McKenna earlier that day to get the names and phone numbers of some of the people who had worked for her father. I confirmed the fact that I could find no obvious reason for her father committing suicide. The farm was doing well. Her parents were in good health. There was nothing to indicate the types of problems that would lead a person to consider ending it all. She told me her mom and dad got along well and seldom argued. When they did, they always made up before going to bed.

"Dad never would have done a thing like that. Never!" she said as I hung up.

McKenna had half a dozen hands working for him at the farm when he died. Grace had the numbers and addresses for three of them. Only one of them, a Sam Zimmerman, was still in the area. The others had already left in search of employment. Bobby had laid them all off the day of his parents' funeral.

Sam Zimmerman lived in a small white house out on the Bob Moffit Road, not far from the McKenna farm. In his mid-sixties, he had worked for McKenna for over twenty-five years. I found him sitting on the front porch of his simple dwelling, watching the cars go by. He was sipping cheap wine from a juice glass, despite the rain and chill of the day. I could tell it wasn't juice by the half-empty bottle sitting on the railing and his red, blood-shot eyes. I could tell it was cheap by the label and his breath.

"Hello, Mister Zimmerman," I said as I came up the steps. "Thank you for seeing me."

"You said you wanted to ask me some questions about the McKennas?"

"Yes, as a matter of fact, his daughter Grace has hired me to find out what really happened to her parents. She asked me to help make some sense out of this terrible tragedy."

He didn't offer me any of what he was drinking, but took a sip and looked at me with watery eyes.

"I just can't believe it," he said, sadly. "I can't believe they're gone like that."

"I know," I said. "It must have been quite a shock. How long did you work for him?"

82

"Over twenty-five years, ever since I got out of the Air Force back in seventy-five."

"What'd you do at the farm?"

"I was his headman, his foreman. I ran the day to day operations. I worked myself up from a hired hand. Bill took good care of me, especially when my wife, Kate, died. They treated me like one of the family. God, I just can't believe they're gone."

"Do you know any reason he would want to take his own life like that? I mean to kill his wife too?"

"Nah, it just doesn't make any sense at all. Why, he was looking forward to getting all the crops planted. He didn't have a depressed day in his life, him or the missus."

"How well did you know them?"

"Like I said, they treated me like family. I ate dinner there almost every night since the missus died, four years ago."

"Have the police questioned you?"

"No," he said, and spat in a can. "Not one damn cop has come talk to me, and I've got plenty to tell them."

"Oh, like what?"

"Well, for starters what a bastard Bill's kid is. That son-of-a-bitchin bastard fired me the day of the funeral. Fired the whole bunch of us who'd been working for his father. Hardly gave us a week's salary. I'd sue the bastard if I had the money. Don't know what I'm going to do now. Most of the others have left town looking for work, but I'm too old to go traipsing 'round the country."

"Did Bobby and his father get along?" I asked, following up on what Grace had told me.

"No, they argued all the time. The kid wanted his father to do more experimenting. He wasn't interested in the business part of it. He didn't want any part of hard work. Shit, he didn't do squat around the farm to help, just doted on his stupid fruit trees. They used to go at it pretty hard sometimes. Bill used to get worked up something awful. A couple of times there I thought they'd come to blows, but Bobby always left the house before things got violent."

"Who's working there now, do you know? I drove past there the other day and there were a bunch of men digging up the place. Did he hire new men?"

"Yeah, I suppose. They're not from around here, though. A bunch of foreigners as far as I can tell. Speak some gibberish. Sure isn't English. Spics more than likely."

Sam Zimmerman couldn't tell me much more, except that Bobby was letting the place go to pot. He gave me an ear full of alcohol-fueled bitterness and resentment, but I had enough of that of my own.

I glanced at my watch as I drove back into town. It was twenty after four. I ran a few lights as I made my way across town to my cousin's, arriving half-past the hour. I knew things were bad when I crossed from the elevator to Pat's apartment and saw the look of desperation on her face, talk about bitterness and resentment. I could hear Little Bud wailing in the background.

"Is everything OK," I said with concern. She was almost in tears herself.

"No, everything is not OK," she said over Bud's insistent squeals. "He's been crying since you left."

"What's wrong? Is he sick?" I said in alarm.

"Oh, he's fine. I'm the one who's going to need medical assistance."

"What's the matter, little guy?" I said, picking him up from the floor, where he sat surrounded by books and magazines and anything else Pat could think of to give him to shut him up. My cousin's usual well-kept apartment looked like a miniature tornado had blown through it. "You not feeling well? Got a tummy ache? Poor little guy."

I carried him around the room on my shoulders. My attention and a familiar face seemed to calm him down a bit. After a few more soothing words, he settled down and closed his eyes. I apologized profusely to my cousin and thanked her for her help. I left the apartment feeling both guilty and annoyed at the same time. Why couldn't things go right for a change? Why did the simplest little things get fucked up? It was bad enough my relationship with Suzy was on the rocks. Now my cousin wasn't speaking to me. I knew she'd recover without too much trouble. I had a feeling that would be the least of my worries before this whole thing was finished.

As I was putting Bud in his kiddy seat, I noticed the doors of a vehicle parked across the street open. Two men got out and walked toward me. I circled in front of my car and met them beside the road. It was Omar from the other karate school and his tall black belt.

"What do you want?" I asked. "I don't want any trouble. I've got my kid in the car."

I noticed that Omar's henchman had a tire iron in his hand.

"I want to kick the shit out of you, douche-bag," he said as he came at me.

He threw a quick left hook at my head. I was ready for him and faster than he was. Evading the punch, I threw a stiff left jab of my own. It snapped his head back. I followed with a hard right, and then a left, the old one-two punch. I have to hand it to him. He didn't go down, but he was rocked. He staggered back across the road.

At the same time, his friend rushed me with the tire iron raised over his head. I stepped into him with a thrust kick that stopped him dead. Then I grabbed his arm with my left and brought my right arm over his. Locking his limb at the elbow, I applied upward pressure with my right, snapping my left down on his lower forearm. The bone at the joint snapped with a crack. He yelped and fell to the ground, writhing in pain as he held his broken appendage.

Omar ran over. I thought he was going to try and attack me again. Instead, he held his arms up and went to his friend.

"You broke his arm," he yelled.

"He tried to crack my skull. What did you expect?"

I made a threatening move toward him. He put his hands up in submission.

"No, please, let me help him."

"You have a lot of nerve coming at me like that. You're both lucky I didn't kill you."

"No, I'm sorry. It's my fault. Don't hurt him anymore. We won't bother you again."

"Get him and get out of here. It better end here or there will be hell to pay. You understand?"

"Yes, sir," he said, dragging his buddy away.

I hoped it was the last I'd hear from them. I had enough trouble without worrying about these 'strokers'.

"You better get that cut on your cheek looked at," I told him as he got back into his car. "You may need stitches."

It was a good thing they were both so inept. It was like they had never had any training. They came at me like street punks. If they had been any good they would have been a lot more trouble.

I jumped in my car and drove off slowly. Little Bud asked me what I was doing. I told him those were two of my students and I was giving them a lesson, which wasn't too far from the truth.

# Chapter 11

I contemplated going to the police and pressing charges against Omar and his partner, but thought better of it. Again, it was my word against theirs, and again, I was the one doing the assaulting. In any case, I didn't want to be distracted from what I had to do.

After dropping Bud off, I decided to do some moonlighting, see what my friend William Riley was up to. The moon was covered by thick gray clouds. I was pumped after my confrontation, and figured I'd put all that adrenaline to good use instead of arguing with Suzy or the cops. If Riley was up to something, tonight would be a good time for it.

I told Suzy I had a lead I had to follow and not to wait up. She told me to be careful, and looked at me with a combination of worry and suspicion. It broke my heart, but I had a job to do. I had to earn my thirty dollars an hour. I got back in the car and drove west out of town toward the mountains

It was a little after ten by the time I got to Riley's place. I parked the car a short distance up the street from his trailer and waited. The rain had picked up. The wind whipped it against my windshield as I sat watching his front door. His car was in the drive and there were lights on inside. I planned to stay a couple hours and see what happened.

To catch a criminal it helps to think like one. It's something I've always been good at. I don't know, maybe I'm really no different than they are, just a little luckier. You know, there but for the grace of God. I could put myself in their heads, and tonight seemed like a good night to howl under the cover of the moonless, wet, windy sky.

It was half-past eleven when he left the house. I had been sitting there about an hour and a half and was just about to leave. He ran to his car, backed out of the drive, and sped down the road as if he was in a hurry. I waited until he had turned the corner leading out of the park before starting my car. I followed with the lights off. He was just turning right onto the main highway when I reached the end of his street. I followed at a leisurely distance, popping on my low-beams.

We drove about twenty minutes down the highway south, passed fields and farms, to a small intersection lit by a yellow flashing light and a convenience store's fluorescent sign. It was ten to twelve. He parked his car along the side of the building and went in. I pulled across the street and waited. I had doused the lights. It was still raining hard, the visibility low. There were no other cars in the parking lot.

It was probably nothing, just a late night run to the store for cigarettes. He must have gotten there just before closing, because shortly after he went in the fluorescent sign in front of the store went out. The tiny intersection was cast in shadow. Someone must be in a hurry to close up. They didn't even wait for the last customer to leave. A short time later, Riley came out of the store. He wasn't alone.

He carried a paper bag in one arm. For some reason it didn't look like groceries. He held his .357 in the other hand. It was pointed at the head of the young woman that walked in front of him. They got into his car and drove off. His lights flashed over my Toyota as he left the parking lot and sped down the highway. For a moment I was afraid he had seen me, but with the wind and rain, he apparently hadn't noticed. He had his hands full. I waited until he was out of sight before starting the engine. I had a pretty good idea where he was going.

Did I just witness an armed robbery and kidnapping? It sure looked like it. Wouldn't you know, I saw the whole damn thing? Call it dumb luck. Call it intuition. Call it what you like, but I had just caught Mister William Riley red-handed, committing a double felony. Now all I had to do was figure out what to do about it.

Unlike most of my fellow citizens I did not have a cell phone. It wasn't that I couldn't afford one. OK, it was partly that, but mostly I just didn't believe in them. I mean, what was so damn important you couldn't leave a message? What was so critical that I had to be connected to a phone every frigging minute? No, if someone wanted to get in touch with me they could call my answering machine. I'd get it soon enough. It wasn't until that night that I actually wished I owned one so I could call the cops and summon help. I guess I could have stopped at a pay phone. For some reason I felt it was important that I kept them in sight, as if someone's life depended on it.

As I followed discreetly, I tried to decide what to do. I figured he'd head back to his trailer, at which point I could call the Staties, but I wanted to keep an eye on him just in case I was wrong. If he got away, another victim might be added to the list of the dead. I didn't want it to happen on my watch. Once was enough. I had to try and help her, but how?

We were almost at his place. I was having second thoughts about taking on an armed man alone. To my surprise, he drove past the turn-off to his trailer park and continued down the road. I followed about a quarter of a mile behind. At the intersection with the main highway back to the 'burgh', he turned left and headed west toward the mountains.

I hadn't been up this road in years, not since those fateful days a decade ago. Back then I had driven up in pursuit of answers to a couple of grisly murders. Now I was following an armed maniac. For all I knew he had more homicide on his mind. I had to find some way to call for help. I felt utterly alone.

I picked up speed as we drove into the hills. I was no longer worried about whether he saw me or not. The long incline we were moving up was a perfect speed trap, but there were no police cars in sight. Where's a cop when you need one?

The road twisted and turned as it followed the contour of the mountainside. At times I'd lose him, only to see his taillights several turns ahead. Past dead-man's curve we drove, where Barry Davids, the crooked prison counselor, went over those many years ago. He would have done better to let me take him in. Hopefully, this little escapade would turn out more fortunately.

The road started to level off. We were on a broad plateau, on the highway heading toward the Canadian border thirty miles away. After a short time, he turned off the highway onto a side road leading to a bowl-shaped lake. I knew this area well. We came up here often with my parents when we were kids. My old friend, John Rothburg, used to work at the observatory on the top of a nearby Mountain. John was long gone, moving on to bigger and better things. I could have used his help right now, if for nothing else than to get me high.

I was starting to get a bad feeling about this, as if the feeling I already had wasn't bad enough. He could only have one thing in mind out here at this time of night. It wasn't June yet. Most of the camps and cottages hadn't opened up for the summer. There was still snow in some deep places in the woods. There wouldn't be anyone up here but rutting deer and hungry bears. I drove past the side road a few hundred yards then doubled back. Slowing down to a crawl, I approached the cut off.

Turning off the highway, I drove down the narrow tarmac lane, looking left and right for any sign of Riley's car. It was as dark as a cave. The rain had stopped at some point while I had been following them. I hardly noticed. The wind continued to howl and blow the branches of the trees about like whips.

There was another road, even smaller and more pitted than the one I was on. It forked off to the right, toward the summer cottages and camps that dotted this side of the lake. Instinctively, I turned and followed it. I hadn't been down here in years, not since my dad used to take us to the lake to go swimming at the small public beach over thirty years before.

I passed cabins and camps I still recognized from those times, although I couldn't have been more than six or seven. I still dreamt about the place. As the road ran down a slope to the lakeshore and the beach, I cut the lights and let the car coast to a stop beside a stone beach house. This guy seemed to have a penchant for beaches. It figured he would come here to do the deed. I tried to calm my breathing. I only hoped I wasn't too late.

I could see the light gray of the sand a few hundred feet away in the darkness. Beyond that, the darker gray of the rippling water lapped the shore. His car was parked just at the edge of the beach, its motor off.

I peered left and right for any sign of Riley. There was no one in sight. All was quiet save for the rustling of the trees in the wind. Cautiously, I got out of the car, listening for the slightest sound or movement.

I did not have a weapon. I didn't believe in guns – more apt to be used on some family member than a real criminal. My samurai swords were hanging on the wall of the dojo, relegated to demonstrations and ceremonies. I had not used them in anger since that day ten years ago when my life depended on it. I felt naked now without them.

I stole down to the beach, crouching in the shadows in case he was there somewhere hiding in the darkness. Reaching the edge of a stone pier, only feet from the water, I scanned the small patch of wet sand for any sign of the kidnapper and his victim. No one was in sight, no maniac with a knife, no body spread-eagled on the beach, much to my relief. There was still plenty of time for that, however. I had to act fast.

The place had seemed much larger when I was a kid, covered with blankets and wall-to-wall bathers. There were no bathers now, not a soul under the single lamp and its pale white light.

I was making my way back to the car when I noticed a flash of light in the trees to my right. It was where the land jutted out into the lake, beyond the far edge of the beach. I remembered that there was a long drive snaking through the trees to a number of small cabins right at the water's edge. I ran down the road toward the driveway entrance. The gate was closed. I went around it and down the road to the first camp, passing through a tunnel of overhanging branches. It was dark, but I could see a light through the foliage. It was coming from the last cottage on the drive.

I snuck up to the cabin silently. My heart was beating like Blue-Man Group garbage cans. Peering through the side window into the small cabin, I saw a pine-paneled room. Riley was standing with his back to me over what appeared to be a wooden framed sofa or futon. A naked girl, around nineteen or twenty, lay on the couch, with her hands tied over her head. She was gagged, her eyes wide in terror. Clad only in corduroy pants, Riley held a knife to the young woman's throat. A bag of money and the gun were on the kitchen table behind him. Although the window I was looking through was to his rear, the door which I had to go through was not, and it was the only entrance into the room. The element of surprise was on my side. He wouldn't be expecting company.

I made my way around the front of the building to the door. Not knowing if it was locked or not, I decided to kick it in and rush him. I didn't have any better ideas. The way it looked, by the time I went for help he'd have her carved up as nice as Thanksgiving dinner. No, it was now or never, and I never say never.

When I kicked open the door and rushed into the room, he was teasing the poor girl's nipples with the blade of his knife. I tried to make it to the table and the gun. He kicked a chair in front of me and came at me with his weapon before I was halfway there. There was no time to think, only react. Even though he wasn't particularly good with the knife or trained in the arts, armed as he was, he was more than a serious opponent. I would not get too many mistakes, but then I didn't plan on making many.

Avoiding his rather clumsy knife thrusts, I circled to my left toward the table. Anticipating my move, he went for the gun himself, using the blade to keep me at bay. Standing in a side-stance to expose as little of my body as possible, I hit him in the ribs with a thrust kick as his arm passed harmlessly by me. The blow sent him crashing into the table, knocking it over. The gun fell to the floor, but he kept his feet and came at me before I could get to it.

I grabbed one of the kitchen chairs just as he was on me, and used it to block the thrust. Before he could react, I jammed the legs of the chair into his face. Pushing his head back, I tried to knock the weapon out of his hand at the same time.

He swept the chair aside and slashed at me again with the blade. I blocked it with a sweeping reverse-crescent kick to his wrist, keeping the inside of my leg, where the large artery is, away from the blade. I knocked it up and away, but not out of his hand. Using the chair alternatively as a shield and bludgeon, I backed him up slowly, but was still unable to get to the gun.

In desperation, he made a lunge at me, forcing me backward while he held on to the chair with one hand. Just before we crashed into the wall behind me, I twisted to the left, swinging my adversary into the pine-board siding. He hit it head first. The chair went flying. Before he recovered I delivered a front heel kick to his lower ribs. He grabbed his side with a groan, but held the knife firmly and looked at me menacingly.

"You again!" he bellowed in rage, recognizing me. "What the fuck are you doing here?"

I answered by snapping a front kick up under his chin. It knocked his head back and staggered him. Kicking his knee with my left heel, I quickly grabbed his right wrist, the one with the knife, as I brought my right up to lock his elbow. It was a simple jujitsu move, but very effective when done correctly. It all happened so fast he hardly had time to cry out as I took him to the floor on his face and locked his arm behind him. Instead of dropping the knife, he twisted away, breaking out of the hold. I didn't have the opportunity to figure out what I did wrong. He got back to his feet and slashed my arm. Warm blood started to seep down my sleeve.

I could hear the girl whimpering in the background through the pounding in my ears. I was breathing hard and disoriented. I fought to gain my equilibrium. He was stabbing at me now, with sharp fast jabs, making it hard to catch his arm without getting cut. I backed away and circled the room staying out of reach, while I kicked his legs. Even though he was an untrained opponent, he was good enough, now that he knew what I was capable of, to pose a problem.

I watched for an opening, waiting for him to make a mistake, while I looked for a weapon of my own. Other than the chair, there was nothing in reach that I could see. But then my vision was narrowed. I was a hundred percent focused on the knife. Then I spotted it, standing in the corner by the door just to the right and behind me, the ubiquitous household broom. To me it was half of a bo staff, one of my favorite Chinese weapons.

Grabbing the broom with both hands, I held it handle forward. Countering his moves and parrying the knife strokes, I struck him in the face and throat. I was faster than he was and able to hit him several times, forcing him backward. I easily knocked the knife aside as he tried to stab me, but I couldn't knock it out of his hand. Still, now that I had something to equalize his blade the tide began to turn. One good strike to his trachea would do the trick. Before I could execute it, however, he turned and dove for the gun, which was lying just behind him next to the overturned table.

Forgetting the knife, I dove with him, lunging for the gun with both hands. We got to it at the same time. Now that we were grappling on the floor, my advantage seemed to slip away. He was bigger than I was, and a little stronger, all elbows and fists.

He dropped the knife in the struggle for the gun, which we both held firmly between us. Somehow I ended up beneath him. He bore down on me with his whole bodyweight, slowly turning the barrel of the gun at my face. Only an inch more to the right and I'd be eating lead.

At the last moment, instead of resisting, I went with him. Crossing my wrists and using his force, I brought the gun quickly across my body. He wasn't expecting the move. The gun went off a moment too late, the bullet digging into the wood floor inches from my head. The sound was deafening.

Just as quickly, before he could react to the first move, I grabbed his hand and twisted the gun under him. I'll never forget the look of surprise on his face when the Magnum went off a second time. This time the barrel was aimed at his chest. Riley crumpled on top of me with a sickening moan. All I could hear was a loud ringing in my ears that seemed to go on forever. It drowned out all other sound for some time.

I rolled him off me and stood up, shaken. He lay on his back with unblinking eyes. There was a dark hole in the center of his chest. It wasn't moving despite the recent exertions. It looked like he was dead. Not exactly what I'd had in mind, but at the moment it suited me just fine. Going over and untying the girl, I asked if she was all right. She wasn't. She started screaming hysterically as soon as I took off the gag.

I calmed her down the best I could and helped her put on her torn clothes. There was no phone in the cabin to make a call, and I didn't have any change for the payphone at the beach house. I ended up driving her to the nearest State Police barracks, where I remained all night explaining what had happened while they confirmed my story.

The girl was less than helpful. All she could remember was the end of her harrowing ordeal. She kept repeating that I had shot the other man. Well, that much was obvious. He had a hole in him the size of a silver dollar. She was heavily sedated under the attending physician's orders. An all-points bulletin had been put out for her earlier that evening. Her parents had reported her missing when the store was discovered broken into and deserted, with her purse still on the counter. Even so, they still weren't going to let me go, until I made my one phone call to Jerry. He had me out of there before you could say dipstick, informing them that I was working with him on a serial murder case. He also told them that the person I had killed was more than likely the murderer they had been looking for. It appeared as if I had saved the day.

Later that morning, after repeating my deposition to Jerry at headquarters, I had to face the real interrogator and explain it all to Suzy. I told her I had been watching the suspect and followed him to a convenience store, where he robbed the place and kidnapped the female attendant. I described how I had followed them up into the mountains and came upon him in the process of raping and tormenting the young victim.

"I'm a hero, so cut me some slack, will you," I said in defense. It worked, kind of.

"Oh, Jay, you could have been killed. You have a family now. You can't keep putting yourself in danger like that. You have to consider me and Bud."

"I do. I did, but I couldn't just let that girl get murdered. What was I supposed to do?"

That started her on her pet peeve about all the other things I could be doing with my life, normal things that normal people did to make a living, instead of running around playing James Bond.

"You mean Matt Helm."

"Heh?" she said, confused.

"You mean Matt Helm. James Bond's a British spy, licensed to kill. Matt Helm's a private detective. He's the one who saves all the beautiful kidnapping victims, not James Bond."

"Oh, Jay," she said in exasperation. "Why is everything a joke to you?"

She was still mad at me when we went to bed that evening.

No one wanted to jump to conclusions about the dead Mister Riley. However, everyone involved, including me, considered the case closed and the serial killer brought to justice. The information was kept from the papers for the time being, but it couldn't be kept under wraps for long,

I called Sheila Patterson that evening and told her the news.

"I think we got him," I said, telling her the whole story. "Unfortunately, he was killed during the struggle to save the girl. It couldn't be helped. He won't be hurting anyone again."

She thanked me, but didn't seem particularly pleased. Maybe the news of the death of someone she had known all her life affected her more than she expected. In any case, it was over. I told her I'd send her a final report.

I was feeling pretty good about myself that night, despite the argument with Suzy. I should have known what happens when you get too cocky.

# Interlude

*Something had happened, something strange and mysterious. 'Jim' couldn't have explained it, even if he'd had more than just the raw sensations of an animal mind. Events occurred without rhyme or reason. Something had happened to trigger a tiny spark of recognition. It brought all the pain and suffering of his life back to him like the piercing ray of a laser.*

*He had been walking in the rain and mist, if walking was what you'd call his bent-back, hobbling gait. It was more stalking beast than human. He was circling the lake as was his want when the wind and rain called to him like this, searching for he knew not what. He took comfort in the vaguely familiar surroundings and the cold bite of the air. It cocooned him in its thick mists. It was then that he saw them, the intruders.*

*The first one made much noise, disturbing the peace with his lights and motor. He broke into one of the cabins by the lake. He had someone with him. The second one moved silently, as stealthy as the night, and followed close behind. There was something about this one, something about the way he moved, the way he looked and smelled, something familiar and disturbing.*

*Creeping closer to the house, he watched the struggle mindlessly. He cared not who won or what the outcome might be. He hardly knew what was happening. The naked, tied up girl barely registered on his consciousness. His eyes were riveted on the smaller man. He tried to remember, tried to recall just what it was the slice of mind that remained to him was trying to tug out of its subterranean depths. Then it struck him. An image, a searing series of sensations so real, so immediate, they caused him to retch. He wet himself like a nervous dog. It was him! This was the one that had caused him so much pain and suffering!*

*The sound of the gun frightened him. The second report sent him running into the woods, snapping branches and crashing through foliage. He soon stopped, however, forgetting what he was fleeing from. His mind jumped to the recent past, the present moment all but obliterated. He felt such pleasure, such power! It filled his senses as if he were there again, instead of standing in the woods.*

*He had been making his way back up the highway to his home in the mountains after finding his old companion, 'Jim'. It gleamed in*

95

his hand. Moving silently along the road, he noticed a flash of blonde hair in the moonlight. Someone was standing on the lawn of a house. She appeared to be squatting by a large opened glass door. 'Jim' silently changed course, cutting across the spacious lawn toward the home. Instinctively, he used the trees to hide his bulk from view. As he paused behind the last tree separating him from the girl and the building, she rose and walked unsteadily back toward the door. She never made it.

To 'Jim', thought and memories were like being there. The past and present, dream and reality were all the same to him. Though it was only a memory the moments came flying back to him like a fast streaming movie. But what he experienced was no mere recollection. It was real. He was there.

He rushed the unsuspecting female just as she was at the opening. Before she knew what was happening a hard hand clamped around her mouth. An even harder blade plunged into her spine. Dragging her back out to the yard, he pulled the paralyzed, staring girl by the leg behind a tree. Again and again the knife sank into her soft flesh, like the teeth of a large man-eating cat. Like a man-eater, he licked the blood from the still, dead body.

Then, just as mindlessly, he lifted the corpse under his arm and carried it back toward the city where he had just come from. He brought her to the place his blood had flowed like wine onto the sand, where all could see her, where all would know what 'Jim' had done.

His mind flashed to others, a young couple lying on a blanket making love. They never heard the monster stalking them, its blade trembling in the night.

Suddenly, the present came snapping back to focus and with it a strong urge, the thirst for revenge. It gave focus to what was left of his mind.

As he circled back toward the lone intruder, the thirst for vengeance rose in his gullet like bile. Yes, he would have his retribution. The thought, if that's what it was, made him feel good, like a stimulating drug being pumped into his brain. He felt better than he had in his short, warped memory.

Gripping 'Jim', he held the bowie knife in front of him like an obscene appendage. The thick, curved blade gleamed in the dim moonlight, a physical extension of his hatred for the world.

*Following the lingering scent of his long forgotten adversary, he loped after the car as it sped down the dark lakeside road.*

# Chapter 12

When news of Billy Riley's death eventually came out, linking him with the series of recent murders, the whole town breathed a collective sigh of relief. My name was mentioned in connection with the solving of the case. The details were withheld, however, as was the name of the kidnapped victim on request of her family. When she finally became intelligible again she was able to confirm my story. I was something of a hero around town for helping to save her life. Jerry was even thinking of giving me a citation. I talked him out of it.

"I don't need no stinking medal," I said. "Just give me the reward, amigo."

"There is no reward. I just wish we could find the murder weapon."

"What, didn't any of the knives at Riley's place match up with the wounds on the murder victims?"

"No, not one of them has ever been used for more than whittling wood. Most of them have never left the case."

"What about the knife he had at the cabin? I can attest it's sharp enough." I felt my arm where a large patch covered my injury.

"No, that was just a kitchen knife he must have picked up there. No, none of the knives in Riley's possession match the wounds on the murder victims. It just doesn't add up."

"Oh, I'd say it adds up just fine. The guy kidnaps a girl at gunpoint, rapes her at knifepoint, at a beach no less. If that doesn't add up to our murderer, I didn't get an A in math."

"When did you ever get an A in math?"

"In the fifth grade, I had a real good teacher. It was all downhill from there."

"Well, I'd feel a whole lot better if we could find the murder weapon."

"Yeah, well, you can't have everything. It'll turn up."

"I hope so," he said. "Oh, by the way, you know that fire out at the Potter farm?"

"Yeah, what about it? Find something?"

"You bet. Turns out it was arson, but that's not the strange part. The old guy had almost 600 pounds of fertilizer in that place, ammonia nitrate. There was enough to blow up the whole county. The stuff must have been taken or moved or something. If it had been there when the place burned down, it would have caused a terrible explosion. Nothing of the kind took place."

"You think someone stole the fertilizer, killed the old guy, and burned the place down?"

"You got any better theories?"

"No, not really, but then I haven't really given it much thought. Been kind of busy, if you know what I mean."

I left Jerry and went to the dojo to work out. After my run-in and less than stellar performance against the knife wielding Billy Riley, I thought I could use some practice. Even though the killer was dead, it wouldn't hurt to hone my rusty knife techniques. Maybe I'd even work out with the swords.

I called my black belts before I left the house. Informing them I was holding an advanced workout session, I told them to be there in half an hour. This meant they had to drop whatever they were doing - regardless of what it might be - suit up and be there at the appointed time. Theirs' was not to reason why, but to obey. This is one of the prerogatives of owning a dojo and taking someone from a fat-bellied 'stroker' to a lean, mean fighting black belt. Anyway, they were always after me for more advanced material, which I seldom had the time anymore to teach them. They were more than willing to come.

While I waited, I stretched out and went through some kata, my most advanced forms - codonqua (man fights himself), and Honsuki. I moved around the room with various kicks and hand strikes, simulating the fighting of multiple opponents as they attacked me from different angles. I did the moves with added emphasis and force, visualizing my adversaries as I did so. Finishing the second form with a flourish, I was already sweating and breathing hard.

Mad that I was winded so soon, I grabbed my samurai swords off the wall and went through my double-sword form – double time. Slashing the air around me with a continuous flowing motion that made the blades blur, I twisted and hopped about the room, whipping the swords high, then low. Peter and Roger, my black belts, came in while I was finishing up.

"That's nice," Peter observed. "You going to teach us that?"

"Not today," I answered. I had other things in mind. "We'll work on some knife techniques and semi-kata."

"I thought you said the best defense against a knife is to run," said Roger.

"You aren't always going to be able to get to a weapon. Say you can't find one. Say you don't have time. It's just you and the knife. What are you going to do?"

I had them suit up and stretch out. I started with the basic techniques they already knew, moving on to more advanced moves that were new to them. We used a rubber knife for safety purposes. Progressing on to free-form exercises, I had the attacker circle around the room like a knife fighter on the street would do, concealing the weapon behind them, slashing and jabbing. In this drill, it was much more difficult to execute the technique and not get stabbed. The Aikido moves were the most effective, though more difficult to master. These techniques used the other's momentum against them to redirect their motion and the knife.

At the end of the session I defended against both of them simultaneously, while they attacked me with makeshift knives. Alternately kicking one, I leg-hawked the other off his feet, knocking them about the room pretty well. I had them running into each other and tripping over each other's feet. I kicked the knives out of their hands and threw them over my hip or shoulder when they lunged or came in off balance. Although I got stabbed a few times, I made them pay for each point they scored. Ending the session by holding one in a choke hold, I stomped the floor just inches from his partner's head. They bowed out and thanked me for the great workout. They were both tired and bruised, but much enlightened.

It was a good, hard session, like the kind we used to have when they first got their belts, something we hadn't done for some time. I promised we'd do it again soon.

It felt good to test myself against these two younger guys, who were both well-trained and in good shape. I could hold my own and then some. I was still as fast and strong as I used to be, if not better, with a good eye and quick reflexes. Best of all, I had killer instinct, that intuitive knowledge of how to hurt my adversary. I needed all the confidence I could muster after my encounter that night in the lakeside cabin. I had survived, but just barely, and for a time there I had felt totally inadequate. Had my opponent been trained or a better fighter, it might have been me lying on the floor gaping at the ceiling with unseeing eyes.

I was playing with the group that night at Kali's gourmet restaurant. I changed and headed home. Suzy and her mother were sitting at the kitchen table chatting over a pot of coffee.

"Hi, Mom!" I said as I walked in. "How you feeling? Better?"

"Yes, Jay, thank you. I couldn't sleep for days, but I'm feeling better now. My back was so sore I thought I'd never walk again. It still hurts when I bend over. My doctor says I won't be able to go back to work for a couple of weeks yet."

"Oh, I'm sorry to hear that. As long as you're feeling better. Just don't lift any more bales."

"It's not funny, Jay. Mom wasn't lifting bags of fertilizer for her health. Some guy made her do it."

"He was so rude," volunteered her mother. Now that they were on a roll, I was in for the duration. "What an arrogant man, just because he had on an expensive suite and a fancy gold watch."

"You said he had an accent and a Middle Eastern sounding name, right?" prompted Suzy.

"That's right. He was dark-complexioned and spoke with an accent. Sounded like those terrorists in the movies. His name was Habeeb or Akbar or something."

"Habeeb? That sounds Jewish," I said, thinking it was just as likely a Columbian drug dealer getting fertilizer for his marijuana plants than an Arab terrorist. "You think he was Jewish?"

"Don't be funny, Jay. That wasn't it. It was something like Abdullah. I can't remember. I wonder if it was one of your new students. They're middle easterners."

"Come on now, honey, don't get prejudiced on me. You know their names as well as I do. None of them sound like the names you mentioned. It's not one of my students. What would they want with fertilizer? They're not farmers."

"Maybe they're building a bomb," said Suzy with a look of triumph.

I tried changing the subject.

"Jerry wants to give me a citation for saving that girl and solving the murders in town. This will be great publicity for business."

This was the last thing Suzy wanted to hear, especially the part about the publicity.

"Publicity for what business? Certainly not the agencies!"

"My business, the detective business."

"Jay, I wish you'd quit that. The work's so uncertain and grimy. And this last episode, you could have been killed. That's not exactly the kind of publicity that's going to help down at the agency. It has to stop. I don't know if I can take you going out at all hours of the night doing

God knows what, getting into God knows what kind of trouble, not even knowing if you'll come back or not. It's just not worth it. If you had gone to computer training school like I asked you to, you could have had your own repair business by now."

"Get real! I can just see me fixing f'ing computers."

"Don't be crude, Jay. Tom Phillips has more business than he knows what to do with at his place. The town could use another computer store. I could sure use that kind of knowledge down at the agency."

"Now, just when things are finally getting good, you want me to quit and start a new career, at my age? What, are you crazy?" I was speaking loudly now, practically shouting.

"You don't have to yell. Bud's taking a nap. You'll wake him."

"Well, I don't know what more you want from me. I'm finally starting to make some money, and you want me to take three steps backward. This is a chance to get established in town once and for all. My reputation has never been better. I'm getting calls from all over the county for jobs."

"I want you to quit the detective business. The dojo is fine, a couple of nights a week for a hobby, but this private-eye stuff has got to stop."

I didn't bother answering, but went down to the basement to start loading my drums into the car for the gig.

She followed me down.

"Jay, we've got to talk."

"OK, but not now. I've got to get ready. I'm late. I'll grab a bite on the way to the club."

I was a hero everywhere but where it counted, in the eyes of my woman.

That night, the restaurant and club were packed. In spite of the crowd, I was in a sour mood. My argument with Suzy boded ill for my ongoing investigative activities. For some reason I just couldn't see myself repairing computers. Hell, I couldn't even see myself owning one. Except for a little snooping and grade fixing like John Rothburg used to do, or booking trips and filing claims down at the agencies, what good were they?

"Nice crowd tonight, eh, Jay?" Paul said as we finished the first set.

"Yeah, what happen, someone lose a busload of rich, well-dressed partygoers on their way to Vegas?"

"You ever consider they might have come to hear the band?" offered Denise, getting up from the piano. "Word's getting around. We're starting to attract a following."

I wasn't convinced.

"Probably has something to do with the college commencements this weekend," commented Paul.

"Yeah," I added. "Town's full of parents come to see their little beer-swilling, barely-passing scholars graduate."

"Well, whatever the reason, it's nice to play to a full house," said Denise, heading for the bar and her first drink of the evening.

The good news was the crowd stayed. Better yet, they drank. The place was jumping by the last set. People were dancing to our upbeat numbers. The floor was packed for the slow songs. Too bad I was in a funk, wondering how I was going to placate my wife. I had been trying to ignore it, but it was pretty obvious our marriage was heading for a crisis. We were drifting further apart, not spending any time together and arguing when we did. Each of us was consumed in our own personal world to the exclusion of the other's, while the very thing that should have brought us together, our child, was pulling us further apart.

After the last set, while I was packing up my tubs, Kali invited us to his house for an all-night party with a few of his friends. Denise and Paul wanted to go. I just wanted to get home to bed. I was still not fully recovered from that harrowing night at the lake and felt weak.

Kali's club consists of two long rooms. The first one as you enter is the saloon, with cozy booths along the walls and a rich mahogany-paneled bar in the center. This is where most of Kali's gay patrons congregated. An archway leads to the dining room, where the bandstand and dance floor are situated. It was now after midnight and closing time. We were seated at a table next to the bandstand. A row of windows and booths made up the far side of the room, which looked out onto the street

The place was still mobbed, the room a blur of activity as people walked back and forth. They shouted over each other with their arms raised, holding cigarettes and half-empty drinks. Others rushed about from table to table or from one room to another. We were sitting in a group, talking about the invitation. I looked up for a moment and saw a strange-looking man staring at me through a front window. He looked like a beggar, but deformed in some way. It was only for a moment, only a fleeting glimpse. My view was half blocked by the intervening crowd. It was there one minute, gone the next, swallowed up by the throng and movement outside as a rush of partygoers swept by.

I looked down at my drink then up again, and the image was gone. In the split moment I had seen it, I had the distinct impression of hostile intent. It's like the feeling you get across a crowded room when someone's staring at you. It's instinctive, honed by millions of years of living together in caves and cities. You can tell in an instant whether a look is hostile or friendly. A second later, after whoever it was had gone, I got goose bumps, in a kind of delayed reaction. I wasn't even sure I had actually seen anyone, or what it was I had seen. Was it real or just a shadowy figment of my imagination?

"Well, are you coming to the party or not?" asked Denise, apparently for the second time.

"I don't think so. I'm still not feeling all that great. I think I'll just go home to bed."

"I can't believe it. The great macho man is turning in already," chimed in her husband.

"Hey, I don't have your constitution, Mister Destructo."

Paul was on his fifth martini of the evening. I on the other hand still had two untouched screwdrivers on the bandstand bought by well-meaning customers, and was more than feeling the two I had already imbibed. Denise and Paul were just getting started. They made me look like an amateur as far as booze was concerned, and I was far from a beginner where booze was concerned. That had been years ago, however. I paid dearly now for every binge, one way or another. I knew my limits and I had reached them that evening, so I passed on the party. Denise and Paul decided to go, and left with a group of partygoers.

I drove home dejected, depressed at finding myself alone after being among friends and revelers all night. I was in a kind of anticlimactic funk. The house was dark when I arrived. Despite all my efforts at being quiet I woke Suzy up carrying the trap-case full of clanking cymbals and hardware downstairs to the basement. She was waiting for me in the kitchen when I came back up.

"We have to talk, Jay," she said.

"It's late Suzy. It's been a long day and an even longer night. Now's not the time. I'm tired and I'm really not feeling well."

104

"That's just the problem, Jay. It's never the right time. There's always some reason why we can't talk."

"Look, Honey, there's nothing to talk about. I'm not going to give up the detective agency to take a course in computer repair. I'm going to do what I've always done, what I've been trained to do, what I know how to do to make a living. It's not like we live in a big dangerous city. This is the 'burgh'. Nothing happens here."

"What do you call what just happened to you? What about all the murders? Why do you have to get involved in all that business?"

"Because that's when people need me the most. That's when I can make the most money. Most guys can't handle that kind of heat."

"And you can, right mister macho man? That's the problem. You putting yourself in danger endangers your family too."

"How's that?" I asked. "Who do you think can protect you better than I can? Anyway, it's over. Everything will be back to normal. Except now people will call *me* when they need help."

"Oh, Jay, you're, you're…"

"What, incorrigible? Is that the word you're looking for?"

"Yes, and if you're not willing to change for your family than perhaps you don't deserve to have one."

"What's that supposed to mean?" I yelled, totally upset now. I hadn't wanted to talk. I hadn't wanted to argue. I had warned her I was sick and tired and now wasn't a good time, but she persisted in her rant. Now it was my turn.

"You want to leave? Now that things are finally getting good? It's not like I'm some deadbeat. I've been doing my best. I'm doing my share. I don't mind hard work, I just want to do it on my own terms, do what I'm good at. Is that too much to ask? Now you're threatening to leave me? Listen to yourself."

"I can't take it any more," she said, now in tears. My heart broke at the sight of salt water dripping down her pretty cheeks. "I don't want to go through that again, knowing how close you came to getting yourself killed like all those others. You're like a moth to a flame, always heading for danger when most people do their best to avoid it. You've got some sort of death wish and Bud and I are not going to share it. You either have to quit the detective business or I'm leaving."

"And where are you going to go, to your mother's? She doesn't have room for you and Bud."

"Then we'll stay here and you can go."

"Fine," I said, getting up and grabbing my jacket. I didn't even bother packing my things as I walked out of the house and slammed the door. It wasn't until I was in the car, idling in the driveway that I realized I had no place to go.

# Chapter 13

That night I walked out was the lowest point in my Dead Sea life. I felt that my life was over. All that was worth living for was back in that apartment. Yet I couldn't turn around and go back. I couldn't live a lie no matter how much it hurt to leave. I couldn't pretend to be happy if I wasn't, and if I wasn't happy, there was little chance anyone around me would be.

The first person I thought of was my old man. I hadn't seen him all spring, since I helped him take his snow tires off the truck. You might find it odd, living in a small town and not seeing your father in months, but I avoided him as much as possible. It's not that I disliked him or anything. I just found it difficult to stomach the fact that he married my old girlfriend, Mary, the town's only female mortician.

It wouldn't have been so bad if I hadn't had such wild, dirty sex with her. The thought of her doing those things to my pop was a bit hard to bear, so I tried not to subject myself. Oh, Suzy would take Bud over from time to time to see Granddad, and I helped him when he asked. For the rest of the time I pretty much avoided them. Now, late at night with no place to go, all I could think about was the warmth of my childhood home.

The house was dark when I drove up a little before 2:00 a.m. I tried the door, but it was locked. Too caught up in my own misery and self-pity to worry about anyone else's discomfort, I knocked and rang the bell, calling out as I did so.

"Dad, Dad! It's me, Jay. Dad, are you there? Let me in! Dad?"

After a few minutes the front light came on and the door opened.

"Jay? Is that you?" he inquired, squinting at me through the crack in the door. "What's the matter? It's two o'clock in the morning, for Christ's sake!"

"Suzy threw me out. We had a fight. She wants to leave."

"What? What brought this on?"

"You going to invite me in? I need a place to stay for the night."

He hesitated for a moment. Then he came out, wrapping his bathrobe tighter around him.

"You having problems at home?" he asked, sitting down on the front steps. I remained standing, a bit annoyed he hadn't invited me in. "What is it, the karate school or the working in nightclubs and bars? Or is it the fact that you don't have a steady income starting to bother her? Don't tell me she doesn't like you staying out all night snooping on cheating husbands and getting shot at?"

Dad always had a way of summing things up.

"How do you know about that?"

I hadn't talked to him about the case. As far as I knew, he didn't know anything about my involvement. Although my name had been in the paper, there was nothing about me almost getting shot.

"Oh, I have my sources. You don't think I'd read about you working on a murder investigation without finding out what really happened. You were lucky you didn't get your brains blown out. But you were always pretty good at that, falling in shit and coming up smelling like roses." This was one of his favorite sayings. I grew up listening to him pronounce it like the holy gospel whenever one of us kids got away with something.

"And for what?" he continued. "Where have all your hobbies gotten you? Now Suzy wants to leave you. Well, I'm not surprised."

"Thanks for all the support!" I yelled. I should have known better than to go there for help when I hadn't said two words to him in months and those not particularly friendly. I expected a little more sympathy than what I was getting, however. "I'll tell you what I'm doing it for, thirty bucks an hour. How else am I going to make that kind of money around here? I don't exactly have a lot of marketable skills, and I'm kind of old to start acquiring them now, especially things I'm not interested in like goddamned computers."

"You could have had a great career with the FBI instead of wasting your time playing private eye. But you had to go and smoke pot at a party."

I should have known not to wake him. It was late and at that moment I realized how old and frail he was. He hadn't thrown that fiasco in my face in years. Ten years to be exact, and he still didn't have the story right.

"Sorry, Dad," I said, helping him up. "You don't want to catch a chill. Why don't you go back to bed. You're right. What was I thinking? Don't worry, everything is all right. I'll get a room at a motel. Thanks for listening. Sorry to wake you."

As I drove off, I could see him in the doorway shaking his head. Mary had woken and was standing behind him, probably asking him who it was at that time of night. They'd probably have sex now that they were up. The thought made me even more depressed. Then in a stroke of inspiration, I remembered Kali's party. It was just two. With any luck at all, it would still be going strong by the time I got there.

I drove back through town toward the street where the club was located. It was closed when I drove by. All the lights were off, the streets deserted. Keeping right at the end of the block, I went over the little bridge spanning the river where it empties into the bay. From there I followed the road to the more expensive area of the city, where Kali's house was located, along the waterfront.

Pulling into Kali's driveway, through an impressive wrought-iron gate, I parked behind the last of an even half-dozen cars. The party was still in progress, although it looked like things were winding down. All the lights in the place were on, but there was no music playing or loud talking as one would expect at one of Kali's bashes. Everything was quiet, almost too quiet. I could hear crickets chirping in the thickets and the rush of waves onto the rocky shore just behind the house.

I walked up to the front door and rang the bell. When no one answered after a few seconds, I knocked and rang again. Still no answer, I decided to walk around to the back of the house. Maybe they were all out there.

Circling around the drive, I came to a patch of grass running along the side of the house. A tall hedge separated Kali's place from the adjoining property. It was dark. The hedge cast a shadow and blocked out most of the light. Groping my way blindly to the rear of the building, I tripped over something before I had gone halfway. It felt like a bag of dirt or woodchips, low, heavy, and unyielding. Not bothering to check what it was, I continued on, calling out as I did so.

"Hello! Hi, it's me, Jay. Where is everyone?"

No one answered. All I could hear was the sound of waves washing up to the shore a few yards away in the darkness. I could just make out a form lying in a splash of light flooding from the large rear windows of the house. If my senses were not deceiving me, I was looking at a prone human figure. It was oddly out of place, unless this was a sleep-in, which I doubted. Then I had a sickening realization. From the way it was lying, arms akimbo, head tilted, it was a dead body. I was then struck by the further realization that the thing I had tripped over in the dark at the side of the house was probably a dead body as well.

Suddenly, the ground seemed to give in around me. I felt I was being swallowed in a deep abyss. I found it impossible to breathe. For a long moment I didn't know where I was or who. I was transported back in time to a rainy night long ago that hadn't seemed real then either. Had I fallen asleep and waken up in a dream? No, I wasn't dreaming. I didn't have to pinch myself to know that this was real.

I forced myself to take a breath. My breathing came back to me in short rapid pants. I forced my mind back to the here and now. For a moment, however, I thought I might never come back to reality. Instinctively, I got into a crouching stance, ready for action. Fighting to control my breathing, I attempted to use the flush of adrenaline to steel my nerve and pump up my strength.

I thought of running back to my car and going for aid, but there was always the chance there was someone inside that needed help. Then I had a chilling thought that made the need for action even more urgent. My friends, Paul and Denise, were at that party. They may still be inside. I didn't hesitate or consider consequences. I became the moment. Each sense was attuned to its surroundings. I scanned the area, listening for the slightest sound. Smelling death in the air, I ran rapidly to the rear door and peered inside. I was instantly sorry.

There, lying on her stomach just visible on the stone floor was a partially naked woman, covered with blood. I realized I should have called for help, but there was no going back now. There could have been a gang of knife-wielding maniacs beyond that room, but I was committed. Actually, I should have been committed for going on.

I entered the house and moved through the room, trying to avoid the sight of the dead woman on the floor. I was sure she was someone I had seen earlier that night wiggling her ass on the dance floor. She wouldn't be wiggling it any more.

As I passed through the building, I searched for a weapon of some sort. Grabbing a poker from the fire place, I whipped it around in front of me in a figure-eight pattern to get the feel of it. I had used one once before to good effect.

There was another body lying by the sofa in the living room. A young, bearded male lay on his back, his eyes staring at the ceiling. Blood covered his chest. He looked surprised. I spun around quickly expecting the killer to come at me any moment from behind some door or chair. The stairway loomed before me dark and threatening.

Suddenly, I panicked and ran toward the front door, wanting nothing more than to get out of that death-house. I had never been particular claustrophobic, but at that moment I felt like I was in a coffin cramped with bodies. I almost tripped over another male lying on his side, one armed raised over his head as if pointing to the door.

There was a grimace on face. His throat had been slit. Then I heard the sirens.

I had been at the police station, in an interrogation room, about an hour before Jerry finally came in. I didn't give him a chance to ask any questions.

"I want to lodge a complaint," I told him as soon as he sat down across from me.

"We find you at a multiple homicide and you want to lodge a complaint?"

"You know as well as I do I had nothing to do with that. Yet your boys drew their guns on me, even after they knew who I was. I was handcuffed, still at gunpoint, brought down here and thrown in a holding cell for an hour. I've been deprived of my rights. The way those cops were looking at me you'd think I had the freaking plague."

"Well, Jay, what do you expect? We get a call about a maniac slicing people up at a party and when we arrive, who do you think answers the door but you."

"I'm thinking of suing. What have you found out?" I asked, changing the subject.

"Hold it, Jay. Suppose you tell me what happened. What were you doing there? Did you see anything?"

"No. I went home early and ended up having a little spat with Suzy. Figured I'd cool off and see if the party was still going. Kali invited the band. I showed up around two. No one answered the front door, so I went around back and discovered the bodies. I was making my way out of the place when you guys showed up. Now tell me what you know. Are Paul and Denise OK?

"They weren't among the dead if that's what you mean."

"Good, they must have left early. Maybe they decided not to go. I'll have to call them as soon as I get out of here. How many were killed. I saw at least five, two outside and three inside. Jesus, five!"

"Try eight. There were two more upstairs and one in the basement. He must have run there to hide."

"What about Kali?"

"Oh, he's OK. He was hiding with some friends in a paneled room behind his bedroom closet, sort of a panic room, I guess. I won't tell you what we found in there. Suffice it to say, Kali has some very kinky habits and a bit of explaining to do."

"You're right. I don't want to know."

111

We sat in silence for a moment, staring at each other across the table with expressions that said it all.

"It's happening again, Jay," he said finally.

"It can't be. That's over - ancient history."

"Then who is it? No clues. No evidence. No motives. Multiple homicides. A single killer with a knife. It sure does fit the MO."

"Kali must have some enemies. Did anyone see anything? What did he say?"

"No one saw anything. A few of the guests got away, apparently escaping during the melee. One made it all the way to the police station halfway across town. Kali and his friends were pretty much hysterical, reverting to their native tongues under the stress. But even the English speaking witnesses don't make much sense. Best I can make out the killing began outside on the lawn, then moved from there inside to the rear rooms. By the time anyone knew what was going on it was too late. Only three, besides Kali and the two with him, made it out alive. They somehow managed to crawl into the hidden room unseen. Other than that, everyone was killed."

"Jesus! Just like on the yacht. How many were there back then, seven?"

"Yeah, that's about right. This guy's no amateur. If it isn't the same person, it's the same type of person, just as dangerous, just as sick. You didn't see anything?"

"No, Jerry. To tell you the truth all I was trying to do was get the hell out of there. If I'd a seen him, I probably would have run."

"That would have been the smart thing to do."

# Chapter 14

It was almost five a.m. by the time I left the station. A pale glimmer of light was beginning to shine in the sky above the peaks in Vermont. Still not having a place to crash, I called my cousin Pat.

"Hi, Pat," I said when she finally answered the phone after about the tenth ring. Her voice was garbled and barely audible.

"Jay, is that you? It's not even five a.m. yet. Is everything all right?"

"Yeah, sure, I, ah, I was just wondering if I could crash there this morning. I've been up all night. There was another murder. It was pretty bad. I'll tell you all about it. And, well, I can't really go home at the moment. Suzy's upset about my working on the case. It looks like that William Riley guy wasn't our man after all."

"Gosh, Jay, that's terrible. Why don't you come over. I'll put a pot of coffee on. I'd be getting up in another hour anyway."

I thanked her and hung up, arriving at her apartment ten minutes later. The coffee was just brewing. The light of the sun had not quite filtered down into the valley yet.

"What's all this about another murder?" she asked as soon as we sat down with our cups at the kitchen table.

"Last night, out at Kali's place. You know, the guy who owns Lilly's down on River Street. There was a party at his house. Someone broke in and killed eight of the guests with a large knife."

"Oh, my God!" she exclaimed. She was a little young to know much about the events of ten years ago, but had read about it in the paper. It must have made an impression. "Sounds like those killings back in the late eighties."

"Yeah, that's what Jerry LaGrande said."

"You were involved in that, weren't you?"

"No," I lied. "Not, really."

"And you're involved in this recent thing?"

"I found the bodies!"

"Oh my God!"

"After Suzy kicked me out, I went there to blow off some steam. I tripped over one of them. Erg!"

"Suzy kicked you out?" Suddenly the multiple homicides seemed less interesting than the family soap opera that had appeared. "What did you do, Jay?"

"Nothing! Why do you assume it was my fault? I'm just doing what I've always done. Things are finally starting to go good and all she does is complain."

"Maybe the fact that you almost got yourself killed has something to do with it."

"It has everything to do with it, but I can take care of myself. It's the cost of doing business. If I want to make it in the profession, I've got to show I can handle myself in a pinch. I think I've done that."

"Listen to you, Dirty Harry. You ever think of how it must have affected Suzy? You have a family to think of now, Jay."

"You think I don't know that? It's my family I'm trying to provide for."

"Well, then you better write yourself a good insurance policy, because you're liable to need it in the line of work you're in."

I didn't answer.

"You think I can take a nap here for a couple of hours? I haven't slept since the night before last, and that wasn't that restful. I'm bushed."

"Sure, Jay, you can sleep on the couch. I wouldn't mind a few more winks myself."

The two cups of coffee I drank didn't seem to have any effect. I was asleep before Pat covered me with one of her spare blankets.

I woke up a few hours later slightly disoriented. I lay on the couch slowly shaking off the cobwebs, and thought about the recent murders. It appeared the murderer was still at large. Riley's abduction and attempted rape of that young woman was just a tragic coincidence. I was having trouble getting my mind around this thought. I didn't want to admit that the wrong person had been killed, and that I had killed him. The realization made me ill. I sat up feeling nauseous. It passed when I remembered what he had been about to do.

Pat was sitting at the table. The smell of toast filled the room.

"Want some breakfast?" she asked. It was almost noon. "I though you'd sleep all morning."

"I guess I did. What I would really love now is a shower," I told her.

"Sure, I'll get you a towel."

After showering, I had a quick breakfast. While spooning some scrambled eggs into my plate, Pat mentioned a bit of the local gossip she had picked up around town concerning Bobby McKenna.

"The local farmers here seem to be having a problem getting enough fertilizer for their spring planting. Seems all the high-grade stuff has been stolen or bought up. They're all using manure, which has also become scarce."

"Please, not while I'm eating."

"Some detective! Don't you think it's kind of strange?"

"Yeah, Jerry mentioned something about it in connection with the Potter fire out on Beekertown Road. He told me the place should have blown sky high due to all the ammonia sulfate he had there, but nothing like that took place. It had all been removed. Only trouble is, no one knows where it is

"Yeah, there have been a number of thefts of fertilizer around the county," Pat confirmed. "The biggest one was out at the Agricultural Training Center. Every single wholesaler and retailer has been bought out, as well."

"I heard about that theft on the radio. Almost 800 pounds, wasn't it? And the other day, some guy in a suit bought all of the fertilizer at Wal-Mart and made Suzy's mom put it in his truck. She hurt her back."

"Yeah, I remember you telling me about it, but wait, that's not all. Your friend McKenna seems to have plenty of manure available for sale."

"Doesn't he need it for his own planting?"

"Doesn't seem to, doesn't seem to be doing any planting by the sound of it, at least that's what they're saying down at the Grange Hall."

"Hmm, interesting. I'll have to look into it. So what do you think is going on? You think Bobby's trying to corner the fertilizer market?"

"Could be, but there's other things you can do with that besides fertilizing crops, you know."

"What, like Timothy McVeigh?"

"Yes, for starters."

I hadn't thought of it before. I had to admit, the whole thing sounded fishy, and not in a kosher kind of way. Pat started me thinking. Whatever was going on, Bobby McKenna seemed to be involved in more than a casual way.

Later that day I called Paul and Denise from the office to see if they were OK. It was Sunday. News of the murders had been splashed across the front page of every paper in town, all three of them. There was also a story about the curious scarcity of fertilizer threatening the spring planting season. Emergency shipments were being sent up from Albany and from across the lake in Burlington.

Paul answered the phone.

"Hear about the murders?" he asked as soon as he recognized my voice.

"Yeah, I found the bodies."

"No way! We must have left just before it happened! If Denise hadn't had a headache, it might have been us."

"God forbid. I'm just glad to hear you're both all right. It was pretty bad."

"You saw it? You were there?"

"Yeah, but there's not much to tell. It was all over by the time I got there. I was just leaving to get help when the cops came. I really didn't see much. There were a few bodies lying on the grounds and in some of the rooms. Not very nice. I didn't really get too close. I was too focused on staying alive myself. The guy could have still been there."

I didn't tell him about the pretty, half-naked blonde in the red party dress I found lying on the floor dead, in a pool of her own blood."

"I guess this means we won't be playing at Kali's club next week," said Paul. "He's probably going to want to close down for a while, with all the publicity."

"Oh, I don't know, it might be good for business."

After talking to Paul, I decided to check-in with Jerry again. I wanted to see if he had learned anything since the previous morning.

"Anything new?" I asked when I got him on the line.

"No, just what I told you last night. The coroner's still working on the bodies. Hey, Jay?" he asked, after a brief hesitation.

"Yeah?"

"Will you do me a favor?"

"Yeah, sure, anything, what?"

"Ah, will you promise me you won't leave town for awhile?"

"What do you mean? I may have to go out of town from time to time to work on a case."

"I mean don't leave the county. You can travel around locally. Just don't leave the area. We still want to ask you some questions about last night's murders. You'll be needed for the inquest as well."

"Ask away, I've told you everything. Don't tell me you pinheads think I did that? Please tell me you don't believe that."

116

"Of course I don't, Jay. You know me better than that. But, well, I'm not the only one who has a say in this. You know what happened last time. There were a few who thought you were involved back then too. Some of them, like the DA, are still around and seem to think it kind of strange you're involved again now."

"They're just making noise. I'll get to the bottom of this."

"That's another thing I need to talk to you about. I don't think it's such a good idea for you to be investigating the murders when you're, well, a material witness."

"I don't see what that's got to do with anything. There's no conflict of interest here. I haven't committed any crimes. That dim-wit DA, Dewitt, can suspect me all he wants. That doesn't give him the right to tell me I can't do my job."

"Well, the licensing board is going to review your license next Tuesday. You'd better be there to state your case."

I gave Jerry a few choice words and hung up. I was sorry as soon as I clicked off the line. After all, he was just the messenger. He knew I had nothing to do with the murders, but his hands were tied. Even the chief of police had to take orders from somebody.

Later that afternoon I stopped by the apartment. Suzy was out, probably at her mom's with Little Bud. I grabbed some necessities, put on a clean shirt and a pair of jeans, and got myself a room. It was in the same fleabag motel out on the lakeshore I had been living in ten years ago when I first got back to town. It was small and rundown, but had a microwave, a coffee machine, and a TV, everything I would need for the duration.

I spent a quiet but depressing evening watching late night movies in my room. This was after sipping gin and tonics in the even more depressing motel bar. The joint was filled with lonely salesmen and truck drivers, who were probably wondering what they had done to end up in this godforsaken, middle of nowhere spot.

I slept late and tried several times to call Suzy. She must have been screening her calls. It was just as well. I was in no mood to apologize. I didn't think I had done anything wrong. Still, I wanted to talk. The way things were going she might get her wish after all. If the DA had anything to say about it I wouldn't be a private detective for much longer.

I couldn't believe I was a suspect. Given the way things were going, however, and the uncanny and disturbing similarity with the events of the past, I guess I shouldn't have been too surprised. After all, I was known around town as a karate expert. I was someone who had actually used his skills to dispatch a knife-wielding murderer. There were probably few other people in town that could have pulled off such a multiple homicide single handedly. By the way, no one had ever found that killer's body. No one had ever seen him, except me.

What was it Jerry had said? Don't leave town. Don't worry, I wasn't going anywhere. I certainly wasn't going to give up the case, not now. Just the opposite, I was just getting started.

I sat in my dingy motel room pondering the recent massacre at Kali's house. Was it connected to the murder of the Patterson girl and the young couple at the beach? Had Riley been responsible for those? We'd never know. If not, there was a new murderer on the loose, one with the same penchant for knives. I'd have to find out if the wounds on these latest victims were made by the same weapon as the earlier ones.

I doubted if Jerry would willingly provide the information I needed, not after his suggestion that I close up shop. I'd have to find another source for that information. I immediately thought of Mary, my dad's new wife, an ex-mortician who used to work with the coroner from time to time. In spite of my scruples – she was my old girlfriend after all - I decided to give her a call later that night.

I went over what I could remember of the crime scene, reviewing each moment, trying to recall each sensation, each sight and sound, each minute detail. Attempting to pull up some clue from the common everyday surroundings, I searched my memory for something unusual or out of place that might give a hint of who had done this terrible thing and why. I wondered vaguely if the recent thefts of fertilizer had anything to do with it, but could find no plausible connection. It was just more noise to complicate an already messy puzzle.

Now that I had been kicked out of the house, there was nothing to prevent me from prowling the night and seeing what I could find. Maybe a few evenings without me warming the bed beside her would be all that was needed to make Suzy more reasonable and accept me for what I was. Whatever I did, I'd have to keep a low profile. I couldn't afford to be caught near another homicide.

With that in mind, and knowing I had late lessons at the dojo that evening, I took a short nap. One needed to rest if one wanted to prowl the night.

# Chapter 15

I had a group class and privates that evening. I grabbed a quick supper at the 'Spoon' and headed to the dojo. A few of my eager new orange and purple belts were waiting by the door with their gi's dangling from their colorful new belts. By the time I opened up and finished my paperwork the place was packed. Several people from the other karate school in town came in to sign up. Word travels fast. It was one of the largest classes I ever had. Usually business slacks off in the spring when everyone gets out of school and goes on summer vacations, but not this night. It was a full house. With the recent murders, self-defense was on everyone's mind.

Figures, neither of my black belts showed up, just when I needed them the most. They were probably still smarting from our advanced class of a few days before. However, there were plenty of green and brown belts to help out with the lower-ranking participants. It was a good session. They were all sweating and breathing hard by the time I bowed them out, an hour and fifteen minutes later. Then just as quickly as it had filled up, the place emptied out, everyone in a hurry to continue their evening or wind it down at home.

I was sitting in the office alone. The last student had left five minutes before, after handing me a check on his way out the door. Stephanie, one of my female students, had cancelled her private earlier. Ali had a lesson scheduled after that. Although he had passed his orange belt test, I had not seen him since his partners, Mustafa and Praveen, came in and apologized. I let them back, but hadn't seen them since. Tonight was their first lesson since before the test. I didn't know what to expect, and doubted they would even show up. If they did, the three of them would net me a neat $120. I was surprised when all three of them came in early.

I hadn't heard them come in. I was just finishing up my bookwork. The three of them barged into my tiny office. It's just big enough for my desk and two straight-backed chairs, but they all crowded in. They had someone with them, by the looks of him another mid easterner. He was dark and swarthy, clean shaven with black hair. Two-hundred fifty pounds if he was an ounce, he stood about six-six.

He had muscles on his muscles. They rose like the hump of a Brahma bull behind his thick neck. He was truly an impressive specimen.

The smirks on the faces of my three students made me wonder if it wasn't payback time. I felt alone and vulnerable behind the desk with the four of them standing in front of me, but I wasn't worried. I had a heavy wooden practice sword hanging on the wall behind me. It was a large, kind of kendo stick shaped like a samurai sword and made of thick, heavy, hard wood, almost as formidable as the sword itself.

"You're early," I said to Ali. "What are you guys doing here?" I asked looking at the others.

"We have someone who wants to sign up," said Praveen, the spokesman for the group. "This is our friend, Hamid."

"Hey, Hamid, nice to meet you," I said. "I think we have room for one more student."

I pulled out a sign-up sheet and slid it across the desk. No one picked up a pen.

"Hamid has studied before, back in Beirut," said Ali as if boasting.

"Oh, what style?" I inquired, eying the big man and gauging how far across the desk he'd get before I bashed his head in with my kendo stick.

"Dante," he replied, glaring at me.

Dante was an American martial artist from Chicago, who professed to teach the true form of the art. He demonstrated the techniques for real in his class using full-power contact without protective gear. He was said to have promoted actual death matches. Somewhere along the line Dante was shot by someone who knew nothing about karate. Hamid threw this information out more as a challenge than an answer to my question.

"Didn't he get shot?" I said, laughing. "It's hard to teach karate when everyone's trying to take each other's head off. I can rip and tear as well as the next guy, but I wouldn't have much of a school left if I let them beat each other up and hurt one another. We teach our students control and respect here, in a safe environment. Troublemakers won't be tolerated." That speech seemed to subdue them a little.

"No, sir," the big man said as he sat down in one of the chairs and began filling out the form. The other three went to change up.

"How long did you study?" I asked. "Did you obtain any rank?"

"No, we didn't have belts in our school. I studied in the mosque for about a year with the local Imam, who learned it while in college in the U.S. He was very kind to me when my parents were killed."

"Oh," I said. This was the first first-hand, face-to-face account I'd had of actual life on the streets of Beirut. Hamid had apparently not come from an affluent family as my other three students had. I'd have to keep an eye on him, although he seemed OK. Maybe the Dante thing was just a macho come-on. We'd have to see.

"Did you bring something to work out in? I have some time. One of my private classes cancelled tonight. I can fit you in for an orientation class before I start the others."

"Yes, I brought sweat-pants. That would be good." He left to change up.

For the first class I usually show them the basic stretches and stances. Stretching is probably the single most important aspects of the martial arts. To deliver high, powerful kicks, you must be stretched, end of story, plain and simple. You need to stretch out prior to working out to avoid tearing and damaging these large muscle groups. However, after years of pulling and stretching, they become permanently pliant in a way, so that when you have to use them in a pinch, you can. I showed him the basic stretches, along with the horse-stance and some punches.

Toward the end of the lesson, I showed him his first kick, something I would normally hold off until later. Since he had studied before, most of this would be familiar to him. I could tell from the way he stretched out, however, that he hadn't thrown any kicks in awhile.

"This kick," I said, demonstrating a snapping front-ball kick. "If delivered to the right target can stop a man in his tracks. It can be delivered to the groin, the knee, the solar plexus, and the chin, using the ball of your foot." Each time I mentioned a target, I'd demonstrate the kick in the general direction of that point on his body.

"One kick like that won't stop a man in a real fight," he announced.

"Maybe not a trained man in a ring, but it might stop someone out on the street who's not expecting it. I've seen a scrawny green belt about Ali's size stop someone as big as you with this kick. And the guy had a cup on! It stopped him in midstride." I demonstrated by stepping forward and showing an overhead strike to an imaginary opponent, only to be halted in midstride by an imaginary kick to my groin. "Don't underestimate the effect of this kick. But you're right in a way. The idea

121

isn't to pulverize your opponent with a single blow. The essence of Kenpo is speed and precision to weak parts of the body. You'll learn to follow up your kicks with hand strikes and take-downs. You'll learn to overcome your opponent with a virtual barrage of offensive moves, while being deft at blocking and eluding his blows. But here we take things one step at a time."

"The only way to teach karate is to do it for real," he said, as if reciting a mantra.

"In here we do it my way, OK? Who's giving the lesson here?"

"I'm sorry sensei, but if I am going to study with you, I have to respect your ability."

"Are you challenging me?" I asked in disbelief. Nothing like this had ever happened before. The other three stopped stretching and gathered around as if this is what they had come to see. "You better damn well respect this belt I have around my waist."

"You think you can bully others around just because you have a black belt?" he said, gaining confidence with his friends as an audience. "You think you can humiliate people, treat them like criminals?"

He was starting to scare me, and that made me dangerous, sometimes deadly. I remembered how deadly and laughed.

"Mister Hamid, I should inform you that the paper you signed freed me of any liability for what may happen to you while studying in my dojo. I'm covered regardless of what happens to you, for broken bones, contusions, abrasions, anything."

I took a step toward him. "And right now you're cruising for a serious accident." I turned and looked at each of the others one by one. "And I won't stop with Hamid here."

They didn't look too concerned. Their friend was twice as wide as me at the shoulders and dwarfed me by almost a foot.

At that moment, my new student rushed me. He was big, but not the biggest opponent I had faced. From his first move he made one mistake after another, mistakes that any trained man would have avoided.

He obviously underestimated me, breaking rule number one. Always consider your opponent as good as you. If they are, you'll have a fighting chance. If not, you'll have a cake-walk. Either way, you'll be prepared for whatever happens.

Apparently, he'd always been able to rely on his size and weight to intimidate and overwhelm his opponent. Instead of coming at me with punches and kicks, he tried to grab me with both hands around the neck. I easily knocked his hands away, opening him up. Then I hit him with a trigger to the Adam's apple. It was just a short, quick jab with the second-knuckle of my index-finger. You make sort of a fist with your second-knuckles and extend the top one as if you just pulled a trigger, bracing it with your thumb. When that little bony knob hits the protruding cartilage of the trachea, it doesn't take much to do some damage. It's excruciating. One has to be careful with this type of strike. If you hit them too hard, the organ could swell and the person could suffocate. That's why I barely tapped him, but it was hard enough.

He froze in midstride, paralyzed, staring in surprise, and holding his throat. He was having trouble breathing. Just to be sure, I stepped into him with a thrust kick to take him off his feet.

Ali actual screamed as if I had just murdered his friend.

The demonstration had the desired effect. The big man writhed around on the floor moaning in some language I didn't understand. He was retching and gasping for air all at the same time.

I immediately felt bad for the big jerk. He had obviously been talked into coming and helping his rich, arrogant friends. They were the ones I was really mad at. They stood there in surprise staring at their oversized and prostrate defender.

"Out!" I bellowed. "All of you get out now! Take him with you!"

"But our clothes..." said Mustafa, the largest of the three, although small compared to his prone champion.

"Fuck your fucking clothes. Get them and get out of here. Don't bother changing. If I see any of you here by the time that clock strikes eight, you'll wish you stayed in fucking Lebanon or whatever stinking shit-hole you come from. Now get the fuck out of here!" I yelled this in my loudest dojo commando voice, building it up from my diaphragm and expelling the words like blows.

They grabbed their stuff, helped their incapacitated friend to the door, and ran out as if their lives depended on it. In a way I guess it did. I was so worked up at that point I'm not sure what I would have done.

As soon as they left, I fell into a complete calm. I meditated, readying myself for the fight to come. I left the dojo soon after, taking my samurai swords with me. Walking warily to my car, I expected an ambush at any moment. I suspected I hadn't heard the last of my Arab friends. They definitely weren't coming back to the school this time and certainly wouldn't get any refunds. They were lucky they didn't get beatings. The nerve of them, thinking they could have one of their pea-

123

brained, gorilla friends teach me a lesson. Well, they'd have to do a lot better than that big Dumbo.

Too worked up to go back to my tiny motel room, I cruised the streets of the 'burgh', seeing if I could track the activity of my four errant students. I was unable to find any sign of them. As a matter of fact, the town seemed particularly deserted this Monday evening. The only vehicles on the street were police cars. Jerry had told me he was going to put on some extra men to beef up the evening patrols. Being their number one suspect, I'd decided to keep a low profile.

The night had turned humid. A warm wind blew up from the south. It was cloudy, the stars and moon obscured. A light mist in the air promised more to come, much like that night ten years ago. It was a good night to prowl.


Main Street closed up after nine p.m. in the 'burgh'. This was especially true on Monday nights when most of the restaurants and clubs were closed, like Lilly's. The place was dark and deserted when I drove by. Kali's house was dark and quiet as well. He was obviously staying with friends. Who could blame him? I sure wouldn't want to spend the night there. I noticed a police car sitting in a small park at the end of Kali's street and kept going.

I was near my motel and had been seen by too many squad cars to risk driving around any further. I pulled in and stopped off at my room to hit the head. Putting on a dark sweatshirt and jacket, along with my black gi pants, I headed back out into the night. I left my swords in the room. I certainly didn't want to be caught with those if the police happened to stop me.

Hamid and the boys made me think. Was there a Mid Eastern connection to the murders? Everyone was a suspect. I needed some way to focus the search. Perhaps the murders weren't the work of a madman after all. Just like the ones ten years ago, perhaps they were only made to look that way to cover up something else, something even more sinister.

To catch a murderer, you have to think like one. Fortunately, or unfortunately as the case may be, I seem to be quite good at this, maybe too good. I tried to reverse the situation. Instead of going out and trying to find the killer, I imagined I was the murderer. Where would I go if I wanted to kill young people in the act? Stalk the college dorms? Most of the students had left for the summer. Stake out some lonely convenience store like that loser Riley had done? That didn't quite fit the killer's MO either. The evening was warm and damp, a good night to make forbidden love under a blanket on the beach. Where would the killer strike? Where was he now?

I walked back behind the motel to the water's edge, where the lake curved in a wide arc to form a bay just outside of the town limits. From there I followed the shoreline back toward the city and Kali's house.

I passed several motels like the one I was staying in. It was easy walking, mostly beaches, until I reached the tall wire fence that marked the beginning of the paper mill. I had to wade out into the water, stepping on stones and drift logs to get by this obstacle without getting wet. I only partially succeeded. Walking in back of the mill, I passed huge piles of sawdust and logs, which blocked my view of the highway.

I was soon in a neighborhood of expensive houses, where Kali made his home. Staying low and in the underbrush, I scanned the area. On a side street, just under a light, was one of Jerry LaGrande's squad cars, sitting like a cat waiting to pounce. I slid back into the shadows and made my way further along the shore. The killer certainly wouldn't return to that crime scene.

So far my luck had held. I hadn't been spotted. No dog had barked out an alarm. But I was having second thoughts. There were cops all over the place. The killer was probably long gone by now. What was I doing out in the middle of the night? How would I explain myself if caught? I had no good answers to any of these questions, but having come too far to turn back, I doggedly kept on my way.

I soon came to a small lakeside park where the river comes into the bay. This seemed a likely spot for young lovers seeking solitude. I decided to camp out in the bushes for awhile.

I still wasn't sure what I was doing. The odds of finding the killer like this were next to zero. There really wasn't much chance of anything happening out here tonight, let alone the killer conveniently showing up. Then again, stranger things have happened to yours truly. Who's to say it wouldn't happen again. I had nothing to lose.

It was getting late. I was trying to decide whether to move on or go back. I had neglected to bring a watch. From what I could guess, it was somewhere between two and three o'clock in the morning.

Suddenly, I felt as if I was being watched. I don't know how to explain it, but I couldn't shake the feeling of someone's eyes on me. My mind flashed back to that moment in the club the night before the murders, when I thought someone was watching me though the front

125

window. Was that the murderer looking at his future victims? The thought gave me an instant chill.

I had the same primitive, instinctive feeling of danger now.

Deciding I'd had enough hiding in the dark, I stood up and walked along the side of the park toward the street. I expected the police to call out at any moment and order me to stop and identify myself, but the command never came. There was no one there, no squad car, no cops, just me, the lonely street lamp, and the sensation of being watched.

I made my way up the road, heading toward my motel, making the three miles in a little under an hour. All was going well until I passed the McDonald's just a few buildings before mine. A police car pulled up alongside of me and stopped. The cop in the passenger seat, holding a sandwich in one hand and a cup of coffee in the other, rolled down his window and asked what I was up to at this time of night. I told him I was staying at the next motel, and being unable to sleep had taken a short walk. I gave him my name and told him where I lived here in town.

"I'm staying at the motel temporarily because I had a fight with my wife," I confessed.

The young officer didn't know me, but his partner, who was driving, did, although he didn't particularly like me.

"That you, Lawless?" he asked from the other side of the car. "What, your wife kicked you out of the house again?"

"Yeah, Frank, it's me, and for your information this is the first time I've been kicked out of the house."

"Out kind of late, eh?"

"Any law against that?"

"No, not unless a bunch of people get cut up tonight."

"Well, if you guys spent less time stuffing your faces and more time out there actually hunting the criminals maybe there wouldn't be any murders."

It was an exchange I'd just as soon not have had, but it was soon over and I was on my way again. Shutting the door to my cheap room a few minutes later, I had a couple shots of the Crown Royal I had bought earlier. Not long after that I was lying in bed dreaming about a tall girl with long legs and a very short skirt. On waking up I identified her with Sheila, the sister of the murdered girl. We were running along a deserted street, with newspapers and debris blowing everywhere, like tumbleweeds. It was as if a huge parade or crowd had passed that way,

126

yet there was no one about. We were looking for something, searching for someone who for some reason we just had to find. The dream soon turned into a sexual fantasy as we stopped to rest in someone's garage, where we made love in a car. I woke up with an erection, smelling upholstery. I made a note to call Sheila that day.

# Chapter 16

Later that morning I was awaken by a knock on my motel room door. When I didn't answer immediately, the knocks became more insistent and louder.

"Mister Lawless, this is the police," a voice said. "Please open the door. We'd like to talk to you."

"OK, OK," I yelled back, annoyed and concerned at the same time. "What now?" I opened the door. Facing me were two clean-cut, raw-faced state troopers in their gray New York State uniforms. They were both big and had crew cuts.

"What's the trouble, officer?" I inquired squinting and momentarily blinded by the bright morning sun.

"We'd like you to come down to headquarters for a few questions, sir," said the one with the cruelest cut. My troubled expression reflected back to me through his iron-rimmed sunglasses.

"Questions? About what? What's the problem? What do you have to drag me down to headquarters for?"

"We really can't talk about it here, sir. Would you please come with us."

"Am I under arrest for something? I have a right to know what's going on before I go with you."

"No, sir, we just need to ask you some questions."

"OK, I'll be right with you." I closed the door and quickly dressed, splashing some cold water on my face in place of a shower. I felt dirty and frazzled from my late night escapades, and didn't feel like I'd gotten enough sleep. I certainly didn't feel like dragging myself down to state police headquarters to answer some stupid questions.

More curious than worried, I followed the troopers back to their station out on the southwestern part of town. Once there, I was conducted into an interrogation room where I only had to sit a few minutes before my interrogator arrived.

Much to my surprise this guy was short like me, with long, rather unkempt hair and a dark complexion. I guessed he was either Italian, Lebanese, or from some Latin country. He introduced himself, but his name wasn't familiar, nor did it sound Italian, Lebanese or Spanish. He told me he knew who I was from some of the other investigators, and said he was from Boston originally. This gave us something in common. I told him I had gone to school there. I didn't mention the drug bust and my rapid fall from grace. After the introductions he got right down to business.

"Can you tell me where you were last night between eleven and five this morning?"

"The same place your guys found me, in my motel room sleeping."

"We have your address as 65 South Catherine Street in town here. Is that correct?"

"Yes, that's my home address."

"If you live here in town, why are you staying in a motel?"

"That's personal," I said, not wanting to go into my marital problems with this airhead.

"Have a fight with the wife?"

"Something like that. Look, what's this about? I have a right to know what I'm being questioned about."

Instead of answering my question, he ruffled through some papers on his desk and asked a few more of his own.

"I have a police report here from last night. You were stopped and questioned about…." He paused and looked down at the fax sheet he was holding. "Three fifteen a.m. this morning? I thought you said you were asleep in your room?"

"Yes, most of the night, but I was having trouble sleeping. I, er, I have a lot on my mind. My marriage is on the rocks. I took a short walk down the street to clear my head, just a few blocks. I was headed back to my room when two of the city's finest stopped me and asked me some questions. Now can you please tell me what this is all about?"

He hesitated, as if having trouble saying what he wanted to say. I thought he was going to hack-up some phlegm and spit. Instead, he hacked-up something even more disgusting.

"There was a double homicide last night in town. Not far from your motel."

"Oh, shit!" I whispered. "Where? When?"

"Some time between the hours of midnight and four this morning. Exactly where did you go for your walk?"

I couldn't tell them where I had really gone. It would have incriminated me for sure. So I made up a plausible story. It wasn't the first time I had lied to the cops.

"Like I said, just down the road. I wanted to think things over. I really wasn't dressed for hiking. I turned around a little way past the McDonalds, just before the mill."

"Do you know when it was?"

"Yeah, around three. I glanced at the clock on my way out the room."

"Did you see anything, anyone that looked suspicious?"

"Except for the cops who stopped me I didn't see a soul. It's totally deserted that time of the evening on a Monday night. I don't even remember seeing a car drive by."

"It says here you were found at the scene of a multiple homicide on the 25th last, out at the Hundouri residence. Is that true?"

"If it's in your report then it must be true, but I'm not a suspect. I'm helping the police on that case. I'm a private investigator working with them unofficially. I went to the party after having a fight with my wife. I must have showed up right after it happened. I told the city cops everything. As a matter of fact, that's why I'm at the motel. My wife objects to my involvement. That's what was keeping me awake last night. It's kind of hard to sleep after witnessing what I saw."

"I'm sure. A bit of a coincidence, you being out and about the same night two murders occur. You're a trained martial artist aren't you?"

"Yes, sir. I own my own school in town, Lawless Academy of Self-Defense. You should get a few of those overweight rookies of yours to sign up."

"Don't worry about my rookies. They can take care of themselves."

"OK, can't blame a guy for trying to drum up some business, but I'm afraid I can't tell you much more about last night. I went back to my room right after I talked to the police and fell to sleep immediately."

"You have quite an interesting history, Mister Lawless," he said after a pause, looking up from more papers he had been perusing. "Most of your files are sealed, but there's enough information here to indicate you were involved in a similar situation a few years ago."

"I was working with the authorities in my capacity as a private investigator. That's why they contacted me again now. I'm on your side. I figure you guys need all the help you can get."

"Is that why you killed William Riley?"

His question took me momentarily by surprise. I hesitated a moment before I spoke.

"He had just robbed a convenience store at gunpoint and kidnapped the attendant. He was on the point of raping her at knifepoint when I interrupted him. In the struggle for his gun, it went off. It's all in the record there."

"Quite a hero, aren't you?"

"Like I said, I'm on your side. Now if you don't have any further questions, I'd like to be on my way. Looks like you have a lot of work to do."

"I'd advise you to listen to your wife and stay out of this, Mister Lawless. You've already been questioned regarding two multiple homicides. I wouldn't go for a third if I were you."

"You have any more questions, officer?"

"No, that's all for now," he said standing up. "Just don't leave town."

I was famished by the time I left the State Police barracks, and groggy from lack of sleep. I hadn't even had a shot of caffeine yet. I stopped at a Dunkin Donuts and scarfed down a couple jelly-filled heart stoppers between gulps of hot coffee. Then I went to the office to phone Jerry

I was wearing the same clothes I had thrown on on my way out the door that morning, the t-shirt I was sleeping in and a pair of frayed-at-the-cuff, wrinkled jeans. I had already worn the jeans five days too many. My hair was overdue for a trim and ruffled. I hadn't shaved in two days. I must have looked pretty scruffy. Alice, the girl at the insurance agency, gave me a concerned look as I came in and rushed to my closet-sized office without saying hi.

"What's this about another murder last night?" I asked when I finally got Jerry on the line.

"Jay, where are you? We've been looking all over for you."

"The State Police grabbed me for questioning first thing this morning. I've been up at the barracks answering questions since seven."

"Yeah, they're in charge of this one. We faxed them all our field reports from last night. You were on one of them."

"Yeah, I know. Thanks for nothing."

"We were looking for you. We need to ask you some follow-up questions after what happened last night. We have an all-points bulletin out for you."

"That's just great! Look, I've answered enough questions for one day. Now it's time someone started answering mine. Can we meet somewhere, just you and me?"

"Sure, Jay, where you have in mind?"

"How about the old ball park, in about half an hour?"

"OK, that ought to bring back memories. See you there."

"Come alone!"

I knew I could count on Jerry. After all, we grew up living next to each other, playing together most of our lives. We were both on his dad's Babe Ruth baseball team, spending many summer evenings on the diamond. Jerry was on first base. I played shortstop. I stopped playing in my final year. It would have been my best year, but I wanted to play drums in a band. His father never forgave me, but Jerry had remained my friend. I once defended him against the neighborhood bully. It was more because I wanted to continue playing marbles, where I had a distinct advantage, than to help him, but he never forgot it.

The park was as good a place as any to meet. Out on the south end of town, where the poorer neighborhoods are located, it was no longer used by the city athletic department. The place was deserted at this time of the day, although it was fine baseball weather. It would be easy enough to see if Jerry was alone or not, not that it mattered. The park was in a sparsely populated area, with a large industrial building and a river behind it. There were several escape routes. One was a narrow footbridge across the river into the woods. If that was blocked, there was always the dam. It was narrow and precarious, but passable. I had the routes planned out if needed.

Jerry showed up in his new Caddy a short time later.

"Nice car, Jer," I said as he got out and shut the door. "Police business must be good."

"Isn't she a beauty? I've always wanted one."

"My dad would be proud of you. He drives one just like it, although it's an older model."

"I really can't afford it, but now the kids are out of the house and on their own, Lisa thinks it will help my image."

"We can't have your image in jeopardy now, can we?"

"What's going on, Jay? We had another murder last night. Two kids down behind the monument?"

"What, down behind what monument? Not the one overlooking the bay? Last night?"

"Yeah, why?"

I hesitated to tell Jerry where I had been the previous evening. I was afraid to implicate myself even further in the murders, but I had to trust somebody.

"Exactly where did they find the bodies, Jerry?"

"They were in the little park across from the monument, near the city water treatment plant. They were in a sleeping bag, naked. We haven't found their clothing yet. Stabbed repeatedly just like the others."

"On the other side of the river from the monument?"

"Yeah, now suppose you tell me where you were last night. What are you doing staying in a motel?"

"Suzy's not too happy about my involvement in this whole business. She threatened to walk out on me if I didn't give up the private investigating agency."

"Well, maybe she's right, Jay. You may have kept your license this time, but the board is split and you might not be so fortunate next time."

I decided to tell him.

"I was there last night."

"What? You were at the scene of the murder?"

The river empties through a narrow channel into the lake just behind the monument, where I had been hiding the previous night. There's another park on the other side of this channel, where people go to fish and picnic in the summer. It's also apparently a favorite spot for lovers. A footbridge, a little further down from where I was hiding, connects the two parks. I had the right idea, just the wrong side of the river.

"Well, not exactly. I was out snooping around, hoping to catch him in the act, like I caught Riley. I snuck down behind Kali's house to see if he'd come back to the scene of the crime. I saw your boys hanging around, so went a little further down to the park. You know, trying to think like the killer. I waited in the dark and watched, but I didn't see anyone. I even looked across the channel occasionally, but couldn't see much. It was a dark night. I didn't want to take the chance of crossing the footbridge in case the place was being watched."

"It was," said Jerry, his jaw clenched. "It happened right under our noses."

"And mine."

We sat on the narrow bench we used to sit on while we waited for our turn to bat. Our initials were still carved in it somewhere, obscured by the carvings of succeeding generations of ball-playing youngsters.

"I could have sworn there was someone there watching me," I told him.

"Did you see anything? What makes you think you were being watched?"

"I don't know. Just an instinct, I guess. The night of the murders, at the club, I thought I saw someone peering in the window. It was unsettling, the way he seemed to be glaring at me. But when I looked again, he was gone. I got the same feeling last night, of someone glaring at me, though I didn't see anyone the whole time."

"Hmm, another murder, and in your vicinity. Maybe someone is following you."

"Who? Why?"

"That I don't know. Maybe it has something to do with the past."

"Maybe it has something to do with a sick fuck who likes to kill people with a knife. It's a small town. If something happens it's liable to be in my general vicinity."

"Well, people are beginning to talk. You'd better keep a low profile."

"Any lower and I'd be a mole. Hey, I was wondering if I could take a look at the photos from the McKenna house that morning. You know, the dead couple out on the Bob Moffit Road."

"Why? That was a murder-suicide. We even found a note."

"A note? No one mentioned that. What'd it say?"

"We kept it from the news boys. It was hard to read with all the blood. It didn't say much. The head-shrinks took a look at it. It was pretty incoherent, but the old man seemed unhappy with life. You know, no grandchildren, spinster daughter, do-nothing son, the same old story. People just get tired of living."

"Well, I'd still like to take a look at those photos. I'm working for Grace McKenna and I owe her some closure. Anything you can do to help will be appreciated."

"OK, I'll see what I can do. Give me a call later in the week."

I didn't find out much more from Jerry, except that the murdered couple was killed with the same weapon as the others. The MO was almost identical to Becky Jo Patterson and the couple found down on the boat landing. It was definitely our man, and he was a sadistic serial killer.

I promised to lay low and keep him informed, ignoring his advice to make up with Suzy. I couldn't very well give up the case now. It wasn't going to let me.

# Chapter 17

Remembering my exotic dream of the night before, I phoned Sheila Patterson from my office. I hadn't talked to her since a few days after the confrontation with the Riley kid. I had told her the case was closed. The least I could do now was let her know it had been reopened and give her the opportunity to rehire me. Much to my delight, she, not her parents, answered the phone. Much to my dismay, she told me she was leaving town.

"Oh, I'm sorry to hear that."

"Well, there's not much reason to stay around. I've got to get back to the City. I've been away from work too long."

"I understand, but, well, I feel bad that we, I mean I, well, your sister's killer may still be out there. I thought you might want me to keep searching for whoever it is."

"I thought sure it was Billy, and for all I know it still could be. You said yourself you found him raping that girl with a knife."

"That's true, but we still haven't found the murder weapon."

"I really don't care any more. Now that Billy's dead it's all over as far as I'm concerned."

"I understand. When are you leaving?"

"I'm driving down tomorrow, why?"

"Oh, I was just wondering if you wanted to have a drink tonight before you go."

There was silence on the other end of the line as she pondered my invitation, delivered out of the blue. It wasn't that I wanted to cheat or anything, or get even with Suzy for throwing me out. I certainly wasn't looking forward to sitting alone in a flea-bitten motel room either. A little conversation with an attractive woman might do my frame of mind some good. I needed some attitude adjustment. Much to my surprise she said yes.

"What do you have in mind?"

"Oh, we could do dinner if you like. Have a few drinks afterward. There's not much happening in town on a weeknight."

My first thought was Lilly's where I worked, but the club was still closed after the brutal murders at the owner's house.

"You like Italian food?" I asked finally, remembering one of my family's favorite restaurants when we were kids.

"Yes, anything would be better than diner food and country music."

"They play Italian music, opera sometimes."

"Sounds perfect."

"Great, how bout I pick you up around seven. Dress casual."

Hanging up, I immediately felt good and guilty at the same time. Good because I had a date that evening, guilty because it could be a further blow to my precarious marriage. I called Suzy at her office next door, too afraid to see her in person, hoping she would answer the phone. She didn't, so I left a message.

While I waited for Suzy to return my call, I dialed my other client, Bobby McKenna's sister, Grace. I hadn't talked to her in a while. I felt bad that I hadn't done much on her case, being tied up with the murders. No one answered there either. I left a message, saying I'd try again later.

A few minutes after that Suzy came in.

"You wanted to talk, Jay?" she asked, walking into my tiny office.

"Don't you think you should shut the door?" I said, concerned about our personal affairs being overheard.

"I told Alice to go to lunch. We're alone. Now, what is it you want to say?"

"How's Bud doing?"

"He's fine. Wondering when his father's going to come home."

"I guess that's up to his mom. Don't you think all of this is a bit silly?"

"Do you know the police had an all points bulletin out on you this morning? They called the house at eight o'clock looking for you. I told them you were staying out at the Beaker, but they said they'd already been there. What's going on, Jay? Are you determined to ruin our lives?" She was crying now, much to my discomfort. I hadn't expected this. She seemed fine when she walked in, all business and no emotion. Now the spigot had been opened. "Why are you doing this?"

"Please don't be upset, Suzy. I'm just trying to help, do my job. I've gotten myself involved in this, now I have to see it through. I don't want to fight. I don't like the thought of you and Bud alone in that apartment with a killer on the loose."

"I'm safer in that house alone than I am around you by the sound of it. No, we'll be fine. Anyway, I've asked Alex to stay with us. He's staying in the rumpus room."

"What!" I yelled. "Booth's there? What's the idea?"

Alex Booth and Suzy had gone to grade school together and were childhood sweethearts all through high school. He still had a crush on her.

"I'll be damned if I'll let that jerk stay in my house with my wife and child. I have rights, you know."

"You lost those rights when you walked out. I'm having a restraining order put on you. You are not to come within a hundred yards of the house. And you'd better not try anything with Alex, you're in enough trouble."

"Look sweetheart, be reasonable. You just can't lock me out like that."

"Yes I can. My lawyer thinks I have sufficient grounds for a divorce."

"Divorce!" This was all coming at me too fast, even if I hadn't been rousted out of bed by two goons in gray at six in the morning after a half-night's sleep. "I thought we were going to try and work things out?"

"So did I, but it appears you've decided to just go your own way without giving a damn what anyone thinks, what those who depend on you think."

"You really want a divorce? After all we've gone through together? I thought you loved me."

"I do, Jay. That's the problem. I love you, but you haven't done a thing to change. You haven't done a thing I asked you."

"I gave you a child!"

"I didn't ask to get pregnant, that just happened. You weren't all that thrilled about it as I remember. You certainly haven't gone out of your way to be a great father to him."

"What's that supposed to mean?"

"Oh, Jay, you can't have a wife and family and live as if you were still a bachelor, at least not with me. I expected more."

"You got just what you saw. You knew what you were getting when you married me. You could have done a lot worse, you know. I don't cheat. I don't beat you. I don't go out drinking with the boys every night. I've been a good husband and a decent father. It's not my fault the kid doesn't relate to me."

"Oh, Jay, just listen to yourself. You're incorrigible."

"You're nuts. And if you want a divorce you can have one. You've already given me grounds by shacking up with that Booth creep. What a loser. You deserve each other."

I was standing behind my desk. I had stood up and pushed my chair back at the mention of Suzy's new roommate.

"We're not shacking up. He's helping us out through a tough time. You said yourself I shouldn't be alone."

"A lot of good that little jerk would do you," I laughed. I walked past her into the main office. "I'm glad we've had this talk. At least now I know where I stand."

"You're not going to do anything to Alex, are you?" she said as I walked to the door.

"You know me, honey. I wouldn't hurt a fly unless he was buzzing around my head. Tell him he'd just better behave himself."

I was smarting after leaving the office, with a hurt that went so deep it made me want to vomit. Instead of crying, I swore and banged my fist against a street sign, making it vibrate back and forth and scraping my knuckles.

This certainly wasn't what I expected. Yeah, I knew Suzy was mad and fed up, but I had no idea she was contemplating divorce. And to take up with Alex Booth, her old flame, when I hadn't even been gone a week, well that was just plain low. The thought of my little boy alone in that house with some other guy made my throat constrict. I felt the full weight of my neglected responsibility. I could no longer be there to protect him. I felt more than helpless. I felt bereft of hope.

I drove back out to my motel in a daze, not knowing where else to go, although I couldn't stomach going back to my lonely room. Instead, I walked to the small beach area behind the building, where the warm sand and sun beckoned. Too many bathers about for my grand funk, I turned left and walked further down the shoreline, away from town.

I was stung with the immensity of my loss and racked with guilt for my failure, my utter inability, to succeed at anything important in my life. I seemed destined to be unhappy, caught in a web of my own devising, a net of lost love and unfulfilled hopes. I couldn't deny it. The emptiness of my life without Suzy and Bud stared me in the face as I trudged the beach looking for a quiet place to scream out my pain.

I crossed a small stream, caring little about my wet shoes or pants, and walked in the sand dunes behind the city dump. Beyond that I passed the cabins and shanties down by the 'crick', a marshland that adjoins the beach. It's a lonely stretch of sand, where joggers and dog lovers go on the weekends to avoid the crowds. It was mostly deserted today. A man and his mutt walked in the distance. I sat on a log and stared out at the lake.

It was a gorgeous day. The sun glistened off the sky-blue water with the movement of the waves, flashing back and forth across the liquid surface like racing fire flies. The clear sky was tinged with the gray and purple of distant mountains. I took no joy from the peaceful scene, only the darkness projected on it from my tortured soul.

I probably should have had a good cry, but I didn't. Instead, I just got madder. I felt betrayed, turned on for no reason. All I had done was try to provide for my family. I had been doing the same thing, after all, for the past ten years without a complaint. Now all of a sudden, when all my hard work and patience was finally paying off, she was dumping me. She was giving me over for that little jerk, Alex Booth. My spirit was beginning to rise with my anger. If she wanted a fight, she could have one. The more I thought about it, the more I was convinced she didn't have a leg to stand on. All I needed was a decent lawyer to state my case. We'd see who came out on top in this.

Of course, I was firmly in denial by now. Not only did I not have the funds to hire a good lawyer, I'd more than likely have to fall back on my hack of a semi-retired brother. Tony would more than likely just make things worse. Not to mention the fact that these cases were almost always found in favor of the mother. This was especially so when the father was a two-bit detective and the wife owned her own businesses. No, I realized after careful consideration, I probably would not do too well in a court of law after all.

The man with the dog was getting closer. I got up, brushed myself off, and walked back toward my motel. At least I had an evening with an attractive, intelligent, young female to look forward to. Perhaps things weren't so bad after all. Perhaps this was just what the doctor ordered. I felt better as I got ready for my date with Sheila.

I picked Sheila up at seven and drove back toward the city. The ride to the restaurant was awkward to say the least. All I could think of to talk about was the case and my wrecked marriage. She obviously didn't want to hear about the former. The latter I couldn't speak of without blubbering like a baby. Things got a little better when I got her on the subject of her work and living in the 'Big Apple'.

"I can't wait to get back," she said after describing her job and her cat, Tabby. "My roommate's taking care of her, but I miss her so much."

"I know what you mean," I said lamely. "I had a dog once."

I wanted to tell her how crappy my life was and that I missed my little boy more than breathing itself.

"I miss my sister," she said suddenly, as if reading my mind. Her words stunned us both to silence for the rest of the trip into town.

Anthony's is on the main street, where it's been since the early twenties, as pictures behind the bar will attest. I parked the car in an empty spot right in front of the restaurant and helped her out. It must be my lucky day, I thought, a date and a parking place in one night. Boy was I mistaken.

We climbed the long flight of stairs to the dining room and stood waiting for the hostess to seat us. There was a good crowd for a weeknight. Anthony's regulars were at the bar. Several couples sat alone, looking into each other's eyes. A few families with their kids, like the Lawlesses in the old days, chattered away by the windows. A group out for a birthday celebration took up several tables in the center of the room. It wasn't long before we were seated.

I should have known bringing Sheila to Anthony's was a mistake. While I hadn't been there in a long time, my dad and his new wife went often. It was one of their favorite places. I never should have invited her there. Just as I feared, as we finished ordering, who turns up but my father and my old girlfriend, Mary, the ex-mortician.

"Oh, Jeez," I blurted out as they were seated.

"What's wrong?" asked my date. "See someone you owe money to?"

"No, just my old man, and I'd rather not talk to him at the moment."

She looked at my left hand and the ring on my finger. I was so used to wearing it, I had forgotten all about it.

"Oh," she said. "Are we doing anything wrong?"

"No, no, not at all, it's just that me and my old man don't get along so well since his second marriage."

"I understand. It's hard sometimes when a parent remarries."

"She's my old girlfriend."

"Oh," she said again, momentarily at a loss for words. She looked at my pop with new admiration.

I was feeling miffed at the way she kept glancing over at them, when my father walked up to our table.

"What, too proud to come over and say hi to your old man?"

"Hi, Dad."

141

"And who's this lovely young lady. I don't believe I've had the pleasure," he said, bending at the waist and taking my date's hand.

"Dad, this is Sheila Patterson. Sheila, this is my father."

"Hi, Mister Lawless. It's nice to meet you."

"The pleasure's all mine, dear," he said, shaking her hand lightly.

"Sheila's visiting from New York," I told him, hoping he would let go of her hand and leave. Instead, he held it and sat down.

"You're the sister of that poor girl they found on the beach last month. I'm so sorry about your sister. That's just terrible. I hope Jay here is helping you."

"Your son has been very helpful," she said, taking her hand from his, much to my relief. "A person's life was saved thanks to him. Your son's a hero."

"You have no idea," said my father, patting me on the shoulder. "Jay here is too modest to brag, but that's not the first life he's saved."

"Er, can we change the subject," I requested, embarrassed and trying to think of a way to get rid of him. "Sheila doesn't want to hear about that."

"Oh, yes I do. It sounds very interesting."

"Hey, I have an idea," he said. "Why don't we get a larger table and all sit together. That's my wife, Mary," he said, waving to her. She waved back from across the room. "She knows quite a bit of the story."

"No, Dad, we'd really rather eat alone if you don't mind. I wouldn't even have come here if I'd known you were going to be here." Lacking anything better, I resorted to just plain rudeness. I was fueled by the memory of his lack of sympathy the night Suzy kicked me out of the house. After all, if he had invited me in that night, maybe I wouldn't have become so involved in the murders. I certainly wouldn't have found the bodies!

"I'm sorry," he said, looking hurt, but understanding. "I see you two want to be alone. Nice meeting you, Miss Patterson. See you around, Jay." He turned and walked away. I felt immediately sorry.

"Well, that was very rude," she said. "That's not a very nice way to treat your father."

"I told you we didn't get along. He's so smug, thinks he's the mayor or something."

"He was just being polite. He seems very nice. Quite a handsome man for his age."

"Yah, everyone says he looks like Paul Newman."

"So are you in trouble now? I mean, well, does your wife know you're out to dinner with me?"

"My wife doesn't care what I do."

"Oh, you don't get along with her either?"

"She asked me for a divorce today. She doesn't like my line of work."

"I can understand why. Didn't she know what you did before you were married?"

"That's the whole point. She knew exactly what she was getting into. Nothing's changed since we met ten years ago. She thought somehow getting married and having a kid would change everything."

"And it hasn't?"

"No, why should it?"

"I don't know. It's just usually when a guy gets married and has a child, they, well, they usually settle down. Stop being little boys and become responsible men."

"I've always been responsible, even when I was a little boy. Responsibility's a frame of mind, not a puberty thing."

"Maybe your wife is afraid for your safety. I mean after all, you are in a dangerous line of work. You could have been killed that night."

"Believe me, I could have been killed on a lot of nights. That didn't stop her from marrying me. Why do you chicks think you can just change everybody to your liking? If you like someone well enough to marry them, why do you have to go and try to change them?"

"Because we see the potential and tolerate the imperfections. Don't you believe in the perfection of man?"

"Hell no," I said, much too loud. A few of the patrons turned to look at the rude, loud-mouthed man. "Just the opposite, I believe in the ultimate evil of mankind. The human race sucks."

"That's a terrible attitude, Mister Lawless. Now I know why your wife has left you."

"You don't know the half of it."

We ate the rest of our meal in silence. The mood was ruined. The date was in shambles. It was all downhill from there.

I looked around the room. The restaurant had slowly filled up since the time we sat down. There was now a line of customers snaking down the stairs waiting to be seated. I hadn't noticed them come in, but sitting at the table closest to the stairway were Praveen and Mustafa, two of my ex-students. They were with another well-dressed man that I didn't recognize. My attention latched onto them like a laser

143

beam, hot and intense. Praveen, the eldest and leader of their little group, was looking in my direction when I noticed them. He quickly averted his eyes, pretending to be suddenly interested in the menu. I kept staring at him as if he were the only person in the room.

"Is there something wrong?" asked Sheila following my stare.

"No, just a couple old friends."

I tried asking questions about her work. She answered in short sentences. She was obviously upset. It was like those dating shows you see on reality TV, where things go terribly wrong, but this wasn't funny or fun. I could tell she was not having a good time.

"I'm sorry," I said finally. "I guess I'm not much fun tonight. This homicide case has got me so messed up I don't know what I'm doing."

"Are you still involved with that?" she asked, surprised.

"I found the bodies at the house party. You must have heard about it."

"Yes, it sounded terrible. That must have been horrible. Do you think it's the same person that killed my sister?"

"I don't know. I don't know what to think. It could be, or it could have been Riley. I just don't know."

Things went a little better after that. At least she was civil and we managed to finish our dinner without any further undue tension. That is until we were on our way out.

We were waiting in line to pay the cashier. I happened to be standing by the table where my ex-students and their well-dressed friend were sitting. The man in the suit made the mistake of looking at me just a little too long, with an expression just a little too arrogant.

"You might want to reconsider the company you keep, buddy," I said, looking down at him. "These two punks you're sitting with are a couple of troublemakers."

Suddenly, I remembered the description of the man in the suit with the fancy gold watch who had made my mother-in-law lift the heavy bags into his truck. I looked at his expensive time-piece.

"Hey, you haven't recently bought fertilizer at Wal-Mart have you?" I asked. "You're not the guy who made my mother-in-law lift some heavy bags lately have you, pal?"

Before any of them could answer, I moved on to the cashier's booth. I half hoped one of them would try something, but they weren't that stupid. "See you around, boys," I said as I left. "Have a nice evening."

"What was that all about?" asked Sheila, obviously unnerved by the whole encounter.

"Oh, nothing, just a couple of troublemakers from my karate school. I had to kick them out for behavior unbecoming a martial artist. One of them was giving me the evil eye, so I thought I'd give them a little piece of my mind."

"Was that really necessary?"

"No, but it felt good."

I drove her home in silence. She barely said good bye to me as I wished her a safe trip back.

I thought about my miserable attempt at a date all the way home and far into the night as I tried to fall asleep. As tired as I was sleep eluded me like a happy moment does a manic-depressive. But then what did I expect?

# Interlude

*'Jim' had followed the scent down from the mountain to a place of lights and noise. He followed mindlessly, like a predator tracks its prey. His only sensation was the anticipation of the heart-pounding kill.*

*The trail led him to a place of pretty people and glistening lights. He blended in seamlessly, unobserved despite his odd appearance and lack of personal hygiene. He was just a bum on a busy street looking for handouts. This beggar sought neither food nor money, however. He was searching for something more elusive, something more ill-defined. He was looking for redemption, and he would only find it in the death of his victim.*

*As he stood at the window peering into the long room filled with lights and movement, a vague sense of recognition began to glow. Like a bright ember beneath a pile of dead leaves, it inflamed his hatred. Just as he was about to bust through the window and kill his prey, a group of revelers rushed out of the building. One of them jostled him in the crunch to get by, distracting him completely from what he was about to do. Forgetting his purpose, he followed the group as if they had been his objective all along. His mouth watered with anticipation.*

*Moving along the sidewalk, he followed the partiers to their cars. Then he ran at a trot after them, as one by one they pulled out and sped down the road on their way to the party. There were half a dozen cars, so it was easy for him to follow. Just as one vehicle pulled out of sight another came into view going in the same direction.*

*He loped over the bridge that spanned the river and around a corner past the park. The last car turned into a long drive further up the street. He followed and came to a circular driveway, where the vehicles had parked. A large lawn separated the drive from the house. There was loud music coming from it, and lights everywhere. People milled about the entrance greeting each other.*

*He watched and waited for an opportunity to strike, his instincts sharpened. His mind was clear of all thought. Each muscle was taut, ready to spring, He was not alone. 'Jim' was with him, glistening by his side*

*Eventually things quieted down. The music became softer, the voices more subdued, the activity less frantic. Instinctively, he knew that now was the time to move. After that things were a blur as he ran from person to person, room to room, in a killing spree. The screams and pleas for mercy were snuffed out like used candles. Only a few got away.*

*After that, he ran north along the lake for a short way. Then he collapsed and fell asleep in a copse of trees behind large piles of logs and sawdust. A giant smokestack belched sulfur into the air.*

*He slept for several days. When he awoke his instincts picked up the scent of his tormentor again, close by. He followed.*

# Chapter 18

I must have been tired because I slept right through most of the day. I didn't wake up until mid-afternoon, almost three o'clock, and was immediately plunged into a deep funk. It was close to five by the time I showered, dressed, and grabbed a bite to eat. Then I drove down to the office. Luckily for me Suzy had already left.

I dialed Jerry's number at the station. He picked up on the first ring.

"Hi, Jay, I was just going to call you," he said, almost as if he was expecting me.

"Oh? Good news I hope. Anything new on the latest murders?"

"No, not really. I wanted to talk to you about your request for the McKenna photos. Sorry, Jay, no can do."

"Why not? I'm not asking to borrow them or anything. I just want to stop by and take a look at them."

"Jay, that case is closed. They've already been looked at by our forensic experts. You seeing them would serve no useful purpose whatsoever."

"There was a time when you would have appreciated my help."

"We do need your help, but not with a suicide case that's been closed for weeks now. We still have a serial killer on our hands."

"I know. I just feel I owe it to Grace McKenna, my client, to leave no stone unturned in trying to find out what happened to her parents. Do you know Bobby is trying to cheat her out of her share of the inheritance?"

"That's rubbish. I happen to know he offered her a very fair price for her share of the farm. She's not a farmer. What does she want with the place?"

"It's her legacy. She has just as much right to it has her brother. How'd you come by this information, if you don't mind my asking?"

"Leo Kruger, Bobby's lawyer, happened to mention it. We've done our homework, Jay. Contrary to what you may think, we happen to have a very good investigative department here."

"Then why haven't you captured the murderer yet? The last murder was right under your nose, for God's sake."

"And yours."

"Touché! So what do we do now?"

148

"You do nothing. This is a police matter. I'll let you know if we need your help. Right now I suggest you lay low."

"Fine, how do you suggest I earn a living?"

"You ever try selling cars?"

I gave him a few choice words and hung up, greatly disappointed in my old friend. Though he wasn't exactly treating me as a suspect, he wasn't showing me much trust either. I sensed a subtle shift in his attitude regarding me and that made my mood even darker.

After Jerry I tried calling Grace McKenna again, but there was no answer. I left a message, feeling vaguely worried about her. Where could she be and why hadn't she answered any of my calls? I made a point to stop by her place. Then I called my dad's house.

I had been putting this off as long as possible. Now that Jerry had turned down my request to see the photos of the McKenna residence on the day of the deaths, I had no other recourse. I needed to talk to Mary, my old girlfriend, and ask her for help.

Hoping she would answer and not my father, I dialed the number. It had been our family's phone number for over forty years, and was indelibly burnt into my memory. I couldn't have forgotten it in a hundred lifetimes, a little piece of life that hadn't changed amidst all the mutations of the years.

Much to my relief, Mary came on the line.

"Hi, Jay," she said on recognizing my voice. "Your dad's out at the golf course. I expect him back in a couple hours."

'Hi, Mary! Actually, it's you I wanted to talk to."

"Me? What can I do for you?"

We hadn't spoken in months and not two words together since she married my father. I hadn't gone to their wedding even though I was invited and I had insulted my father only the previous night. Now here I was asking for a favor. But I was on a case, being paid thirty-bucks an hour to get information and information was what I was going to get, even if I had to grovel in the dirt. In spite of all this, Mary was more than happy to help. It was then I remembered what a loyal friend she had been.

"I'm helping Grace McKenna look into her parents' deaths, and need to look at the photos of the scene that morning. Jerry, down at the station refused my request. I'm afraid I won't be able to get a court order either."

"Hmm, wasn't that a suicide?"

"The police think so, but I have contradicting information."

"I thought that was kind of funny when I heard about it. I thought it might have something to do with the theft of ammonia nitrate around town. You know, that it might be some kind of terrorist plot."

"I hadn't considered that, sounds kind of farfetched. I don't think there's been any fertilizer stolen from McKenna's farm, just the opposite. They seem to have plenty."

"Interesting. Well, it struck me as strange nonetheless. What do you think I can do about it? I'm retired as you know."

"Yeah, but you still carry some weight downtown. I was hoping you could get your old friend at the coroner's office, Doc Sharp, to release the pictures to you."

"I don't know, Jay, I haven't talked to Phil in ages, but I'll see what I can do. How do I get in touch with you?"

"Just leave a message on my answering machine." I gave her the office number. "I check it everyday."

"OK, Jay, I'll do it for old time's sake, if you promise to bring Suzy and Bud over for a visit."

"You get me those photos and I'll cook you and dad dinner."

"It's a deal. Remember, you promised."

I had no intention of bringing the family over for a visit, let alone cooking my father and my old girlfriend dinner. At that point, however, I would have said anything to get what I wanted. I uncrossed my fingers when I hung-up the phone.

I sat in the office doodling on a notepad as the early evening sun slanted further into the western sky on its way to the other side of the world. As I drew, I thought about the case. It was only a matter of time before my thoughts began to get tangled in my mind like the doodles I was drawing. Maybe it wasn't that farfetched after all. The whole series of murders that had baffled the authorities ten years earlier had been a cover-up for a terrorist plot to steal a B-52 and drop an H-bomb on Washington, DC. Maybe this was no different. Perhaps the murders at Kali's were more than random. What if it was payback or part of a drug war? Maybe there was more to my ex-employer than met the eye. I decided to follow-up and ask him some questions.

Calling the duo from my trio, I asked if they knew where Kali was staying. They were having dinner. Denise, who answered, didn't know, but Paul was able to tell me he was staying with friends out on the north shore of the lake. I got the address from him and headed up old Route 3 toward the Canadian border.

A few miles out of town, I turned right onto the road that heads toward the lake. It passes through flat farmland to the shore. Summer homes and cottages crowd the water's edge. I found the house without much difficulty, an old converted farmhouse with a long front porch overlooking the lake.

A rather large gentleman in shorts and no shirt sat on the porch in a rocking chair sipping a drink. I pulled into the drive. There were three cars, all Hondas of one sort or another, parked in front of me. I got out and approached the man on the rocking chair. He was dark, with curly black hair matted on his chest that trailed along his ample shoulders to his back. I wished he'd put his shirt on. He didn't bother to get up let alone dress.

"Hi, is Kali around? I'm Jay. I work in the band down at the club. I was told he was staying here. I wanted to talk to him about something."

"Kali's very upset. He already talked to the police. He's not seeing anyone right now. Why don't you call later."

"I'm a friend, not a cop. I need to talk to him. It's important. I drove all the way out here to see him."

"Well, you can turn around and drive all the way back."

"What are you, his keeper?"

"Something like that. Now please leave before I call the cops."

"I'm working with them, investigating the murders. That's why I'm here. I can get a court order if you want to do it the hard way. Would you rather I bring the whole bunch of you downtown?"

"You're not a cop. You can't do that," said the stubborn baboon.

"Look, don't give me any of your..."

"Frankie, who's that?" said a familiar voice from inside the house. "What's the matter?"

"There's someone here to see you. I told him you weren't taking visitors."

"Who is it? Jay, is that you?" said Kali, recognizing me through the screen door.

"Yes, Kali, I just stopped by to see how you were doing."

"Not too good," he admitted, stepping out onto the porch. "I can't sleep after what happened at the house. I keep having these terrible nightmares."

"I can imagine."

"They told me you came to the party and found the bodies. The killer must have still been there."

151

"You think?"

"Oh, it was so horrible. All those beautiful people killed. Oh!"

I thought he was going to start crying. Instead, he threw himself in another chair and wrung his hands. "I don't think I'll ever open the club again. I couldn't face the people."

"Why, you didn't do anything."

"Yes, but the stigma of what happened will never leave me."

I didn't bother responding, but started asking him some questions.

"I know you've probably already told the police everything, but I was wondering, Kali, do you know anyone that would want to do this to you?"

"What, kill all my friends?"

"No, maybe they were after you and the others just got in the way."

"Who would want to kill me?" he yelled.

"That's exactly what I want to know. Who would want to kill you? A competitor? A business associate?"

"What, are you crazy, another restaurant owner break into my house and kill everybody in sight? That's nuts."

"Maybe someone from your other line of work," I offered, trying a hunch.

"Heh, what other line of work?"

"Suppose you tell me. This can't be a random incident. Someone was after you and they must have had a good reason. Did you owe anyone money?"

"Just what are you insinuating?" said Kali's fur-backed protector from his rocking chair.

"Nothing, it's just that, well, I know about what they found in your little hideaway. Jerry, the chief of police told me. You're not exactly as clean-cut as you'd like everyone to believe. Maybe your elicit life of kinky sex and designer drugs caught up with you."

"That's not true," said Kali, standing up and taking a few steps forward.

"That's enough," said his large friend, also standing up.

"Whoever did this is still out there and probably still holding a grudge. You can tell me things you can't tell the cops. It won't go any further than this and it might help save your life. Mister Muscles here sure ain't going to protect you."

"I don't know what you're talking about, Jay. No one's after me. I have no enemies, honest. What you're talking about is harmless fun, not a sinister drug ring. No, there's nothing like that."

I didn't exactly believe him but there was nothing more I could do.

"OK, Kali, if you think of anything give me a call."

I gave him my card and drove off, promising myself to keep an eye on my ex-employer. It looked like the gig had ended. I'd have to call Paul and Denise to see if we could find another place to play on the weekends. Figures, just as things were getting good, they were starting to unravel again.

The next few days went by uneventfully. I made little progress on the McKenna case. I spent more time trying to recover my lost finances. I put up some fliers to drum up more business for the karate school, and called some agents to find a gig for the band.

Now that Sheila had left town and I could not get in touch with Grace McKenna, my funds were running low. A few more weeks of this and I wouldn't even be able to afford the flea-bag motel room I was living in. That all too familiar feeling of desperation was creeping in around me and I felt helpless to do anything about it.

I tried calling Grace McKenna several more times over the next few days, leaving messages each time. None of my calls had been answered or returned. My visit to her residence turned up nothing. The place was shut up tight. None of her neighbors had seen her in days. I was definitely worried about her, and ended up having Jerry put a missing person bulletin out on her.

After leaving the station, I went to the office to check my messages. Hitting the 'Play' button on the machine, to my surprise, I got a message from Suzy to call her. It sounded urgent.

I ran next door to the travel agency and rushed into her office. She wasn't there.

"Where's Suzy?" I asked her partner. "I got an urgent message from her."

"She didn't come in today. She's not feeling well."

I ran to the car and drove to the apartment. Dashing up the stairs to our second-story flat, I knocked on the door. I hadn't been there in awhile and didn't feel I had the right to just barge in. It wasn't my place. Suzy's name was still on the lease. After all, she might have been in the sack with her little friend, Alex. I didn't want the image of them together to ruin my already lousy day.

"Who is it?" said a voice that I recognized as my mother-in-law's.

"It's me, Jay. Is everything all right?"

"Oh, hi, Jay. Suzy, Jay's here," she yelled into the room, stepping back to let me in. "Suzy will be glad to see you. She had some trouble down at the agency."

"What's wrong? What happened?" I asked in alarm.

"Nothing," said Suzy coming into the room with a mug of coffee in her hand. "Just a little scare down at the agency, nothing serious."

"Someone assaulted her," her mother informed me.

"What happened?" This time I asked the question in a voice that said I'd better get a straight answer or I'd be the one they were complaining about.

"It was nothing, really," explained Suzy. "I was closing up. It was around five-thirty. It was probably just a wiseass kid. Someone ran by and hit me in the head with something. It wasn't that hard, like a rolled up newspaper, but it surprised me and knocked me down. By the time I got up, whoever it was had run around the corner. I never got a good look at him."

I was livid, seeing red at the thought of someone attacking my wife.

"Did you call the police? I'll see if Jerry can't put some extra patrols on your street. Better yet, I'll keep an eye on the place for the next few days just in case whoever it was tries it again. I hope he does."

"I don't want any trouble down there," Suzy replied.

"Don't worry, if there's any trouble it'll be over before you even know it started."

"I've already talked to the police. They'll take care of it," she assured me.

I was less than assured.

Are you sure you're OK. Did you see a doctor?"

"No, it's not necessary. I was more surprised than hurt, although I banged my knee when I fell. I'll have to take it slow for a few days."

"Fuck!"

I punched the wall, making a hole in the plasterboard, which just upset Suzy and her mother even more.

"I'm sorry, sweetie," I said after her mother left the room. "I'll try not to get upset. It's just that I don't like the thought of someone hurting you. I want to protect you."

"Don't worry, Jay. I know how to take care of myself. I studied self-defense with the great Jay Lawless."

"Very funny. Can we talk about things?"

"There's nothing to talk about, Jay. You made that clear last time we spoke."

"No, you made that clear when you invited Alex to sleep over."

'He left. He's not staying here any more. Mom's staying with us for now."

"Then why can't we talk? I miss you and Bud and want to come home."

"Not now, Jay. I've got too much on my mind. I'm not ready. Anyway, I don't hear you saying you're going to give up the detective business."

"The detective business is giving up on me. I haven't got any clients. One's left town the other's disappeared. The band lost the gig down at Kali's and I lost my three best paying students down at the dojo. I'm open for suggestions."

"We'll talk about it later," she said when her mother came back.

"Fine, there's not much more I can do here. Call me if you need me. Later."

I was upset that someone had assaulted Suzy, but also at her for not letting me help, for not trusting me. On top of that she didn't want to talk about our problems. I was still her husband, after all. I deserved some consideration for that, didn't I? I had never felt so useless, like a discarded piece of rubbish.

I hadn't gone three blocks when I noticed I had a black-and-white tailing me. They followed a few more blocks before they turned on their flashing lights and signaled for me to pull over.

"What's the problem, officer?" I asked the uniformed man who approached my open window.

"Chief LaGrande wants to ask you a few questions down at the station if you don't mind."

"I do mind. What's this about?"

"I don't know, sir. He just told us to pick you up. Do you want to follow us or do you want to go to the station in cuffs?"

"Lead the way, officer, lead the way."

I followed them downtown, curious about what was going on now. Jerry was pushing his weight around if he thought he could just haul me down to the station whenever he wanted. I was about to give him a piece of my mind when he told me why he had me brought in.

155

"We found Grace McKenna. Her car was in a ditch out on the mountain road. She must have been there over a week. Look's like she died on impact."

"Oh, no! I've been trying to get in touch with her."

"Yeah, we know. There are a number of calls from you on her cell phone. Why were you calling her?"

I looked at him in disbelief. Maybe the job was getting to him.

"I told you, I was working for her. I was trying to contact her about her parents' case."

"And what about it?"

"Not much, since you won't let me see the photos of the crime scene."

"It's not a crime scene. It's the scene of a suicide."

"Well, the old lady sure as hell didn't commit suicide."

"Jay, that case is closed."

"What about Grace? Are you going to close that case too?"

"That was an accident. She went through the guardrail and into a ditch. She died almost instantly."

"There's been an autopsy?"

"I guess. I only know what the state boys told me. When was the last time you saw the McKenna woman?"

"Why? I thought you said it was an accident."

"No reason, just wondering why you were the only one she had messages from. You were the one who reported her missing, weren't you?"

"Yes, that's right."

"Awful interested in her whereabouts, weren't you?"

"Like I said, I was working for her. I wanted to get paid. You got any more stupid questions for me you can talk to my lawyer. I'm out of here. Don't bother getting up."

"Wait Jay, that's not all," he said as I got up to leave. "Have you seen Kali Hundouri lately?"

"No, why?" I lied.

"Where were you last Wednesday evening, around midnight?"

"I don't remember offhand, probably asleep in my motel room. Jerry, what's going on? What's this about?"

He hesitated a moment and looked at me hard, as if trying to see if I was hiding something. It's a look I've seen on countless law enforcement personnel over the years.

"Mister Hundouri was murdered a few nights ago. We just found the bodies this morning. There were three of them, your friend and two other men. The estimated time of death was Wednesday evening or early Thursday morning. They were mutilated pretty badly. We're keeping it out of the papers for now."

"So someone *was* after him."

"That's what it looks like, Jay. We know you were asking around about him."

"Yeah, I talked to a few friends of his, got his address, but didn't get a chance to see him. I was going to go out there tonight. You've saved me the trouble."

I left the station after answering a few more questions and promising again not to leave town. The whole episode left me shaken, though I tried not to show it. They must have been killed right after I left. Maybe my hunch was right, and the murders had something to do with drugs, which Kali was obviously involved in. Or was it something else, something more sinister. I wondered if what Jerry had said earlier was true. Was I being stalked? It seemed wherever I went, death followed.

# Chapter 19

I headed back out to my motel room, trying to assimilate everything Jerry had told me. I felt bad for Grace McKenna, worse because it meant I probably wouldn't get paid for the work I'd already done. For some reason I didn't think it was an accident. It also looked like Jerry suspected me of foul play. Something was fishy here and it wasn't the lake trout. I decided to pay Bobby McKenna another visit.

I drove out to the Bob Moffit Road, where the McKenna farm sprawled along the highway. Slowing down as I approached the turn-off to his drive, I pulled along the side of the road just short of the gate and stopped. It was closed across the entrance, with a no trespassing sign attached to it. Bobby was standing behind the gate arguing with another farmer, who had pulled up in his pickup truck.

"All's I want Bob is to buy a few hundred pounds of manure to fertilize my fields. I hear tell you got plenty."

"Well, you heard wrong. I've got just enough for my own crops."

"What crops? I just drove by your west field and there's nothing planted there but crows."

"Never mind what crops. I'm only planting the back fields this year. I'm not planting corn anymore."

"Well, whatever you're planting, you're the only one around here that seems to have fertilizer."

"Any extra I had I've already sold off. Sorry Barney, I don't have anything for you."

The other farmer gave Bobby a long look.

"You know if your dad was still around, he'd…"

"He's not still around. This business drove him to suicide."

"I doubt it was the business," said the disgruntled farmer as he walked back to his truck and drove off in a cloud of dust.

"Hey, Bob," I said as I walked up from where I was standing discreetly out of the way by my car. "I just heard about your sister. I'm so sorry. That's terrible."

"If you say so. I told her her drinking would be the death of her." He did not sound the least bit sorry she was gone.

"She drank?" I asked. This was news to me.

"Like a fish. What do you want?"

"Nothing, just to tell you I'm sorry, see if there's anything I can do."

"What, like help someone else try to get my inheritance from me?"

"No, like helping you find out what happened to your sister."

"Nothing happened to her. She died drinking and driving. It happens all the time. It was her own damn fault."

"That's funny, the coroner didn't mention anything about alcohol. Are you sure she was drinking? Did you see her the night she disappeared? When did she go missing?"

"Fuck you, Lawless. I don't have to tell you shit."

The vehemence of his words struck me. He seemed as if he was going to jump over the fence and attack me. I took a step toward him, my composure a sign how utterly un-phased I was by him.

"No need to be rude, Bob. I understand completely." I knew he was hiding something and I was going to find out what it was. I stuck my card on the gate. "Give me a call if you want to talk. Until then…" I looked at him hard for a moment. "Take care."

Later that night, after going back to the motel for a few hours sleep, I returned to the McKenna farm. It was just one a.m. when I left the room. I parked my car by the side of the road, beneath a line of tall poplars where it wouldn't attract attention, and headed back toward the farm. Sprinting up the highway, I pulled the hood of my sweatshirt up against the rain. It was coming down hard. So far it had been a wet spring. The wind and bad weather would keep everyone inside and cover any noise I might make.

When I got abreast of the McKenna place, I jumped the gate and continued up the dirt track. Jogging past a fenced-in pasture and an empty corn field, I made my way toward the house. I was familiar with the road from the time I was there with Bud, and made my way well enough without a light. As I approached the barn, I stopped and listened for any sign of someone about. As far as I knew, McKenna didn't own a dog. So I wasn't too worried about that possibility. Still, I didn't want to get caught trespassing.

I walked across the driveway to the patch of yard they had been working on during my last visit. What I thought would be a row of exotic fruit trees, however, was now a smooth grass lawn. Although it was hard to tell in the dark, I could have sworn this was where they had everything dug up for planting.

Sneaking along a row of bushes that clung to the farmhouse like ivory, I peeked into a window. The room was empty, but I could see some men in the next room. They appeared to be playing cards. A

159

television was playing somewhere in the house. Nothing seemed out of place, except none of the men looked like Bobby McKenna. They looked like the crew I saw planting trees that day. Perhaps the boss was upstairs sleeping. I decided to check out the barn.

I crept back along the hedge to the edge of the building, at its closest point to the barn. A couple of large oak trees spread their leaves like a tent overhead. I darted across the dirt drive, which had been splattered to mud by the rain.

The barn was large, at least three-stories high, and as long as half a football field. I had been in it a few times as a kid. I remembered how the cows had turned and stared at me as I walked by, freaking me out.

There was a small door within the larger barn entrance. The larger door, when opened, was wide enough to drive a tractor or backhoe through. The small door was just wide enough to let me through. You had to step up and duck your head when you entered. There was a faint light filtering through the entranceway, and a low hum of some kind of machine. I tried the latch. It wasn't locked, so I slowly opened the door.

I entered a wide cavernous room with stalls and bales of hay, but no cows. The smell of petroleum filled the air. That's all I got to see. I was grabbed from behind and thrown backward out of the barn, knocking my head on the side of the door. I landed on my ass in the mud. A large dark form ran at me through the mist and rain. I only had time to make it partially to my feet when he was on me. His right fist whistled by my ear. I grabbed his extended arm as I fell back and rolled. Sticking my right leg into his midsection, I straightened it at the last moment, sending him flying over my head as I rolled to my feet.

God, I loved that move. Although it's something I've never been taught, I've been using it on bullies since I was old enough to get picked on. And I was picked on a lot, being the adorable little, smart-mouthed runt that I was. It's just something that came naturally to me one day when I was being rushed by a kid twice my size, just instinctive.

My first impulse was to run, to just get out of there. I didn't want to get caught trespassing and was hoping to exit stage left. My attacker, who was just getting to his feet, and as usual, must have outweighed me by a considerable amount, had other ideas. He tried to cut off my retreat. He looked vaguely familiar, but I didn't get time to place the face.

The rain was pouring down, the footing bad. I would have to be careful or I'd be on my back. By the looks of this guy that would be a very bad position to be in. He probably wouldn't fall for that little alley-oop trick again.

He approached me cautiously, throwing jabs and hooks at my head that I easily eluded and blocked. I hit him with straight, hard left-right combinations that cut his face and rocked his head back. He blocked a hand-sword I aimed at the side of his neck and hit me with a grazing right. Even though it only partially landed, it sent me reeling, but I kept my feet.

As he pulled his arm back to unload another right to finish me off, I nailed him with a short, powerful thrust kick to his floating-ribs. Stopping in midstride, he grabbed his side and bent forward, grunting in pain. I immediately snapped a round-house kick to his downturned chin. It sent him flying back. He hit the ground hard. His head snapped back when he landed, sending his brain bouncing back and forth in his cranium. He laid there concussed, with a dazed, surprised look on his face. Grasping for breath, he tried to sit up and suck in air. Not giving him time to get his breath, I hit him with a stiff right as he raised his head. Lights out!

I ran back to the car. I was disconcerted and breathing hard. I wasn't sure what had just happened, but I didn't want to stick around to find out. I normally wouldn't have finished a guy off like that. But this dude was pretty scary, especially coming out of nowhere like that. I didn't want to give him a second opportunity to give me brain damage. I certainly didn't need any more hospital bills or lawsuits.

I got to my car and looked up and down the highway. It was empty. The rain was coming down harder than ever. It would make my getaway that much easier.

Getting into the car, I started the engine and checked the rearview mirror before pulling out. All I saw in the red glare of my taillights was a rush of metal coming at me out of the darkness. A fraction of a second later a pickup truck smashed into the rear of my car. It jerked forward and snapped my head back like a whip. Without hesitating, before they could ram me again, I slammed my foot on the gas pedal and spun out of there spitting mud. They rammed me again, but I was moving now. It only resulted in knocking me further out of range. I sped up and started to pull away.

I was momentarily confused, out of my element. I didn't know what to do. Part of me wanted to stop and confront them. Another part of me – probably the saner part – wanted to get away. I was moving up the highway as fast as I dared in the rain, west out of town. The speedometer was past seventy-five, inching toward eighty. The truck was only seconds behind and gaining. I could see the flashing lights of an intersection about a quarter mile ahead through my rain-splashed windshield. I was thinking of stopping again, when my rear window was shattered. It only took me a second to realize I was being shot at. I sped up even faster, throwing caution to the wind.

As I approached the intersection, I could see a car coming toward the junction from the north. I tried to gauge who would reach it first. My initial impulse was to speed up so I would beat him there and zoom through the lights. It didn't matter that the road we were on had the flashing red light and the stop.

I was going ninety as I approached the lights, the truck only a car length behind and gaining. The other car had sped up too. It was a race. It looked like we'd get there about the same time. The truck pulled up to my blind spot, as if to pass. As he did, I let my foot off the accelerator and jammed on the brakes. It wasn't hard enough to send the car into a spin, but just enough so the other vehicle whizzed past as my brake lights flared. I decelerated from ninety-five to forty-five in four seconds.

There was a small diner at the intersection, where my Dad and Mary went for breakfast. The wide parking lot was empty at this time of night, lit only by a single street lamp. As my pursuers sped past me and through the intersection, I turned the car sharply to the left into the diner's driveway. Speeding across the parking lot, I narrowly missed the side of the building. I was going fifty miles per hour, and crossed the short piece of tarmac in a fraction of a second. Bouncing over a curb, I barreled down the road heading back to the main drag west out of town. Fortunately for all of us, the driver of the car coming down the highway had braked hard to avoid the three car collision. It had pulled up on the side of the road and stopped. The coast was clear.

I was a good distance down the road before the pickup turned around to follow. I had gained thirty or forty seconds on them. Hopefully, that would be enough.

Thinking desperately, I wondered how to lose them. Pushing the pedal to the metal, I sped down the highway. Maybe I could elude them as I got closer to the city, or at least get help.

I had to make a decision soon. I was coming to another intersection. This one was much bigger and busier than the one I had just blown through. It had an array of stoplights to control traffic through the four-lane highway. A left at the junction would take me back toward town and possible safety. At least there might be places to hide. Right would take me up toward the mountains, where I'd had my recent run-in with the late William Riley. Straight would take me through twisting back roads and small villages, which I didn't know well, but might offer some means of escape. Again the damned truck was advancing on me. They must have had some extra horsepower in that rig. My secondhand Toyota had never been driven past eighty. I was now doing ninety-five and was down to a quarter of a tank.

The lights were green as we approached the crossroads. A few cars sat on the main drag waiting for the signal to change. The truck was right behind me. I wouldn't trick him again. I slowed down as we came to the light, which was just turning red. As I did, he hit me from behind, pushing me forward through the intersection. I slammed on the brakes and turned the wheel sharply to the right, narrowly missing a station wagon that was just starting to pull out. It swerved wildly to get out of my way, and got sideswiped by the pickup, which veered off just a fraction of a second too late behind me.

For a moment I thought it was all over, that I would roll over and over until I ended up crushed and mangled on the side of the road. That little Toyota actually stood on two wheels for a few seconds. Then it wobbled down on all fours and skidded violently back and forth across the highway. Somehow I kept it under control, and sped up the road toward the hills and the mountains beyond.

I had a slight advantage. I had gained precious minutes on my pursuers as they careened off a few other vehicles before continuing the chase. It was only a matter of time, however, before they caught up to me on the long, slowly rising highway. My only hope was to try and lose them in the mountains. The bad news was, out here, where civilization was sparse and law enforcement sparser, there was little likelihood of finding help.

I managed to elude them by taking advantage of my knowledge of the roads in that area. My car also had quicker acceleration on the turns, even in the rain. Thank goodness I had used some of my recent short-lived windfall to purchase new tires. They hugged the road like claws. In spite of my endeavors, however, the pickup was right behind me as we sped past the massive walls of the prison in the little village at the foot of the mountain. I was running out of ideas and gas.

Then I saw it up ahead, a state police car coming in the opposite direction. It was about a hundred yards up the road. As soon as he saw me speeding down the highway, he turned on his flashing lights. I slowed down, but still passed him going sixty-five. The pickup had slowed to a crawl. I looked back in my rearview mirror to see the trooper turn around and speed after me. He completely ignored my pursuers. I pulled over to the side of the road.

"Boy, am I glad to see you," I yelled, jumping out of my car as he pulled up.

"Hold it right there," he ordered, pulling out his revolver and pointing it at my chest.

"Wait, you don't understand. I'm being chased. That truck right behind me, you must have seen it."

"I said hold it!" he shouted with a voice of authority. It was a tone he didn't need with the large gun he pointed at me. "Don't move. I didn't see anyone else but you going through town there. You must have been going near a hundred miles an hour."

"I told you, I was being chased."

"Give me your license and registration. Leave it on the seat and move to the other side of the vehicle."

I looked up and down the road. It was dark and deserted. The rain had let up a little, but still pounded the pavement. Not wanting to give this trigger-happy rookie an excuse to shoot me, I did as he instructed. Placing my license and registration on the seat, I moved to the other side of the car. As I did, I kept up my pleas for help. He looked at my license briefly. Then without checking any further, he looked at me ominously.

"You're under arrest," he announced. "There's a warrant out for you, for trespassing, and assault and battery."

"What?" I said. "This must be some mistake. I was being chased and shot at. Look at my car."

The trooper looked at me as if I was some demented child molester, and pointed the gun at my chest again.

"Up against the car."

"Wait, call the chief of the police in the city, he'll tell you who I am."

"Look, buddy, he's the one who swore out the warrant. It says you are dangerous and violent. So you better just shut up and do what I say."

164

As he said these words, he walked toward me with the gun still pointed at my chest, and pulled a pair of handcuffs from his belt. It was then that I noticed the pickup truck moving slowly up the highway in our direction. Its dim lights cast an eerie glow in the downpour.

"There, there they are, right in back of you. Those are the guys who are chasing me. Look!"

He glanced back quickly in time to see the other vehicle pull up behind his squad car. He kept his attention and his gun pointed in my direction, however.

"You just hold it right there," he said to me. "Don't try anything."

He turned to see who had pulled up.

"Can I help you?" he yelled over the hiss of the rain. "You'd better keep moving. There's nothing to see here. This is police business. Keep moving."

I edged behind my car.

"Officer, you'd better watch it, they've got guns," I warned.

At this point the trooper didn't know who had guns and who didn't. He was starting to get nervous.

"Get moving there!" he shouted again over the rain.

There was no response from the pickup. Then there was a flash. A spray of bullets shattered the glass in the open door of the squad car. The officer was standing right next to it. Diving behind his front fender, he returned fire, sending two or three errant bullets careening over his assailants' heads. It gave them the time they needed to take aim and fill him, and the front of his car, with lead. As all this was happening I jumped into my Toyota and sped up the highway. The road rose up a steep incline. I jammed my foot into the floorboard to gain speed. By the time they were moving after me, I had reached my cruising velocity of ninety-five mph, and was heading into the final peaks of the mountain range.

Higher and higher we went, the road hugging the curves around the side of the mountain. At one point I glanced in my rearview mirror. They were right on my bumper. Another glance showed me the gas gauge was on empty. I looked up just in time to see the curve. I vaguely recognized where I was. I had no idea what to do. Just at that moment, they hit my rear bumper, trying to knock me off the road. I fought to gain control. We were at dead-man's curve, the hairpin turn at a scenic gorge that Barry Davids went over with me chasing him ten years before. It looked like it was my turn to go over the gorge this time. I hit the guardrail and careened across the highway to grind against the cliff

165

face on the inside lane. Then I was flung back across the road like a pin-ball. Smashing through the guardrail, I went over the 300 foot drop.

I've had some intense moments in my life, like the time I went out of that B-52 as it crashed in flames in the Potomac with its nuclear arsenal. I was lucky to live through that. I'd be luckier to survive this. Obviously I lived or I wouldn't be telling you the story now, but it was close, as close as I ever want to come to the other side.

Somehow, as my car lurched toward the guardrail, before going over the cliff, I was able to open the door and jump out. Actually, I didn't exactly jump as much as duck-and-roll. I landed on a soft spot of leaves and grass before tumbling head-over-heels down a short embankment into a grove of trees. This more or less broke my fall, though I felt like I had dislocated my shoulder. It took me awhile to get to my feet. I stood swaying for a moment, and had to hold onto a branch until I got my equilibrium back. My car had exploded in flames at the bottom of the gorge. I glanced back up the embankment to see the headlights of the pickup briefly spray over the broken guardrail and disappear. I guess I wouldn't want to hang around too long either if I had just shot a state trooper.

I made my way back up the slippery slope with great difficulty. I had to grab on to tree branches with my good arm as I painfully pulled myself forward. Once on the road, I made my way back down the highway until I could see the red and blue flashing lights of the rescue vehicles on the road below. The body of the unfortunate trooper had obviously been discovered. Not wanting to explain my involvement in a cop killing, I made an about face and headed back up into the mountains. It was time for Jay Lawless to disappear.

# Chapter 20

I remembered my dad had a hunting camp up here on the mountain. It was nothing fancy, not like the big camps along the lake. This was just a plywood shack stuck in the middle of the woods, with an outhouse in back. He and his well-heeled buddies used to go to bond and recall the days of their youth. They drank and caroused, and oh yeah, occasionally hunted for deer.

Dad invariable came home empty handed every year. My uncle would bag two or three deer a season, but my father never shot a thing, although he had a sharpshooter's medal from the Marines. I guess he just didn't have the heart to shoot them, especially a big, proud, handsome, twenty point buck standing in the wild just minding his own business. Still, he loved the days at the camp with his buddies.

He would take us out to the cabin once in a while in the summer, although he never took us hunting. The camp was usually the starting point for an all-day hike. Sometimes we stayed there overnight, sleeping on musty-smelling army cots. As far as I knew, my father hadn't been there in years. I hoped the place was still there and unoccupied. I doubted there would be anybody around this time of year, in the spring.

I needed time to think and a place to recoup. I didn't plan on hiding out for long. I had revenge on my mind. Things had gotten real personal, really fast. Someone had shot at me and run me off the road. I wanted nothing more than to return the favor. That would be difficult, however, without transportation. Mine was a burning wreck at the bottom of the chasm. No doubt that's what happened to poor Grace McKenna. Not only had they tried to kill me. They had guns and weren't afraid to use them against the police.

Who the hell were these guys? I wondered as I made my way up the highway. Instead of staying on the road, which wound its way around the mountain, I cut through the woods. My plan was to go directly over the intervening peak. It would be light soon and the place would be swarming with Staties looking for whoever killed one of their own. Traveling through the forest at night would be a risk, but I'd been over these trails before as a teenager. Anything was better than walking along the road like a dumb duck.

There was a well-known spot up the highway where a small wooden shack had been built to house a cold-water spring that ran out of the mountain. From there I scrambled up an embankment and pushed through the pine leaves into the forest, to the entrance of a well-marked trail. I was immediately plunged into darkness, but the path was wide at this point and easy to follow, at least at first.

It had been over thirty years since I'd been here last. I was with my older brother, Tony, and his friend. They only let me go with them because my dad demanded it, and pretty much ignored me the whole time. I stuck to them like glue. I was actually the one who climbed a tree to find our bearings when we got lost. The bowl-shaped lake we had been heading for was the same one where I had my fatal encounter with the Riley kid. It was again my target tonight. It had taken us all afternoon back then, over three hours, to reach the lake. I knew I'd make better time now as a man, although in the darkness that was proving difficult.

The trail became a narrow path, which threatened to disappear at every step in the darkness. Soon, however, the sun rose in the eastern sky and shined directly on the mountainside I was hiking on.

I knew that if I kept the sun behind me, I would hit the lake. The first hour I'd be climbing, the next, I'd be descending down the other side of the mountain. From there it would be another half-hour hike around the lake, along country lanes and dirt roads to my dad's camp.

I was exhausted from lack of sleep, and drained from the strain of my life and death car chase. Anger fueled my legs, however, as I labored up the mountainside. Hoards of black flies buzzed in my eyes, nose, and mouth constantly, making the trek more difficult. Cutting off a couple fern leaves from a bush, I stuck them into the back of my shirt so the fronds dangled over my head. They swished up and down as I walked and brushed off most of the pesky little insects. I tried to put things together as I hiked.

Bobby McKenna was definitely up to something, but what? My adversary of that morning had looked familiar. Did he know me? How could they have recognized me so quickly? They must have known who I was. And the thing with Suzy at the agency, was that connected, or was that my three mid-eastern students getting payback? I couldn't ignore the possibility. I wondered if it had anything to do with the stolen fertilizer. Maybe all my conspiracy-minded friends were right after all. Suppose someone was trying to make a bomb, a big one!

Why would someone try to kill me for snooping around a barn? What were they, the cow police? I wondered if my errant ex-students were involved. All these thoughts collided in my brain as I walked through the silent forest to my father's camp.

As hoped, the lake came into view only an hour after I got to the top of the mountain. It must have been around eleven or twelve noon by the time I reached its shore. I came out to a little clearing at the far end of the lake from the beach. I had stumbled onto what appeared to be a small fishing camp. There was a good-size tent set up on a square wooden platform. It was raised slightly above the ground, probably to keep it dry when the lake, which was only a couple feet away, kicked up. A stone hearth stood in the middle of the clearing. It had been used recently, probably the previous weekend. Hopefully, whoever owned the place wouldn't be back for awhile.

Dropping to the ground next to the lake, I splashed cold water on my face. I was so thirsty I could barely keep from slurping the lake water like a dog. I unlatched the tent and looked in. It was musty, but dry and inviting. I crawled in and lay down. I only intended to rest for a moment. The hum of the insects and the lapping of the water on the shore soon lulled me to sleep, however. I awoke with a start late in the afternoon.

My shoulder, where I had hurt it in the fall when my car went over the gorge, ached with pain and stiffness. I rose and staggered out of the tent into the late afternoon light. The sun was now on its way down behind the next mountain. The slope rose behind the lake to form a broad, square ridge. My dad's camp was located at the foot of it. I would have to hurry if I wanted to make it by nightfall. I prayed my luck held out, as I started my hike around the semi-populated lake.

Walking along the shoreline, I soon came to a dirt road that circled the lake for several miles. Little used except by fishermen and hunters, it would take me to my father's cabin. I didn't expect many vehicles to be on it, at least not cops. I knew I'd hear anyone driving along before they'd see me.

I made good time and was soon walking along a narrow, paved country lane. There was nothing but trees and fields around me, the lake on one side, the mountain on the other. A farmer in a pickup truck, which I hid from as it drove by, was the only traffic I saw.

It was late by the time I reached the turn-off to the hunting camp, a dirt road with four or five wooden signs nailed on a tree. The signs announced the names of the camp owners. The Lawless sign had long since eroded to a blank white nub.

My stomach growled as I walked down the road, glad to be at my destination. My first order of business would be to try and mess up some grub. That wouldn't be easy out in the middle of nowhere. I hoped there'd be something at the camp.

I found the cabin in a clearing at the end of a short, partly overgrown track leading from the dirt road. My dad's name was still nailed on a tree. I tore it down as a precaution as I walked by. I assumed they were after me. I wasn't sure why. What did that trooper say, trespassing and assault? Now it would be for killing a cop. No sense making it easy to find me. Not that I intended to hide for long, but I definitely needed a place to gather my thoughts.

The door to the square, tarpapered lodge was padlocked. I kicked it in without a problem. The place smelled mustier inside than I remembered. It probably hadn't been slept in for half a dozen years, but the cots still had blankets and the windows still had glass. The wood-burning stove looked like it still worked. However, there was no food.

I gathered firewood for the stove. As I did so, I checked out some of the nearby camps, hoping to find something to eat. As luck would have it, in the next cabin, which I also had to break into, there were a couple cans of Spaghetti Os and a packet of instant soup. I brought this back to the camp along with an armful of wood. I left a note and ten dollars. I didn't have anything else in my wallet.

After lighting the stove and stoking up a nice warm fire, I was able to heat up the can of Spaghetti Os and have a hearty, much needed meal. Lighting a kerosene lamp, I lay on the same cot I had slept on as a kid, and considered my next move. I was planning to take them by surprise. Now all I had to do was figure out how.

By now the authorities would have probably figured out I hadn't died in the crash. They'd also more than likely have every cop, Statie, and paramilitary goon in the county out looking for me with orders to shoot on sight. For some reason I felt certain the killing of the trooper would be pinned on me. It seemed that Jerry had convinced himself I was a dangerous criminal. The unfortunate rookie had just enough time to radio my license plate number into headquarters before being riddled with bullets. Never mind I didn't own a gun. I was the last person to see him alive. I'd be the fall-guy if past experience was any indication.

If my assumptions were correct and the police were after me, I wondered how long I'd have before they started looking up here in the mountains. With my luck, it'd probably be the first place they searched. I'd have to be careful. A fire would be out of the question. I'd have to stay out of sight. I crashed most of the next day and woke up in the late afternoon.

Who could I call for help, even if I did somehow manage to get to a phone? My dad? He certainly wouldn't turn me in, but would he help me? I could just hear him telling me to go to the authorities and trust the system. I'd just as soon trust a poison adder. I needed to call Suzy, if for nothing else than to let her know I was OK. I prayed she and Bud were all right. My anxiety rose as I lay there thinking about them. Even though it was beginning to get cold, I got up sweating with concern.

If my assailants knew who I was, and from all evidence they did, then my family could be in danger. Suddenly, hiding out in the woods no longer seemed an option. I had to get to them. I had to protect my wife and child.

I waited until dark. Taking an army blanket from one of the cots for warmth, and an old Swiss army knife from a shelf in the camp, I ran out into the night. It must have been around ten. The sky was clear. Millions of stars peeked down through the gaps in the trees. The moon was low in the eastern sky. I knew I could make the twenty or so miles back to the city by five a.m. I had no idea what I was going go do after that. Nothing mattered except making sure Suzy and Bud were safe.

I walked back to the highway, keeping well off the road. After a couple hours or so I was back at the spot where I had started my hike over the mountain. The underground spring bubbled out of the rocks. I slaked my thirst with the ice cold liquid, and filled an empty coke bottle with it, after cleaning it the best I could. I didn't know where I would find more. I needed to keep myself hydrated if I was going to jog back to the 'burgh'.

I planned to keep up a good pace, running where I could and walking as fast as possible. I looked down into the village in the valley below. I could see roadblocks on the highway leading into town. I'd have to steer clear of the roads if I didn't want to be seen. At this rate, it would be long after daylight before I'd get home.

I started across the road to the gulley that led through the woods and down behind the town. As I did, a lone car came around the curve and slowed down. I darted back into the trees and out of sight as it pulled into the parking area. It came to a stop right in front of the small shed and spring.

It was dark. I couldn't make out who was in the car. It sat there for some time. No one got out. Finally, the driver opened the door and exited cautiously. There was something familiar about the way he moved, but he was engulfed in shadow. He stood by the car unmoving for some time. Whoever it was hadn't come here to hike. It didn't look like they were taking a leak either. Maybe he was looking for someone. Maybe he was looking for me! On an impulse, I stepped out of the trees and approached the man rapidly. I was taking a chance, but something about the guy's silhouette seemed recognizable. I was two feet away from him before he finally reacted. I could hardly believe my eyes.

"Is that you, Jay?" he said, peering at me in the darkness. It was my father.

"Jesus, Dad, what are you doing here?"

"Whoa, you scared the hell out of me, coming out of the woods like that. I thought you were a bear or something."

"Dad, what are you doing here?"

"Looking for you! What do you think, I'm out here at this time of night to get a drink of water? I knew you were in trouble. When they found your car at the bottom of the gorge without a trace of you, I knew somehow you got away safe. I also know you wouldn't shoot a cop."

"Yeah, the only gun I own is in your closet."

"I figured you'd be up here, maybe holed-up at the hunting camp."

"You guessed right. I was just on my way to town to check up on Bud and Suzy. I have a feeling they may be in danger. I was run off the road and shot at by a bunch of McKenna's thugs last night. At least I think they're his men. They found me snooping around the barn. I don't know what's going on, but it must be big for them to react like that to a little trespassing."

"Slow down, Jay. We need to get you off the highway. They've got road blocks all the way back into town and up toward the border. We'll have to travel the back roads, but even those are being watched. It wouldn't do to be stopped with you in the car."

"We could go back to the camp, try tomorrow night."

"No, they know about the camp. They questioned me this morning. It's pretty common knowledge. I used to hunt with several of their fathers. One of them asked about it. I had to tell them. That's why I came, to warn you in case they followed up on it. No, we've got to get you back to town. I'm worried about Bud and Suzy too."

We got in his car and drove back up the highway in the direction I had just come from. A short distance past the turn-off to the lake we took a right down a small country lane. It snaked through the hills and circled back eastward. After a few more miles we were in deep woods, surrounded by trees.

As we drove I told him what had happened, from the time I entered the McKenna farm to the time I drove off Lookout Gorge. At my description of the trooper's murder he just shook his head and swore.

"There's something in the barn they didn't want me to see," I said, summing up my latest theory.

"Maybe you just pissed somebody off. Sounds like you gave that guy a pretty good beating."

"He attacked me from behind. He didn't ask any questions. He just started whaling on me. I nailed him with a couple of kicks and took him out. Next thing I know there's a bunch of goons after me in a pickup truck shooting guns. No, there's something going on there they don't want anyone to know about."

"Do you know who it was who attacked you?"

"He looked like one of the guys working for McKenna."

"You need to go to the police."

"Jerry put the warrant out for my arrest. He's been acting funny. There's something going on."

"Then go to someone else."

"Who, like the State Police? They'd just as soon shoot me as look at me. No, I've got to handle this on my own. Even if they listened to me, I have no evidence. It's my word against theirs."

We argued for a few more minutes. I told him about the missing fertilizer and the terrorist angle.

"Sounds pretty far-fetched," he observed. "And you think it has something to do with the murders?"

"It wouldn't be the first time something like this has happened. Look what was behind all the bloodshed last time."

We sat in silence the rest of the trip.

Somehow we managed to avoid the roadblocks and stakeouts. My dad grew up in this area and knew these roads like the veins of his hands. It took all night, but by daybreak we were driving down the familiar streets of the 'burgh'. I had even managed to doze off for

173

awhile. Only time would tell what the new day would bring, but there was a good bet I wasn't ready for it.

# Chapter 21

Not knowing if my place was being watched or my phone bugged, we decided to call my cousin Pat. Jerry knew we were related, but I guessed he hadn't put her under surveillance yet. It was a little after five a.m.

"Hello," she answered, woken out of a deep sleep for a second time by her errant cousin.

"Hi Pat, it's me, Jay. Sorry to bother you again so early, but I need your help."

"Jay, where are you? Are you OK? What happened?" she asked in a rush. "They're saying you killed a state trooper. They found your car at the bottom of Lookout Gorge!"

"I know. I'm with Dad. I'll tell you all about it. First I need to get in touch with Suzy. Can you help me?

"Sure, Jay. Are you going to the police?"

"Not right now. I'm not sure who I can trust down there. Remember what you were saying about someone stealing fertilizer to make a bomb?"

"Yeah?"

"Well, I think I stumbled onto something like that at the McKenna farm, but before I could tell anyone they were chasing me down the road shooting at me. The Statie got in their way."

"That's terrible. You've got to tell the police."

"I would, but there's something fishy going on. I'm afraid they'd shoot me on sight. Can we talk? Has anyone contacted you?"

"No, I only know what I've read in the paper or heard on the radio."

"Good. It's funny the cops would have known about my trespassing and the fight at the farm so soon. I mean, why would those guys call the cops then chase me in their pickup, guns blazing? It doesn't add up. That trooper was looking for me. He had my name on a warrant less than twenty minutes after the incident. Someone tipped him off. He mentioned Jerry's name specifically, like the chief of police himself had issued the alert. It's all just plain strange. Makes me a little reluctant to waltz down to the station. You should have seen the way they gunned down that trooper. It was as if they were above the law."

"That's awful," she said again. "What are you going to do? What do you want me to do?"

"Give Suzy a call. The cops may be watching the house and monitoring her phone, but they won't suspect you. You could say you need a hand shopping or something. She'd be glad to help. You know her. Then get her to your place where I can talk to her. Tell her to bring Bud."

"You need a place to stay?" she asked helpfully. Good old Pat, I knew I could count on her.

"We can talk about that later. Right now I need to make sure Suzy and Bud are all right. If whoever is after me knows who I am, they could be in danger too."

"OK, it's early yet. Why don't you and your dad come over. No one will be up or about at this time of the morning. I'll give her a call at six, tell her it's an emergency. I need my medicine and the van is in the shop, which is true by the way."

"You're great, Pat! Thanks a million. You may have just saved my life."

"I hope it doesn't come to that. See you in a bit," she said and hung up.

I told my dad and we made our way through town to her place without being spotted.

When she let us into her apartment I smelled the aroma of coffee and toast. She cooked us a breakfast of bacon and eggs, and listened as I told her my story. I was going on pure adrenaline. Sleep would be impossible until I knew that Suzy and my son were all right.

At six o'clock on the dot, Pat dialed our home number. No one answered, which was unusual. Suzy would normally be up by now. It was a workday and she had to open the office by eight. In any event, the phone was right by her bed. She would have answered if she were there. I had all I could do to stop from grabbing the phone and yelling for her to pick up. Instead, Pat left a message that she needed someone to take her to the pharmacy. As an afterthought, she told Suzy she was sure everything would be OK, and suggested she bring Little Bud over for the day.

"Bud'll be all right here. It'll give you a chance to rest. I'm sure you need it after what's happened. Don't worry, dear, you know Jay. I'm sure he'll be OK. He has a way of turning up when you least expect it."

Then she hung up.

"Thanks, Pat" I said. "That was perfect. I wonder where she is. I'm worried about her. She should have been there and answered the phone."

176

"Any chance she's staying with friends?" asked my dad. "After all that's happened, she probably didn't want to stay there alone."

"Yeah," I replied. "We can try and get in touch with some of them, her mom, the girls at the office, maybe Alex, her old flame. She might have left a note. We've got to locate her."

"Calm down, Jay," my dad said. "We'll find her. I'm sure she's all right, staying with friends. We'll find her.

Pat and Dad took turns calling Suzy's friends and acquaintances. The first on the list was her mom. No one had seen Suzy since the previous day when she left work early to pick up Bud at daycare. As far as the girls in the office knew she had planned to spend the night at home. She was upset at the news of my accident and disappearance, but wasn't worried about her own safety, or Bud's.

"What did her mom say again?" I asked Pat.

"That she called last night around seven, but no one answered. She thought they might have gone out to McDonalds or some place for dinner. She was going to call back, but by the time she remembered, it was too late, around ten. She was going to call first thing this morning, but we beat her to it. She was a little worried as well, under the circumstances."

By 7:15 that morning I was frantic with concern.

"Where could she be?" I asked for the tenth time.

"I wonder if the cops have a tail on her," said Dad. "At least then she'd be safe."

"Yeah, that is if Jay's hunch about the chief of police is wrong," Pat reminded us.

"We've got to check out the apartment," I insisted, hardly able to contain myself. "We can't lose a minute."

"How we going to do that in broad daylight?" asked my cousin.

"I can't, but you can. We keep a key under the planter by the rear door."

"How? I'm in a wheel-chair, remember? And my van's in the shop."

"Where's the shop?" I asked.

Forty minutes later, my father drove Pat to my apartment. I sat by the radio and TV waiting for news. Well, not exactly sat as much as paced the small apartment like a cat in heat. I was too nervous to stay in one spot for more than a few seconds. There was little of immediate benefit on the airwaves, mostly weather reports and disc-jockeys

177

playing the same mindless crap. When I did find a news channel all they talked about was the murder of the state trooper. I listened spellbound as they described the murder suspect, the fugitive who was still at large. I heard my name mentioned as if in a dream. I hardly believed they were talking about me. They had found the murder weapon, a semi-automatic .45-caliber handgun next to the burning hulk of my car.

Finally, after what seemed like an eternity, but was only a half-hour, Pat and my dad returned. Suzy and Bud were nowhere to be found.

"Where could they be?" I wondered out loud. "She's not at her mom's. None of her friends have seen her."

I called my office phone and ran the messages. There was nothing except an old one from Jerry LeGrande asking me to stop by the station. I was frantic.

"We found this," Pat said finally, as if she did not want to give it to me. "A note."

I grabbed it from her hands and read it eagerly, my heart a throbbing, pounding piece of lead in my ribcage. I read it in spite of my shaking hands, which made the letters dance before my eyes. All there was on the slip of paper was a phone number.

"Where did you find this?" I asked, unsure what it meant.

"In the middle of the kitchen table beneath a salt shaker," said my dad. "You couldn't miss it."

I looked at the number again and had the immediate overwhelming urge to grab the phone and dial it. I hesitated as my father began to speak.

"I think it's time to call the authorities. Kidnapping is a matter for the Feds. Maybe we can get the FBI involved."

"So is attempted murder and cop killing. These guys aren't fucking around."

"That's all the more reason to go to the FBI. We can't take a chance with your family's lives."

"That's just why I'm not going to the authorities. For all we know they could be in on it."

"Don't be crazy, Jay. You've got to keep a cool head in this situation."

"I am fucking crazy. And the last fucking thing I'm going to keep is cool. I'll be cool all right. I'll kill them all in cold mother-fucking blood."

"Calm down now, Jay," Patsy begged me, looking worried. She had never seen me riled before. Well, she hadn't seen anything yet.

I paced the room as I thought out some sort of strategy for getting my wife and child back. I had a good idea where they were, but had to be sure.

"Do you know anyone in the phone company?" I asked my cousin.

# Interlude

*'Jim' had been following the trail for days. Sometimes the scent was strong, sometimes weak. Now it was gone, but his thirst for vengeance still burned fiercely.*

*He had followed it to a white house by the lake, and even though he didn't catch his quarry, he had found others to assuage his terrible hunger for blood. He watched as three men engaged in some type of behavior that he vaguely recognized as sex. 'Jim' butchered them like seals.*

*He found the scent again late one night as he walked the shore of the great waters, north of the city. Moving out of his hiding place, he loped in the direction the odor was coming from. He was downwind from a cluster of buildings he could see in the distance. There, silhouetted against the setting sun, stood four large silos.*

*Getting there, he found two men struggling. He watched in dumb fascination, not caring who won. His head moved back and forth with the action. One, the one he wanted, got the better of the other one and ran off. That which had once been Daniel followed. There was a crash. One machine rammed the other. Then they disappeared down the road. He sniffed the air in confusion. Then he crawled into a ditch with his companion, his Bowie knife, and fell asleep.*

# Chapter 22

Twelve hours later I was crawling on my belly through a field of tall, wet grass toward a barn I couldn't see. Instinctively, I knew I had to act. I had to gain the initiative, do the unexpected.

Earlier that night after a supper of soup and bread – the only thing I could keep down - I phoned the number. I called from a payphone at the mall. A friend of Pat's that worked at the local telephone office traced the call for us.

The conversation chilled the very marrow in my bones.

"Do as we say or your wife and child will be killed," said the voice on the other end of the line in a Mid Eastern accent. "Turn yourself into the police and admit to the murder of the state trooper, and we will let them go."

"How do I know you haven't killed them already?" I replied. "Let me talk to them."

Instead, the speaker gave a command in some foreign tongue. I immediately heard the high-pitched screams of a woman and a child crying in the background.

"Is that good enough for you?" asked the voice. "I hope so. We are not playing games, Mister Lawless. Do as we say or we will kill them both."

With that the connection went dead.

As difficult as the conversation had been, it was enough to give us the location of the receiving phone in the vicinity of the McKenna farm. That was close enough for me. My suspicions were confirmed.

So there I was, alone, an army of one, the marine had landed. No matter I had never been in the military or in battle. Like that time before, my intent was strong – kill or be killed.

The hardest part of the day, besides waiting for darkness, was persuading my dad to stay out of it. When he found out what I had in mind, he went home to get his hunting rifle. He was insistent on accompanying me.

"You'll need someone to watch your back. You can't take them all on alone. They've probably got dozens of men out there watching them."

"I've already thought of that. This is a commando raid not a frontal assault. The less men the better. You can't do what I need done."

"The hell I can't! What do you think this is?" He patted the gleaming barrel of his well-oiled 30-30. "Chopped liver?"

"That may be good for bringing down a buck in the woods. But I've got an idea these guys have a lot more firepower than that. If we get into a shootout with them it'll be all over, especially for Bud and Suzy. If they're in there, they wouldn't stand a chance. No, I have to go alone, silent and deadly. I'm trained for this type of thing. I need stealth and invisibility, not guns blasting and bravado. I've got to go alone."

This conversation lasted most of the afternoon, and nearly exhausted me before I was able to get him to accept my reasoning. I had to promise to take his cell phone and call him if I needed help. As it was, I was only able to snatch a couple hours of half-sleep during the long day.


I parted the long grass and peered at the huge silhouette of the barn rising in the darkness before me. I could see two men walking back and forth in front of the building. It confirmed my suspicions that Suzy and Bud were most probably inside.

Surveying the surrounding area from my vantage point at the edge of the field, I could see the four massive silos. They ran along the side of the barn, but in the darkness it was difficult to make out details. Besides the two men at the front, between the barn and the farmhouse, I could make out another one patrolling the perimeter of the structure. They certainly seemed to be on high alert. I wasn't going to just waltz right in like I did last time.

While I lay in the grass watching, I began to think about who might be involved. I was convinced it was some kind of terrorist plot, and that Bobby McKenna was in on it.

And what about Jerry LeGrande? Was he just a local cop doing his job, or was he one of the conspirators? At this point it didn't matter. One way or another, I was on my own. My family was in jeopardy. If what I suspected was true, their lives weren't worth a raccoon's tail.

It was a clear night but cool. The quarter-moon was hidden beneath the eastern horizon. I'd had an overwhelming need for action. Now here, however, I was at a loss for what to do. I could try to take them out one at a time, but the odds were against me. In any case, without knowing exactly where Suzy and Bud were, whatever I did would be highly risky. I had to find out where they were being kept.

Crawling on my belly toward the rear of the building, I kept to the long grass until I was opposite the rear wall. Again, I surveyed the area, making sure there was no one watching. Then, waiting until the man on patrol had passed, I sprinted to the rear of the building, where a low shed squatted next to the barn. Quickly stepping up on the lid of a metal barrel, I pulled myself onto the roof and lay still. Moving along the roof to the back of the barn, I began looking for a way in. I missed having my samurai sword tied over my shoulder, like I had that night ten years ago. I could have used it now.

There was a row of windows about six feet above where I stood. They didn't appear to be open. A shuttered hatchway stood above the large double-doors, which entered the barn next to the shed. It was a good twelve feet away and at least four feet above the roof I was standing on.

Whoever was in charge of security had been a little lax. There were enough boxes and crates stored on the shed's roof to form a convenient staircase. I leaned a wooden skid against the barn and stood it on top of two sturdy crates. Using it as a small stepladder, I was able to reach the window directly above me. I peered in. I could just make out a loft filled with hay. The window was not made to open, just to let in light. I would have to risk breaking it if I wanted to gain entry that way.

I went to the edge of the roof and peered up at the entrance hatch above the large barn doors. Although it was out of reach, there was a post directly above it, with a pulley to lift bales of hay for storing. If I could get a rope, I might be able to swing myself up and in. I was contemplating these alternatives and others when the sentry returned on his rounds.

I lay flat on the rooftop in the shadows of the barn until he disappeared around the corner. Realizing that I couldn't easily gain entry from here, I dropped down to the ground and tried the shed door. It was unlocked.

Thinking there might be a way into the barn through there, I entered the shed. It was filled with farm equipment. There were crates of various sizes, and what looked like oil barrels. I couldn't make out much in the dark. Edging my way along the inner wall looking for an entrance to the barn itself, I almost stumbled over a low sawhorse. When I straightened up I saw something that almost made me lose my meager supper.

There in the middle of the room, tied to a chair, was the headless body of Bobby McKenna. I knew it was Bobby because at his feet was his head, glasses, long hair, and all. It stared at me through the darkness.

Retching, I turned away, knocking over an empty can in my haste to get out of the shed. I didn't care who might see or hear me. No one appeared to notice.

I hid in the shadows behind the barn, trying to gather my wits. In spite of everything I had witnessed those ten years ago, the sight of the headless corpse of Bobby McKenna shook me to my very core. Despite my shock, or maybe because of it, I was even more determined to save my wife and child. I steeled myself to do whatever it took to get them back unharmed.

Trying to keep my head, both figuratively and literally, I appraised the situation and my alternatives. It didn't look like I'd be able to get in through the windows at the back of the barn without breaking glass. That would more than likely alert anyone in the vicinity. The opening above the doors would have been difficult even for someone with acrobatic skills. It would have been impossible for me. The shed seemed to offer no means of entrance, even if I'd had the stomach to enter it again. I had to find another way in.

Edging along the side of the barn, I saw the guard moving away. He must have made another circuit while I was in the shed. He disappeared behind the outcropping of the silos that stood like huge conning towers next to the barn. As I approached them, hidden from the guard by their bulk, I noticed two things.

There, on the nearest of the large red towers was a wooden ladder built into the wall of the silo. At the top, a good fifty or sixty feet above me, was an opening large enough for a large bag of grain. Just looking up at it gave me vertigo. I hate heights!

I stood there for the longest time. I knew what I had to do, but didn't have the will-power to move. Finally, after getting my breathing under control again, I started up the ladder, one rung at a time.

It was nothing more than two sets of boards nailed in pairs straight up the side of the silo to the hatch. There was just enough to grab and place a foot on. My knees were shaking before I had gone twenty feet. I went slow, one foot at a time, keeping my eyes straight ahead on the wall in front of me. I tried to concentrate on my breathing, but my progress was excruciatingly slow.

I stopped at each rung to catch my breath and collect my courage for the next step. I was three-quarters of the way up when the guard returned on his rounds. I froze and pressed my body into the side of the silo. Holding on for dear life, I prayed he wouldn't look up at that moment and see me plastered there like a bug on the ceiling.

After making the mistake of looking down, I became frozen in fear. It took me a long time before I could move again. By this time the guard had swung around the front of the building and disappeared. Finally, I made it to the opening at the top, which was much larger than it had looked from the ground. It was boarded up. The wind, which I hardly felt at ground level, whistled past my ears. I clung to my precarious perch sixty feet in the air like my life depended on it, which, of course, it did.

I tested the board over the opening tentatively, but it was nailed shut from the inside. I hit it a little harder with a forearm and felt it give slightly. I would need more force if I was going to open it. From my position, however, I couldn't get much leverage for fear of falling. That fear was almost overwhelming. I kept my eyes locked forward and concentrated on my breathing, which came out in loud, harsh exhales.

Holding on with my left hand, I leaned back as far as I dared and smashed the plywood panel covering the hatchway. I hit it as hard as I could with my right forearm, almost falling through the opening when it gave way abruptly. I caught myself and looked down. The wooden stick, which had been nailed to the inside as a latch, had given way and fallen into the void. I heard it land moments later at the bottom of the silo, which appeared to be mostly empty of grain. It was pitch black inside. Immediately after the sound of the wood landing, I heard the unmistakable cry of a woman. It was Suzy calling out. She was at the bottom of the shaft! Moments later a light flashed in the darkness. A split-second after that a shot rang out and wood splintered by my arm.

Pushing myself back out of the opening, I almost lost my grip as a bullet smashed into the wall next to me. Without thinking, I descended rapidly. Forgetting my fear of heights in the hail of bullets that splintered the hatchway, I went down the makeshift ladder as if it were a fire pole.

I lost my grip about twelve feet from the ground and fell the remaining distance, landing flat on my back. In the last instant before impact, I tucked my head and slapped the ground with both arms. I lay stunned for several moments, not knowing whether or not I had broken my back or would ever move again. The sound of feet pounding toward me motivated me to try. The men from the front of the building were running toward me. I was able to get to my feet and start running, but I hadn't gotten up quite fast enough.

Before I had moved two feet I was tackled low from behind and thrown to the ground. I landed on my face with the guy holding me around the legs. It was the guard who had been circling the barn. I twisted around and was able to elbow and punch his head and neck. I could hear shouts and more men running in our direction. I didn't have time to tussle with the guy. I turned and plunged my thumbs into the sides of his eyes, partly succeeding in gouging them out. He screamed and stood up. I stood up with him and knocked him away with a thrust kick. He sprawled on the ground, crying and holding his eyes, one of which was dangling by a tendon.

Without stopping, as three men came around the edge of the silo, I dove down a small incline into a field of tall grass. I did a shoulder roll, and did it so fast that none of them saw me. They stopped to help their fallen comrade, who was still screaming uncontrollably. It had an immediate effect. They were outraged and scared at the same time. They paused for a long moment while they discussed what to do. Then they took off in three directions, one with the injured man, and two after me.

# Chapter 23

I crawled unseen through the field in the direction of the road. I wanted to make it to Pat's van before anyone saw me. I had borrowed it after getting it out of the shop. It was parked at the diner a half mile up the highway, the same one whose parking lot I had used in my earlier escape.

I expected a bullet in the back any minute, but it never came. They obviously hadn't spotted me yet. I didn't think they were worried about attracting attention. That hadn't stopped them before. I was certain they would kill anyone who got in their way, including Bud and Suzy. I was filled with the terror of what might happen to them. I had to save them. I hoped that as long as they were looking for me, my family would be kept alive as leverage against me.

Somehow I managed to elude them in the dark and reach the highway. Circling back toward the van, I could see it still where I had left it. Now if I could only get to it unseen. The area was abuzz with activity, men running back and forth, all looking for me, I presumed.

A group of men ran across the field behind me. A couple of pickup trucks tore down the drive to the highway. They sped off in opposite directions, one toward the diner where Pat's van was, and one toward town. I ran through another field of turned-up dirt and across a few well-cut lawns, making for the van.

Stealing across the yard of a private dwelling, I looked through a high hedge. Directly across the street, on the same side of the road as the diner, was a line of oak trees. Behind the trees there was a wire fence enclosing a broad field. The field bordered the restaurant parking lot where the van was parked. Looking left and right, and seeing no cars, I crouched low and ran across the street. Hiding in the shadow of the trees, I scanned the area to see if I'd been spotted. No one called out. No alarm was given. I was invisible, or so I thought.

The quarter-moon had risen part way up the eastern sky. It cast a faint glow over the land. I moved along the trees to the last one. From there the fence took over and marched within a few feet of the diner. I slipped over it and into the field. From there I could crawl close enough to the van to spit on it. Now all I had to do was make it there without being seen.

Suddenly, I was body-slammed from behind. Thrown violently forward to the ground, I tucked and rolled, coming up on my feet in a fighting stance..

My agility gave my two assailants pause. I noticed that they were both armed. One of them had a crowbar. The other carried a baseball bat. At least they didn't have guns. Either there weren't enough to go around, or they actually didn't want to call attention to what was going on.

They circled around me cautiously. I moved through the field toward the diner's parking lot. As I did, they took turns taking swats at me with their makeshift weapons. The lights of a pickup truck, parked not far from the van, flashed on. They were there waiting for me. I had to take care of these two before others arrived.

Turning unexpectedly on the two men coming up warily behind me, I darted at the nearest one before he had time to react. He sliced at me with the crowbar as he back-peddled away. I dodged the first stroke and ducked the second. The third came down at my collar bone. I twisted my body and grabbed his arm as it passed harmlessly by me. Using a sticky-palm technique, I pulled him into a cross-hand strike to the throat. Without stopping, I nailed him with another hand-sword to the side of the neck, hitting the large artery bringing blood to his brain. He blinked and dropped unconscious to the ground. I had a feeling he wouldn't be getting up for awhile.

Reeling around on my second attacker, I had just time enough to duck the bat as it whizzed at my head. Blocking another strike with my forearm, I swung his arm down and around forcibly. This not only minimized the force of the blow, but forced his body to bend. His forehead dropped forward. As it did, I kicked him in the face. His head snapped back, but he didn't go down. He responded by whistling the bat by my nose as I moved away. I had bloodied him, but hadn't stopped him.

My assailant was tall and lean, and moved fast. He struck with short, quick whips of the bat that were difficult to counter. It was then I noticed it was my student, Ali. I tried to talk to him, make him see it was me, his friendly instructor. I endeavored to get him to listen to reason, to come to his senses before it was too late. He didn't say a word, but came at me as if in a frenzied trance, slashing the bat from all directions. Finally, learning his pattern, I stepped in with an upward block. At the last moment, however, he swung the bat to the side and smashed it into my ribs.

I wrapped my arm around his, locking his elbow and the bat in the crook of my arm. I had to react quickly and take him out before the effects of his blow could reach my brain. Once it did, my nerve endings would be flooded with pain. I would be helpless and at their mercy. I couldn't let that happen, whatever the consequences. My wife and child depended on it. Good news was I hadn't been hit on the head. Bad news was my ribs had been cracked, if they hadn't been broken. I'd probably pass out soon.

Before any of this occurred, I grabbed him by the throat and locked my fingers around his trachea. Then, as I stood staring him in the eyes, his face not more than three inches from mine, I squeezed and pulled. The small area of bone and cartilage that forms the organ snapped out of place. As I dropped to my knees from the pain of the blow to my ribs, I heard a sharp, ragged intake of breath. It sounded like someone had squeezed a can. I hadn't worked on my grip all these years for nothing. I didn't stop to think about it. That would come later.

Rolling away still clutching the bat in the crook of my arm, I saw Ali grab his throat and reel back in shock. His eyes registered the horror as he realized the certainty of his death. A moment later he fell to his knees, rolled over on his side, and lay perfectly still

I tried to take in air and get to my feet, but the pain in my side was excruciating. It almost made me pass out. I concentrated on my breathing, as if I was on a tightrope over a thousand foot gorge. Every breath was an eternity. I took long, slow inhalations from my diaphragm and tried not to move my ribcage. As I lay there, I heard the pickup truck, which had come rushing down the highway toward me, skid to a stop. I managed to drag myself into the tall grass just as the door opened and someone jumped out.

I stumbled and crawled my way through the field. Every breath I took was an exercise in endurance, an event both dreaded and longed for. I made my way, staggering toward the van. I was halfway there when my pursuer got to me. I could hear him huffing and puffing behind me. The truck, which had made a u-turn in the middle of the highway, was heading back toward the diner.

I turned toward my assailant as he came at me, hiding the bat behind my body. He had a sickle in his right hand, which he twirled menacingly side to side. Without warning, he raised the sickle over his head and attacked me with a yell. As he came in, I extended the bat with both hands and jabbed it hard into his forehead. It stopped him dead, but he didn't fall. Without hesitating, I swung the bat up from the ground and hit him under the chin, knocking some teeth out and fracturing his jaw. Using the bat like a sword, I stepped in and blocked the sickle with an upward stroke, hitting his wrist sharply on the bone. The short, lethal farm implement flew out of his hand. Without stopping, I snapped the head of the bat at him, hitting him between the eyes. He staggered back. He was stunned, but still on his feet. Swinging the bat around 360-degrees, I delivered a blow, low, to the knees. He dropped his hands to cover his damaged leg and started to go down. As he did, the bat completed another circuit and hit him square on the side of the head. It was a homerun swing delivered with both hands. His skull cracked like a walnut. He went down without a sound.

I fell to the ground, holding my side in pain. I gasped for breath, dimly aware that there were at least two more still out there waiting for me. I had to get to the van if I were to have any chance of saving Suzy and Bud. That thought spurred me toward the parking lot.

When I got close to the tarmac, I dropped to my hands and knees in the tall grass. Someone called out softly. It was one of the terrorists. He was calling to his buddy, the one lying in the grass with his head split open. I moved toward the sound of his voice. I could hear others coming up further behind me in the field.

When I was just ten feet from the caller, I answered in a muffled voice. I used a word of Arabic that I had heard my students use to greet each other. I called out weakly as if I were hurt. The man moved to the edge of the pavement and called out a name. I answered back with the same phrase I used earlier. He came closer. As he did, I leaped up with a yell, slashing at him with the sickle, which I had picked up. He stepped back and dodged it. Then he reached into his jacket and pulled out a pistol. I guess the no gun rule had just ended.

Not having a second to think, in desperation, I leaped toward him with a flying double-front ball kick. Forgetting my ribs in a rush of adrenaline, I covered the five feet between us in an instant. He was taking aim.

As I came down on the gunman, I struck his gun arm with the sickle, almost slicing his hand off at the wrist. I followed up with a slash to the collarbone, cutting a deep gash in his shoulder. I had become that demon I had known once before. The dogs of death had been unleashed. I both dreaded and relished it.

190

My opponent was out of the game, bleeding profusely, the gun lying beside him. I didn't bother picking it up, but dropped the sickle and ran for the van. Shots rang out somewhere behind me. The man standing by the pickup truck was firing at me. I ducked, but had no idea where the bullets were going. I expected one to hit me at any moment.

I managed to get to the van and open the door, diving in to the sound of bullets pinging on the metal hood and bumper. They were getting closer. Taking the keys from my pocket, I started the engine. A bullet crashed through the rear window. It dug into the upholstered ceiling inches above me as I sped out of the parking lot and down the highway back to the barn.

Another truck was coming down the street from the opposite direction. It was headed right toward me. The vehicle behind me started in pursuit. Just as I was about to hit the oncoming truck head on, I swerved to the right. Hugging the side of the tarmac, I skidded past fence posts and knocked over road signs. Turning sharply at the last minute, I smashed through the gate and sped down the dirt drive toward the McKenna barn, hitting two men on the road who tried to stop me.

I tore down the dirt track toward the farm. The lights of my pursuers were right behind me. Putting my foot to the floor, I approached the building at high speed. I had every intention of smashing through the large barn door. Just at the point in the road where it turned toward the entrance, someone jumped out of the bushes and spayed the front of the van with bullets. I leaned to the side, lying flat on the seat as the windshield was shattered, showering me with glass. More bullets tore into the upholstery just where my head had been. The truck veered to the left heading right for the first of the huge silos, but not before hitting the gunman and knocking him into the bushes he had just emerged from.

As I had done when I went over Lookout Gorge, I yanked open the door and jumped out. Rolling on my shoulder, I landed in the grass as the van crashed into the side of the silo. The tower was solidly constructed and reinforced with wire. The area where Pat's van hit it, however, was in disrepair and unreinforced. The boards were rotting. There were gaping holes in the wall. Instead of crunching up, the heavy vehicle smashed through the silo and knocked down the beams holding up the silo floor. This started about six feet from the base of the structure where the truck went through. The floor collapsed on the roof of the van, covering it with grain.

To my surprise and relief, Suzy appeared in the hole where the floor fell in. Her hands were tied behind her. Screaming, she jumped onto the roof of the van. A thickset man wearing camouflaged dungarees and a black t-shirt, jumped after her.

Seeing Suzy, I climbed up onto the van to help her down, putting myself between her and the man chasing her.

"Get Bud!" she yelled, before I could untie her. "He's still in there."

I nailed the guy with a spinning back kick as he rushed at me. It was perfectly timed. Like the heavy bag hanging on a hook in my dojo, the kick hit him just as he reached me. It knocked him back into the silo, onto a pile of grain. Just then the other trucks arrived. The occupants jumped out to join the fray. I saw Bud out of the corner of my eye, cowering against the side of the silo.

"Daddy, Daddy!" he cried out when he saw me at the opening. I didn't have time to answer back.

One of the men coming at me, the biggest of them, grabbed me by the neck with both hands. Before he could get a hold, I punched him in the floating ribs with a tight right hook and knocked his hands away. It was a good body-shot. I put my whole weight behind it, snapping my hips in time with the strike. He bent over in pain and dropped his arms. As he did, I grabbed both of his ears and pulled his head down into my knee, which I snapped upward. Holding onto his ears as his head flew back, I yanked them downward. They came off like clip-on earrings. It doesn't take much to remove a person's ears. They came off in my hands.

He held his head and fell to the ground, writhing in pain and screeching. Blood spurted out of the holes that used to be his ears. Just then another attacker burst into the room. I threw the first guy's ears at him. He stopped and slapped them away. Without hesitating, I stepped into him with a thrust kick and knocked him back out of the silo. He fell into two other men who were rushing in behind him. I could hear Little Bud screaming in the background.

"Run," I yelled. "Go to Mommy."

Just then everything went black as I was hit on the back of the head with the butt of a rifle.

# Chapter 24

What happened is difficult to recall. Not so much because I can't remember as that my mind doesn't want to accept the horror of it. It comes back to me in disjointed snippets, like a vague dream only half remembered. I have no way to connect the events or tell what went first or what followed.

I was being held with my arms behind me by two terrorists. Suzy, who still had her hands tied, stood nearby, next to Little Bud. Our abductors were discussing what to do with us, when a shot rang out. One of them, the one nearest the road, jerked and dropped. The one next to me, holding my arm, was spun around when another bullet slammed into of his shoulder blade. The rest scattered for cover. Bullets pinged off the silo walls. A voice cried out of the darkness.

"Grab Suzy and Bud and get in the van!"

It was my father.

I managed to untie Suzy and get her and Bud in the vehicle. All the while my father kept up a heavy fire with his trusty .30-.30. I turned the van around and sped down the drive, skidding to a stop when my dad stepped out from behind a tree. He told me to keep going while he held them off. As I was arguing with him more shots shattered the night. The terrorists had grabbed their own guns and were returning fire.

I jumped out to help. I vaguely remember Suzy driving off in the van, while my dad and I crouched behind a tree. Bullets bit into the bark around us. We decided to make a dash for the highway and his Caddy, which was behind us and to our left. There was a ditch that led in that direction that would give us some cover. As we made for it my father went down with a yell.

"Dad!" I screamed. I bent down to help him. He had been hit in the head and was bleeding badly. "Dad, talk to me. Are you OK?"

I remember leaning over him, yelling at him in this way, when for the second time that night, I was hit on the back of the head with the butt of a rifle.

I woke up sometime later sitting in a chair with my arms tied behind me. The rope was wrapped around me like a coiling snake. I realized, with a sickening feeling, that I was in the shed at the back of the barn. Even worse, I was probably sitting in the same chair I had seen holding the headless body of Bobby McKenna.

My senses were reeling, my head pounding. My ribs ached, and my throat was sore. There were four men standing around me. A bare bulb glared directly overhead, casting shadows into the corners of the room. Bobby's body and head were gone. They must have removed them to make room for another headless body - mine. At least Suzy and Bud were safe, but for how long? Then I remembered my father.

"Dad!" I yelled, recalling his terrible wound and how still he lay. "Where's my father?"

"He's dead, like you are going to be," said one of my captors. He slapped me hard across the face. I recognized him. It was Mustafa, one of my ex-students.

"You killed Ali, ripped out his throat like an animal," he said.

"Yes, he killed Mahmud too," said another. "He smashed his head in with a bat."

"He tore Ahmad's ears off, and blinded Yousef," added a third. "He is a beast from the pits and will die like one."

"They have gone to Allah, as good warriors should," uttered a fourth, who I recognized as the well-dressed man in the restaurant. He was apparently their leader. "Our friend here is very dangerous. Well, the world will see how well he dies.

"There is nothing you can do, Mister Lawless. You and your whole family will die, as will many more unbelievers before we are through. It is too bad you won't be around to read about it, to see the results of our little operation. It will be the biggest thing to happen in a hundred years. It will be talked about for generations. How a few defeated the many. How the powerless overcame the most powerful. We will bring this country to its knees. America will pay for all you have done to our people."

"He killed Ali," shouted Mustafa again, punching me in the side of the head. "He was only twenty-one."

"Ali is getting his reward in paradise," said their leader. "Just as this one will get his in everlasting torment, each as he merits in this short life. That is all that matters. And that our cause succeeds and lives on beyond them. Do not damage him any further. We need him to look presentable."

It was then that I noticed the small movie camera on a tripod facing me six feet away.

"I don't know what you bastards are up to, but you'll never get away with it," I said, trying to put off the inevitable with lies. "This place will be crawling with cops in a few minutes. They know all about your plans. Don't make it worse for yourselves. You better run."

"Oh, it's going to get worse, much worse, especially for you, Mister Lawless."

He said something to his compatriots in Arabic, which prompted a further rush of foreign words in response. An argument ensued, which I could not understand. I think it was over who was going to have the honor of beheading me.

Although my arms were pinned behind me to the chair, my legs were free. Still, I was in a bad way. I could barely move. It looked like my days as a private investigator were about to end, along with my miserable life. While they argued, I struggled against the ropes that bound me.

Someone switched on several bright lamps. They bathed the room in blinding light. I closed my eyes in pain. Mustafa produced a long, slightly-curved knife from beneath his cloak. They all put on black hoods. I thought things were bad a few moments before. They were really looking bad now.

Fear overcame me. It made it impossible to breathe. I almost passed out, but knew I somehow had to keep my senses until the last possible moment. As hopeless as it looked, as long as I was breathing I still had a chance. The leader stood facing the camera and spoke again in Arabic. After reading his statement, he translated it into English.

"Too long have the strong oppressed the weak and helpless. Too long have the Godless held sway. Today, those who have been wronged will be avenged. You will learn that you reap the bitter seeds of destruction when you murder innocent women and children. Their only sin was to cower in their homes, while your bombs and missiles fell from the sky. Your sky will soon fall. You will soon suffer like this unfortunate fool, who tried to stand in the way of our just revenge."

As he talked, I flexed my legs. I couldn't believe they hadn't tied them, and almost laughed. Mustafa, at least, should have known better.

"They're at theMcKenna farm on Bob Moffit Road," I yelled. "They've got silos full of explosives. They're going to blow up the pentagon!"

I shouted this with all the fury I could muster. Then I burst to my feet, the chair still tied behind me, and hit the speaker with a short, quick snapping kick to his backside. He flew headfirst into the camera, which went crashing with him to the ground. For a moment there was pandemonium as everyone scrambled to grab me or get out of my way.

Stepping back, I jabbed the legs of the chair into the groin of one of my captors. He went down, but not before the other two tackled me. They knocked me back onto the chair, breaking it beneath us. I sprawled on the floor pinned beneath them.

"Enough of this!" yelled Mustafa, who was still incensed over the death of his friends at my hands. He'd had enough formalities. The other two yanked me to my feet and held me between them. Yelling something in Arabic, Mustafa came at me with the large knife. I'm sure he was intent on beheading me on the spot. I wasn't going to give him the chance. Using the two men who held me for support, I swung my body up, kicking him in the groin with my left foot as he came in, and in the face with my right, heel first, as he bent over involuntarily. It sent him flipping backward, landing on the back of his neck. I was aiming at his throat. Too bad I missed, because that about spelled the end of my offensive.

The other two terrorists knocked me to the ground again and held me there, punching and kicking me as I lay beneath them. I was helpless at this point. Even though the ropes binding me to the chair had come off when it broke, my arms were still tied behind me. Mustafa got up dazed, and started toward me with the knife again.

Their leader was also on his feet with the camera in his hands, yelling something like, "Kill him! Kill him! Kill the little bastard! Cut off his fucking head!"

One of the men grabbed my hair and yanked my head back to expose my throat. The blade was only a foot away. Mustafa kneeled on my chest and pressed the knife to my neck. He wasn't going to chop or hack my head off. He was going to saw if off slowly like a log. I closed my eyes and struggled for all I was worth, but could not move. This was it, I thought, as my life came flooding back before me.

Just then, just as I felt the cold sting of the bland on my throat, there was a loud, splintering crash. The door of the shed burst open, torn from its hinges. Into the room rushed a vision from the grave. It was a large bearded man. He had long, matted hair, and was dressed in what looked like rags and ragged squirrel pelts. In his hand he held a large Bowie knife.

Even though I recognized him instantly, my mind denied what my eyes were telling me. It just couldn't be, but I could never forget that face. It was the same face that had stalked me ten years ago on the beach of St. Petersburg. The same face on that boat landing staring up at the rain-splattered sky telling me his secret. It was him, the same one who had been killing all those people back then and was more than likely killing them now. He had returned from the grave.

Before these thoughts had time to register, the intruder had crossed the floor to the person holding the camera. With one vicious swipe, he cut the man's throat from ear to ear. He went down gurgling, the camera still whirling, catching it all. Before my three assailants had time to rise to their feet, he barreled into them, knocking them to the floor. I struggled frantically to get free. For some reason I knew he had come for me. That thought scared me more than the terrorists who had almost hacked off my head.

There was a brief struggle as the intruder fought off my three remaining captors. They had grabbed assorted weapons of their own, but it did them little good. They had forgotten all about me at the sight of the large, knife-wielding madman.

Moving quickly and expertly, he kicked one as he stabbed the other, darting about them like a leopard. Even Mustafa, a trained opponent with a knife of his own, didn't last long. He was rapidly forced backward. Knocking over assorted barrels and boxes, he died in anguish in a dark corner of the shed.

Somehow, by twisting and turning at my knots, which were already partly loosened, I was able to get free. I got to my feet just as the killer finished off his last opponent. Now he was coming for me!

# Chapter 25

I ran out of the hole where the door used to be, into the clear night air. The killer was right behind me. As he came up to me, I turned to face him and skipped away backward. He came in with a wide, arcing strike aimed at my neck. I leaned back and ducked away. It missed me by an inch. It was too close for comfort. I circled to his left, looking for a weapon.

Why did this all seem so familiar? I dodged to the side to avoid another slashing strike, and dove away. Rolling on my shoulder, I came to my feet running. I moved at full speed along the side of the barn, looking for something to defend myself with, anything to even the odds. A machine-gun would have been nice.

Where did he come from? Where had he been all this time? What was he doing here? How could he have survived that night? I had practically disemboweled him. His guts were spilling out onto the sand. I saw him die!

He had inadvertently saved my life. Now he was just as intent on ending it.

He caught me near the front of the building, where the driveway opened up into a large dirt parking area. The place was deserted. I wondered if he had dispatched the remaining terrorists.

He had no respect for my kicks or punches, which seemed to have little effect. Cornering me against the huge barn door, he walked up with the knife in front of him as if he were coming to shake hands. There was no hesitation. I tried sweeping the knife aside with a reverse-crescent kick, and followed up with a hard heel thrust to the midsection. Neither kick achieved much. The first kick hardly moved his thick arm. The second one barely stopped his forward momentum.

I kicked him in the groin as he raised the knife to stab me. It was a hard, full-power, well-aimed strike. I broke boards with that kick. He looked at me malevolently, unfazed. However, it stopped him and made him take a step back. It was all the time I needed.

The small barn door was directly behind me. As he thrust the knife at my heart, I threw it open and propelled myself backward onto the floor. I landed on my back and kicked the door shut. His knife thudded into the wood as it closed in his face.

I noticed a rake leaning against the wall. Getting to my feet, I grabbed it and made a stand at the door. I poked the long stick at him as he tried to bull his way in, going for vulnerable areas. Finally, after receiving some vicious blows to the face, he grew a little more cautious. He started using the knife more effectively to force his way in. He had learned his lesson and approached with more respect. He jabbed and stabbed, and countered my attacks, throwing kicks of his own. In this manner, he worked his way forward. It was like he had remembered some long forgotten training. He was no longer giving me any openings. He was adapting, like I would have to if I wanted to survive.

As we moved further back into the barn, along the empty stalls, I looked for something more lethal than a rake to equalize the odds. It was like facing a raging grizzly. The same cold hungry look was in his eyes. There was nowhere to go but back, but I was able to keep him at bay with the rake, using both ends to good effect. Where was a scythe or a sickle when you needed one? They had all probably been used on me. I wasn't sure how long it would be before he gutted me.

Midway down the hall he cornered me again. This time he came at me with a combination of kicks and slashing knife attacks, which I was just able to avoid. I had already been cut in several places. Nothing more than scratches that I didn't even feel until later, but each time he got me I thought I was dead. I reacted to another downward stroke by instinctively raising my arm to block. The blade cut into my forearm causing a searing pain and slicing it to the bone.

The blood seeped out and quickly spread along the sleeve of my sweatshirt. I didn't have time to worry about it. He thrust the knife at my midsection. Twisting away, I sucked in my gut just enough to avoid being stabbed, but I was cut as the blade nicked my stomach. I kept wondering when I was going to drop dead, but was determined to keep on fighting until I did.

I snapped the end of the rake into his eye. It stopped him in midstride, but he grabbed it and tore it out of my hand. I grabbed his knife arm at the wrist and elbow, locking it, but he muscled free and came at me again. His next blow just missed me, the knife sticking into the side of the barn. He ripped it free and came at me again as I circled around out of the corner.

Things were getting desperate. Weak from my ordeal with the terrorists, I was going on empty, the tank bone dry. Still I fought on, controlling my breathing and trying to build the chi.

I worked my way to the back of the barn, where a number of large pieces of farm equipment were parked. We moved among them, him stabbing and slashing, while I ducked and dodged. Finally, he cornered me again. This time it was against the rear wall, near another large door that was shut and bolted.

Just when it looked like there was nowhere to go, I noticed a wooden ladder leading up to the loft. At the same time, I saw a pitchfork. It was lying on the floor not far from where I stood. Finally, a weapon I could do some damage with!

Feinting in one direction, I dove for the pitchfork, rolling on my shoulder. Picking it up as I came back to my feet, I brought it up just in time to block another knife thrust. Jabbing it into his face and belly, I slowly began to back him up. I flashed it forward and back so fast he was not be able to grab it. He growled and crouched low, trying to adjust to this new situation. Like that time long before, he decided to rush me. Some people never learn. It was just what I was hoping for. As he came in, I thrust the sharp, pointed farm implement into his stomach, shoving it in as far as I could.

He grunted, but instead of going down, he stood grinning insanely at me. Pulling the pitchfork from my hands, he held it by the handle as it stuck in his gut. Then he pulled it out with a yell and threw it at me. It thudded into the door and stuck quivering, where only moments before I had been standing. By then, I was almost to the ladder.

By the time he reached the bottom rung, I was halfway up. By the time he got to the top, I was waiting for him. He held on to the ladder with one hand as he slashed the knife at me with the other. I hit him with a series of thrust kicks, smashing my heel into his face and forehead. I kicked him so fast that he was unable to block them or cut me, one kick after the other with no pause in between. Every time I hit him, I added more power to the strike, so that each one was harder than the last. I hit him five or six times in succession, snapping his head back further each time. Finally, spinning around 360 degrees, I delivered a full-power back kick square between his eyes. He tried to block it and let go of the ladder when it landed. It sent him flying backward like an Olympic diver off a high platform.

I looked down cautiously over the edge of the loft to see him lying below. He was tangled in the sharp steel blades of a harvester that had been parked beneath us. As I watched, he tried to pull himself off the machine that impaled him in several places.

Slowly, I descended the ladder. I kept my eyes on him all the way to the hay-strewn floor. He didn't make a sound as he struggled, but continued trying to pull himself free of the impaling blades. It was inhuman, the way he kept attempting to get up. At one point he almost got free, only to fall back again impaling himself even further.

I stood at the bottom of the ladder and watched his death throes in fascinated horror. He jerked one way, then another, as he tried to tear himself off the blades that held him. One pierced his belly. Another cut into his groin. One went through his thigh. A forth sliced his shoulder. Try as he might, he could not free himself from the death grip of the steel harvester. All the while, as he struggled, he stared silently at me with bloodshot eyes, gnashing his teeth in hatred and aguish. That look scared me more than anything that had happened that fear-filled night.

I couldn't leave. I had to watch him die. I had to make sure this time that it had ended once and for all, but it took way too long. I thought of putting him out of his misery like a dying animal, but I hadn't the willpower to move, let alone carry out that desperate act. He would get to the point of almost pulling himself free, only to fall back again. Each time he did so he would impale himself deeper. It took twenty-minutes for him to stop moving. At the end he feebly pawed the air. It was only then that I found that I could move myself.

I slowly limped toward the front of the barn, holding my bleeding arm. I kept looking back, expecting him to jerk up again at any moment, but he lay where he was, half suspended by his bed of steel.

As I approached the front of the barn, the large doors were thrown open. The dark interior was bathed in the bright light of several vehicles. A voice through a loudspeaker told me to raise my hands and drop to my knees. I hardly understood the command. Before I could comply, half a dozen large men in riot gear and helmets rushed into the barn and pointed as many automatic weapons at me. I was forced roughly face first to the ground and handcuffed. I didn't resist.

"Take him with the others," said the man holding the bullhorn.

"I'm not with them," I protested. "My name is Jay Lawless. This is a terrorist cell. They killed the owner, Bobby McKenna, and were using the place to build a bomb or something. They kidnapped my wife and kid. I…"

"What did you say your name was?" asked the man with the bullhorn.

"Jay Lawless, I…"

"You're wanted for the murder of a state trooper. We've been looking for you for days. Jim, take him down to the station for interrogation. The chief wants to question him personally."

201

"Yeah, I bet the Staties would like to question him too," said Jim.

"They'll get their chance. Keep him separate from the others," replied the guy in charge.

"Captain, you ought to see this," said another fully armed SWAT team member running up. "In the back."

"That's the killer you've been looking for," I informed them. "He's the one who killed Becky Jo Patterson and those kids out at the beach. There are more terrorists out back in the shed. They were going to behead me."

They just looked at me dumbfounded, not knowing what to believe.

"Take him downtown and notify Chief LeGrande we have him in custody."

I was taken out of the barn and put in the back of a squad car. The place was ablaze with activity. There were police vehicles and ambulances of all descriptions. Both the Sheriff's department and city police were there, as well as the state police. When the latter heard who was sitting in the backseat of the city patrol car, they stood around staring at me with unconcealed hostility. I'd rather face the terrorists any day then the bunch of lawmen looking at me that night. After about ten very uncomfortable minutes, one of the ambulance drivers came over to patch up my arm and tape my ribs. Then one of the city cops took me to the station.

I didn't waste any time trying to convince him of my innocence. Instead, I closed my eyes and tried to wipe my mind clean of the images that bombarded it. They were images I wouldn't have believed had I seen them in a movie, but which I had lived through only minutes before. It was all so unreal. How, I wondered, would I ever live a normal life again? Not that what I had experienced so far was that normal to begin with. At least Suzy and Little Bud were safe.

# Chapter 26

I must have passed out. The next thing I remember is two officers shaking me awake in the back of the patrol car. It took me awhile to remember where I was and how I had gotten there. I appeared to be in a garage at the back of the police station. My hands were still cuffed behind me. The cop shaking me was calling my name. That reminded me of my father.

"Dad!" I exclaimed, realizing he was probably still lying in the field. "He was shot back at the barn. You've got to help him."

I was overcome with worry.

"Calm down, Mister Lawless," said the officer. "You can tell it all to the chief."

"But you don't understand. My father's been shot. We've got to go back and find him. Now!"

"Don't give us any of your crap, cop killer," said the second one, taller and heavier than the first. He yanked me out of the car, bumping my head in the process.

"Watch his feet," said Jerry LeGrande, who had just driven up and gotten out of his car. "He's a tricky little bastard."

"Jerry," I said, recognizing his voice. "They shot Dad. He's back at the farm in the side field there. You've got to help him. Please!"

"Don't worry, Jay," said my friend the chief. "We found him and brought him to the hospital. He's hurt, but will be OK. The bullet grazed his head. The doctors will know in a couple of days whether they need to operate or not. We'll keep you posted. In the meantime, you've got a lot of explaining to do."

He ordered the two officers to take me up to the conference room where he could interrogate me."

They took me through a rear door into the station and up a flight of stairs to a large room. They sat me in one of the many chairs situated around a long table, and un-cuffed me. There were white boards and a large mirror along the far wall that I assumed was made of one-way glass. A clock on the wall said 5:55 a.m. One officer stood by the door, while the other went out to get the Chief. I waited for about five minutes before Jerry walked in carrying a manila folder filled with notes and pictures."

"Tell me what happened, Jay, from the beginning."

"What do you know?"

"Nothing, just what we found at the farm. What the hell was going on up there?"

"Try international terrorism. Those bastards were making a bomb. That's where all your stolen fertilizer has gone. I stumbled onto them while investigating the McKenna murders."

I told him how I had gone there one night to check the place out and was assaulted.

"You were trespassing!" he insisted.

I told him how they had chased me up into the mountains, shooting at me all the way, and how I was stopped by the trooper.

"They shot him in cold blood, Jerry!"

He looked at me in silence. "We still have to work that out, Jay. Right now it looks like you shot the trooper."

"Why would I do that?" I yelled. "I don't even own a gun."

"I don't know, Jay. Suppose you tell me."

"I just did. Check the bullets with the weapons you confiscated tonight at the farm. I bet you'll find the gun all right."

"We did find it, with your car at the bottom of the gorge. Just tell me what happened."

"Then they must have planted it there."

I told him how I had hid in the mountains after the car crash, in my father's old hunting camp. I described how I had made my way back to town, keeping my father's involvement out of it.

"I didn't know what was happening at first. But it had to be something pretty serious, the way they reacted to my snooping. Then when they kidnapped Suzy and Little Bud, I realized I had stumbled onto something big."

I explained how I had located them at the farm and gone there to rescue them. When he asked me why I hadn't gone to the police, I told him because they would have brought me in for questioning, just like he was doing now.

"I'm sorry, Jerry, but I didn't trust anyone with my family's life but me."

"You could have gotten them killed."

"Not as surely as you would have. I've got to make sure they're OK."

We stared at each other across the table.

I described the whole harrowing evening to him. How I had found the body of Bobby McKenna in the rear shed, hogtied and headless.

How I had located my wife in the silo while trying to gain entrance to the barn. How they shot at me while they chased me through the fields. I told him where to locate the bodies of my four tormentors. He told me they had found them in the back shed, and were wondering what had happened to them. They also found the bodies of the more unfortunate of my assailants, the ones I tangled with in the field. One had been suffocated with his throat swelled up like a frog's. The side of one's head was bashed in. One looked like he had been hit by a car.

"You did that?"

"Some of it, but I had no choice, Jerry. It was them or me. I was trying to save my wife and child. The ones in the shed were the killer's work."

I told him how my father had rescued us at the last minute, only to be shot. I also explained how I had been captured and tied to the chair in the shed.

"It was the same chair I found Bobby's headless body in. They must have killed him when they didn't need him any longer. They were going to do the same thing to me. They had a camera. They were going to film the whole damn thing. When I heard them read their manifesto, I finally understood what was going on. It all started to make sense. They were on some kind of holy jihad against the United States. They were going to blowup a building or something, like in Oklahoma City, only bigger. They must have been stockpiling that fertilizer to use as a bomb."

He shook his head in disbelief. "That's a pretty incredible story, Jay."

"It wouldn't be the first time something this crazy has happened here in town. But wait, that's not the craziest part."

I told him how the killer had burst through the door and hacked down my four would be assassins.

"I somehow managed to untie myself and get away. Well, not exactly escape, but I survived to tell the story. That's more than I can say for the other guy."

"Is it him?" he asked, getting to the real point of the interview. It was the thing he had wanted to know since seeing Becky Jo Patterson's dead naked body on the beach.

"If you mean is he the one who was murdering young men and women around town ten years ago, I would say that's an affirmative. He's also probably the one who's been killing people around town recently. It has to be him. His knife should be at the bottom of the ladder. It should match the wounds on the murder victims to a 't'."

"Did you recognize him?"

"Yes," I said, still not believing it myself. "But I don't know how he could have survived his wounds. He didn't seem human, Jerry, the way he kept trying to get off that harvester. It was like he was impervious to pain. I never saw anything like it. Pure evil was looking out of those eyes at me, pure evil."

I shuddered involuntarily as I recalled the look on his face as he struggled against the sharp blades of the dangerous farm machine.

Jerry asked me a few more questions and promised to follow up on everything I was telling him. Then he said I'd have to spend the night in jail.

"It's just as a precaution, Jay, for your own protection."

I objected violently.

"My wife and child are out there all alone. There may still be terrorists on the loose. They've already been kidnapped once. It's not going to happen again. I've got to be with them!"

"Well, I just can't let you walk out of here like that, not after what you've told me. You just admitted to killing three men. You're still wanted for killing that trooper, for Christ's sake."

"I told you *they* killed that cop! I killed those guys in self-defense. It was five against one. They were armed."

I tried to argue with him, but it was to no avail. There was no way he was going to let me go, terrorists or no. Even so, I wasn't ready for what they were about to do to me.

Jerry left the room and came back soon after with four beefy guards. One of them was carrying wrist and ankle shackles. They weren't taking any chances.

I wasn't sure whose side Jerry was on. I could understand his precaution, but he appeared to completely discount my story of the terrorists. Maybe he just needed more time, but I felt like my time was running out. What if Jerry was in on it? If one old childhood friend like Bobby McKenna could be involved in the plot, than why not another? It still seemed funny they had that alert out on me so soon after my first encounter at the farm. I couldn't stop to figure it all out. I had to act fast or the time for action would be over.

I sat calmly in the chair as they came into the room and divided. Two of them came around one end of the long table. Two came around the other end. Suddenly, they rushed me in unison. Just as they were on me, in one fluid motion, I stood and leaped onto the table.

Jerry was standing by the door. As I jumped off the table, I nailed him with a flying thrust kick to the chest. It sent him crashing backward over a chair. Poor Jerry! A string-bean who probably weighed a hundred and forty pounds wet, he didn't get up.

I was out of the room and down the hall before the four guards could untangle themselves. The two officers who had pulled me out of the squad car were still in the corridor. They looked up in surprise as I dragged a heavy bench in front of the door. Someone ran out of the space adjoining the conference room yelling in alarm. He had probably been watching through the one-way mirror.

The two guys in the hall made a grab for me. One was standing in front of me. The other one was standing beside me. I nailed the one facing me with a thrust kick to the midsection, making him bend over. A split second later, without touching my foot to the ground, I hit the guy next to me with a side kick in the ribs. He bent and grabbed his side. Before the first cop could straighten up, still without dropping my foot, I snapped a front-instep kick to his face, breaking his nose. He flipped over backward and landed on the back of his head.

The second man charged me with his fists raised. As he came in, I ducked the punch and clothes-lined him off his feet with a ridge-hand under his chin. He went horizontal five feet in the air and slammed to the ground on his back. They were both down for the count. It was over in seconds.

The one who had rushed out of the room to raise the alarm was right behind me. He went for his gun. Without turning, I hit him with a back kick in the solar-plexus. It knocked the wind out of him and made him drop the gun. Just then the four beefy guards with the manacles burst out of the conference room, knocking over the heavy bench I had put in front of the door to block it.

By then I was at the glass doors at the front entrance, where another paper pusher tried to stop me. I quickly overpowered him with a rapid series of hand strikes that had him backed into a corner with his arms up in submission. Then I was out the door on the almost empty street. There, I surprised still another patrolman stepping out of his squad car. It still had its blue lights flashing. I hit him between the legs with a front kick and followed up with a half-power hand-sword to the side of his neck. I didn't want to hurt him. Then I jumped in his still running squad car and drove off.

I saw them in the rearview mirror. They ran out to the street after me as I drove away, their hands raised in the air. Some had guns. Fortunately, no one shot at me, but I wasn't sure how long that would last. Fortune was smiling at me for some reason. There were no police vehicles out front. They had to run to the rear of the station to get their squad cars before they could pursue me. Because of this delay, I managed to get out of town without being seen, flashing lights and all. Not knowing what else to do, I headed west out of town to those same familiar mountains. A crude plan was beginning to take shape in my frazzled brain.

I couldn't believe what I had just done. Had I really assaulted five city policemen and their chief? They would probably have an all-points bulletin out on me, with orders to shoot first and ask question later. Well, it wouldn't be the first time.

I was sure they would have roadblocks up in a matter of minutes. I knew I'd have to ditch the car. I didn't want to do that, however, until I was safely out of town and in the mountains, where I could leave it as a decoy. First I had to get there. I figured my odds were less than fifty-fifty, but I'd played those odds before and won.

# Chapter 27

I was surprised how easy it had been to get away. When this was all over I promised myself I'd tell Jerry how badly his men had performed. Granted, I had the element of surprise on my side and the four beefy guards in the riot gear had been slow to react. They might have presented more of a problem had they actually caught me. The men I did face, however, went down from one or two blows, which none of them had been able to avoid. I'd have to see if I could get those guys to sign up for lessons.

Here I was fighting for my survival and the lives of my family, and I was still thinking about how to make a buck. Old habits die hard. I hoped I'd die even harder.

I soon figured out how to turn off the flashing lights and made my way to the west end of town. I knew it was only a matter of time before they'd be on my tail. With the main roads sure to be blocked, I made my way along the back roads that my dad knew so well.

I drove back up into the mountains, to the spot by the underground spring, where I had met my father by chance that morning a few days ago. It seemed like a lifetime, so much had happened.

If I was lucky they would find the car and think I had gone over the mountain like last time. Maybe Jerry would remember my story and start the search up here, while I circled back to town.

I had been pondering how I was going to make the twenty miles back to the 'burgh', when I remembered something John Rothburg had told me. It was during one of our all night sessions of caffeine and conversation. He was talking about how some of the greatest scientific discoveries of all time were made by recognizing the obvious. Often it was something that had been there all along, but seemed so insignificant, so ordinary, it was overlooked. It had been the key to the puzzle and everyone was looking right at it the whole time. In that idea lay the means of my escape.

It was a hot, steamy morning. Summer had finally come to the North Country with a vengeance. It was already ninety degrees by nine o'clock. I headed into the woods across the road from the spring, where I had ditched the car. Instead of going up into the mountains as I hoped the police would assume, I headed down into the valley behind the village and the state penitentiary. While still in the woods at the edge of town, I stopped to take off my dark sweatshirt.

I assumed they would have a description of me, including my clothing, my height and weight, and my hair color. I took off the sweatshirt, along with my gray sweatpants. I had borrowed a pair of jogging shorts from my dad to wear underneath the longer pants for my expedition. Without the sweat suit, I looked like a jogger in my white t-shirt and blue shorts. Now all I had to do was get rid of the mustache and cut my long hair.

I was stiff and sore as I started jogging down a side street. It ran beneath the thirty foot high concrete prison wall. I tried not to breathe too hard because of my sore ribs, although I didn't think they were broken. I was weak from loss of blood from where my arm had been sliced.

Running out to the main thoroughfare in town, I turned and headed east down the street, jogging like a typical yuppie on a Sunday morning. Everything seemed normal. There wasn't any undue police activity yet. No one paid any attention to me.

Seeing a hardware store across the road, I jogged over and went in. Looking for something to remove my mustache, I bought a small pair of scissors and a plastic razor. I had a few dollars and change stuffed into my pockets, which my dad had given me. Good old Dad. I had told him I didn't need it where I was going. He evidently had more foresight than I did, and insisted. On the way out of the store, I grabbed a pair of cheap sunglasses. I then continued on my way down Main Street. The clerk at the checkout counter had eyed me suspiciously at first, but relaxed when I told him I was camping up at the lake.

Observing a small filling station at the east end of town, I crossed the intersection and tried the door to the restroom. It was open so I went in, locking it behind me. The facility was at the back side of the station. No one appeared to notice me.

First thing I did was cut my hair, trimming the sideburns and the back the best I could. I then worked on removing the mustache, which had grown quite long in the last few weeks. I used the razor to remove the remaining hair from my upper lip, and grinned at the stranger looking back at me in the mirror. Then I put on the shades and left the restroom to continue my jog down the street.

An attendant pumping gas noticed me as I jogged by, but didn't give me a second glance. Now all I had to do was make it to the city twenty miles away without getting stopped by the police.

Where it had been quiet when I went into the restroom to perform my transformation, things were buzzing when I left. State police cars had formed a roadblock at the end of town. Sheriff's cars patrolled the streets. One drove past me as I jogged easily out of town. No one seemed to give me much thought.

As I ran I thought about the previous night. I was worried about my father in the hospital with a head wound, and about my wife and child. I had no idea where they were or whether or not they were safe. I wondered if Jerry was somehow involved. In on it or not, he now had every reason to arrest me, if not shoot me on sight.

I had slicked my hair back with water on leaving the restroom, disguising my appearance even more. I wondered if my friend the chief of police would recognize me now. I wasn't sure what I was going to do. Hopefully, the police were looking for me in the mountains. That would give me the time I needed.

Several patrol cars whizzed by in both directions, but no one stopped. The last thing they were looking for was a yuppie weekend jogger. It was around two o'clock in the afternoon by the time I made it back to the 'burgh', without incident. Even the cops at the roadblocks didn't pay me any heed. No one expected to me to come jogging back into town.

The sky had turned grey. Thick clouds promised afternoon thundershowers.

By this time I had been up almost fifty-four hours, with only a couple hours sleep. I was going on pure adrenalin. I went to the closest place I could think of, the McKenna farm. The only thing I wanted to do was lie in a nice soft pile of hay and go to sleep. My stomach was growling, but I couldn't worry about food, not now. I only hoped it wouldn't give me away.

I don't know why I went there, maybe instinct. Normally I would have gone home to check on Suzy, but I was so exhausted I couldn't think. As it turned out, someone or something was doing my thinking for me, guiding me to where I needed to be.

I left the highway and walked along the ditch approaching the McKenna barn. Crossing the west field, I crawled through the long grass just like the night before. Or was it many nights before? I couldn't quite decide.

The place was jumping with activity, but not exactly the kind I expected. Instead of teams of forensic experts combing the area for evidence and police confiscating weapons of mass destruction, there were half a dozen decidedly Mid Eastern looking men dressed in camouflaged fatigues. They were loading what looked like fertilizer from the silo into a huge tanker truck.

What was going on now? There was a second tanker truck sitting in front of the one being loaded. It was already filled and waiting to go. A van was parked in front of the barn. Beside it was a city police car. Next to the car stood Jerry LeGrande. He was talking to my only remaining ex-student, Praveen. He always did seem like the smart one of the group. He must have been. He was still alive.

I crawled through the grass toward the front of the barn, hoping to hear what they were saying. All my suspicions were confirmed. I just had to make sure.

Darting across the dirt drive unseen some distance down the road, I made my way back toward the front of the farmhouse, where Jerry and Praveen were standing. The thick bushes along the side of the house and an unkempt hedge concealed me from view. When the noise of the loading operation and diesel engines was carried away by the wind, I could just make out what they were saying. It was only snippets, but enough to give me the general picture. I guess I should be used to this type of thing by now, with my sordid history. For some reason, however, it was just as shocking as the first time I learned of a terrorist plot. I couldn't believe Jerry was involved.

"When you get to New York, bring both trucks to the base of the first tower," said Praveen to another man in overalls, who I assumed was one of the drivers. "Say you're delivering heating oil. Understand?"

"How far will you be able to escort them?" he asked Jerry, while the other man scurried off to the cab of his truck.

"All the way, but it'd be better if you had a state police escort. My jurisdiction only goes as far as the city limits. However, I have papers signed by the Governor that give us the authority we need, as long as no one looks too closely. If anyone asks, I'm escorting a prisoner. We can put Lawless's wife and kid in the back of my squad car when you're through loading the tankers."

They had Suzy and my kid! I almost bellowed out loud.

"Don't concern yourself about them," answered Praveen "They are going in the van with me. Just do your part."

"I will. Just don't..."

212

His words were drowned out by the sound of two large diesel engines revving up their motors.

I had only wanted to find a place to sleep, a warm corner to curl up in and forget the last harrowing three days. Even more than that, I was worried about Suzy and Bud. Now it looked like I had found them and they were in trouble again. Not only that, my best friend was involved in the abduction.

If I wasn't mistaken, they were taking two tanker trucks full of high explosives down to the World Trade Center buildings in New York City, masquerading as oilmen. That didn't sound too reassuring. If I wasn't a paranoid-schizoid, they were planning on blowing up the 'Big Apple'. I wasn't sure what to do and almost let them drive off, but something urged me to action. This was my last chance.

As I watched, they hustled Suzy out of the barn and into the van. One of them carried little Bud and hopped in next to her. That was all the motivation I needed. The van sped off behind the first truck, which was following Jerry's patrol car down the drive. As if I were another person, I watched myself running after the rear tanker as it pulled, like a straining beast, around the barn and down the dirt drive.

Leaping up on the rear bumper, I grabbed the metal ladder that ran to the top of the tanker, and pulled myself up. As I did, the truck bounced down the dirt drive and accelerated toward the highway. Reaching the top, I dragged myself over and laid flat. Clinging to the rungs, which continued along the top of the tank, I crawled forward, keeping as low and out of sight as possible.

Even though I knew where I was going, and what was happening, I didn't know what to do about it. I only knew I had to do something. My only chance of stopping it and saving my family was to hitch a ride. So that's what I did. I'd figure out what to do once we got there, if I survived that long.

213

# Chapter 28

The caravan made its way across town to the entrance of the thruway, I87, to Albany. Once on the highway, they picked up speed. It started to rain lightly, but the sky held promise of more to come. I held on for dear life, clinging to the top of the tanker, wondering for the second time in my life what I had gotten myself into. Even though I was on the top of the truck, hidden from the view of the terrorists, I was sure to be spotted by other motorists. It was only a matter of time before I was discovered and apprehended.

We were going at a good clip, about fifty-five or sixty miles an hour. Rain splattered in my face every time I looked up. We were going too fast for me to attempt anything, but time was running out. I considered trying to attract the attention of some passing motorist, but thought better of it when I calculated the odds of Bud and Suzy living through the consequences. Like last time, I was on my own. And like last time, I would have to act fast if my family were to survive. Surprise was my best weapon. Now all I had to do was figure out some way to surprise them and stay alive doing it.

We drove for some time, through the broad fields and flat farmland that made up the valley between the mountains and the lake. Soon we were in the mountains themselves, the tall Adirondacks.

At one point, beneath the cliffs of Poke-O-Moonshine Mountain, the road ascended a particularly steep, curving hillside. The trucks had to slow down to forty miles an hour to negotiate the turns. The driver of the one I was on was inexperienced. He ground the gears several times trying to downshift. As he did, the distance between us and the van increased. At some points the vehicles in front of us were not visible at all, but hidden behind curves in the mountainside. It was now or never.

Making my way slowly along the top of the tanker, I crawled toward the cab. I had played the move out in my mind a dozen times during my short ride. Now, as the time came to do it, I froze. Cars had been speeding by the whole trip. Some of them beeped and pointed, but my driver and his companion didn't seem to notice. They were too concerned with keeping the large tanker truck moving up the steep grade. It was raining harder now, in a steady, drenching downpour. It splashed in my eyes, making it difficult to see.

Reaching the cab, I began breathing mechanically, in through the nose, out through the mouth, like I did on the silo to steel myself. Concentrating on placing my hands and feet, I grabbed the slippery metal hand-hold just above the passenger side door. Put there to help gain entry to the high cab, I was planning on using it to swing myself in through the partly-opened window.

I placed my feet between my hands, which were spread apart holding the bar. My ass was sticking up as if I were mooning Poke-O-Moonshine. Without hesitating, I swung myself feet first into the cab, smashing the window. I caught the occupant of the passenger seat unaware and hit him square on the jaw, landing on the driver's lap. The truck lurched violently to the left over two lanes of highway, almost going off the road. The driver jerked the wheel quickly to the right, just missing several cars, and brought it squealing and rocking back to the right lane. We careened back and forth on the shoulder as the driver tried to fight me off.

The other man was unconscious for the moment. My entry had caught him just on the right spot with sufficient force to knock him out. He wouldn't be out for long. In the meantime, the driver was giving me a rough time, even while he managed to keep his vehicle somewhat on the road.

He was a big man, trained more for fighting than driving a rig. At close quarters and seated as he was, however, there wasn't much he could do against my attack. I went after him with short, hard jabs and elbows, which I aimed at his head and neck. His arms were large and muscular, but he could only use one of them. He tried to fend me off with his right hand, punching and pushing me away. I blocked his strikes and countered with forearms and more elbows.

The other terrorist was coming to. As he woke and went to grab me, I nailed him with a backhand. His head bounced against the side of the cab. He slumped back dazed. By this time we had reached the top of the steep incline and were headed down the other side.

The truck picked up speed as I continued to struggle with the driver. So far he had managed to keep us on the road. By now we were approaching fifty-five mph, swerving back and forth dangerously across the wet highway. He was doing a good job keeping me at bay, and had hit me with a few rights. It just made me madder. I attacked him with increased fury, pummeling him with hard rights of my own. I hit him over and over, with quick, fast punches to the temple, ear, jaw, cheek bone, eyes, and nose. When he put his arm up to block, I hit him in the ribs and kidneys with vicious body shots. I didn't let up. My knuckles chewed into his skin.

He tried to hit me with a backhand, but I blocked the strike easily and grabbed his wrist at the same time. Before he could react, I reached across the steering-wheel and took his other hand. Then I twisted his arms together so they were held immobile in his lap. I was almost sitting on him and had him pinned. Problem was, there was no one driving the rig.

The tanker picked up speed on a stretch of road that ran down a steep incline and slowly curved around a large outcropping. Instead of following the highway as it turned, the truck went straight toward the narrow median-strip and the opposite lanes of the thruway. Only empty space and treetops were visible beyond.

Bounding across the median, the truck bounced over a ditch and through some small trees, making the grass and dirt fly. I held the other man's hands tightly in his lap as we skidded across the opposite two lanes toward the guardrail. It looked ridiculously insubstantial compared with the several ton Mack Truck heading for it at fifty miles per hour.

My opponent struggled anew, with even greater exertions, as we scraped along the railing. He managed to slam his foot on the brake. That only caused the truck to skid closer to the side of the cliff.

The heavy tank was careening forward now and almost even with the cab. It made a loud scraping noise that sounded like a building was crashing down on us. The other man had gained consciousness. Instead of trying to grab me, he pawed frantically at the passenger side door, trying to escape before we went over.

I was still sitting on the driver's lap, facing him. The truck crashed through the railing and over the side of the 200 foot cliff. At the same time, the other man leaped out of his side of the cab and was crushed by the tank, which was tumbling and turning down the hillside right beside us.

I struggled with the driver for a few moments more as we both tried to get out of the cab at the same time. We were totally tied up with each other. Our arms intertwined. I was looking straight into his eyes. I knew that only one of us was going to get out of there alive. I was determined it was going to be me.

The truck lurched forward and seemed to hang perpendicular in the air. The door flew open. Even as I fought with him, my mind was clear, almost calm. At that moment I realized I owned him. As he fought against me, pushing and jerking, I moved my arms in a fluid, circular motion. The move knocked his hands off me. Using that momentum as leverage, I flung myself backward out of the cab. The door slammed shut behind me, sealing my adversary to his doom.

I was facing backward, so I couldn't see where I was headed. I saw the cab fly past and disappear. I seemed suspended in midair, but it was only an instant. Then I was falling through space. Losing all orientation, I screamed like a banshee. I fell for what seemed a very long time, but could only have been a few seconds.

Unbelievably, I landed in a tree. Still screaming, I smashed through a few light branches before some of the heavier ones slowed me down and eventually stopped my fall. I was in a broad pine tree. Its wide, soft branches had saved my life.

Moments later the ground was shaken by a gigantic explosion. It sent me falling the last ten or so feet to the ground. I landed face down. Slapping with my forearms, I tried to spread myself flat, kia'ing as I landed. The force of a second blast lifted me off the ground and actually flipped me over, where I lay stunned and dazed.

The valley below filled with fire and smoke. Flames leapt into the sky, singeing the tops of the trees right beneath me. A huge black mushroom cloud rose a hundred feet in the air. Turning back around, I buried my head under my arms as debris and smoking chunks of metal rained down around me.

Looking up, I could see the brush burning around me, where bits of smoking wreckage had landed in the trees. I had fallen into a clump of fern bushes that covered the ground below the pine tree. It was thick with pine needles and rotten leaves. I was about twenty yards below the lip of the highway where the truck had gone over. It was still raining but not as hard as before. I stood and looked up at the embankment.

I was just about to climb it when I saw someone lean over the slope carrying what looked like a small submachine gun. I swore under my breath and ducked behind a tree. A second man, carrying an identical weapon, appeared at the guardrail a littler further along and peered down.

"See anything?" he yelled to the other.

"No," said the first man, who started down the slope only twenty yards away. "Look's like they had an accident. That was one hell of an explosion. Just keep watch until I see if anyone's alive."

217

I ducked into the bushes and lay flat as he made his way past me and further down the slope into the now burning valley. Hoping the van was right around the bend, I stole along the wooded hillside in that direction, eluding the two armed men. After a few hundred yards, I moved toward the lip of the road. The path was wet and slippery, but after a short time I reached the top. Peeking over the edge of a boulder, I saw that my hunch was right. The van had halted at a rest stop a short distance beyond the turn where we had gone off the highway.

I was slightly above and behind them. Four lanes of pavement and a median strip separated me from the rest stop and the three vehicles. The van was parked behind the tanker, which was behind the chief's car. The driver of the van was standing near the rear of his vehicle. He was looking anxiously back down the road where his two buddies had disappeared. They had obviously seen or heard the huge explosion when the second tanker hit the bottom of the gorge. Two of them had gone back to investigate.

Unfortunately, he was looking in my general direction. This would make approaching the convoy from where I was hiding very difficult. The accident had already disrupted traffic further down the thruway, where the police were stopping cars. They would be too busy to bother with the vehicles parked in a rest area further up the road. With the police on the scene, the two armed terrorists would probably be returning at any moment.

Remembering how I had eluded the authorities by jogging right past them, I thought I'd try the same stunt again. Still in my white t-shirt and blue shorts, I stole across the highway unseen, and started jogging up the road. It was only drizzling now. Not enough to call the game. The guy at the van spotted me as soon as I rounded the bend. I kept going, as if I didn't want to break my stride. He stiffened as I jogged off the highway toward the rest stop. It looked like he had something under his jacket, which his hand moved toward ever so slowly as I ran toward him.

I must have been a sight, covered with dead leaves and pine needles, scraped and scratched, black with soot.

"Hi," I said, coming up to him smiling. "Boy those back trails are murder. Hey, you should see the commotion back there. Someone must have gone off the cliff. What an explosion!"

The man didn't answer, but grunted and glared back at me with a hard-eyed stare. It was a look meant to tell me to just keep on truckin'.

I noticed Suzy out of the corner of my eye, sitting with her back to me in the van. At the same time, the man pulled a snubbed-nosed machinegun out from under his jacket. Before he could bring the weapon up I cross-stepped into him with a side kick. It hit him square in the chest and sent him backward into the van. The gun flew out of his hand and went off as it landed on the pavement.

I was on him before he could recover. I kicked him in the head as he began to rise. Then I dropped my knee onto his sternum. I brought it down with full force. He was a big, well-built guy, but the thick bone of his chest cracked like the branches of that pine tree I fell through, driving shards of bone into his heart and lungs. Before I could get to the gun, however, which had been thrown to the side, someone yelled from behind me.

"Hold it, Jay. I'll kill you if you make another move."

I stopped and slowly turned. Facing me with his .357 drawn was my old friend, Jerry LeGrande.

"Jerry!" I yelled as I stared at the muzzle of the large gun. "What are you doing? You can't be with them."

"Is he dead?" Jerry asked, ignoring my questions. He motioned to the man lying by the side of the van with his chest crushed and his eyes staring at the sky.

"Yeah, I think so. He was going to shoot me."

"That's murder, Jay, yet another murder. You've been busy, haven't you?"

"It was self-defense. These guys are terrorists. Do you know what they're planning to do?"

"Yeah, blow up the World Trade Center in New York City. At least that was the plan until you showed up. Where the hell did you come from?"

"Jerry, what are you doing? Why are you doing this? You can't be involved in this."

"I have no choice, Jay. They've got Lisa and my three year old granddaughter. They'll kill them if I don't help them. If this truck doesn't get to the city on time, they're dead."

"What about Suzy and Bud? Are you going to let them be killed?"

"I'll take care of them."

At that moment, another man got out of the tanker and came back to see what was happening.

"Is everything all right?" he asked coming up to Jerry and noticing his dead comrade. "What happened?"

"Never mind," said Jerry, with a tone of authority. "Get back in the truck and tell the driver to be ready to pull out as soon as the other two return. We can't afford to have the police asking questions. I'll take care of this troublemaker. Now get going."

The man looked at his fallen comrade and back at me before slowly going back to the tanker.

"Jerry," I said. "Lisa and your granddaughter are probably already dead. Once they don't need you anymore they'll kill them both and you too. You've got to help me stop them."

"No, Jay, I'm their only chance. I'm sorry, but I can't have you interfering."

"You're going to kill me in cold blood?"

"No, they are," he answered, pointing behind me where his two compatriots came running up.

"Where'd he come from?" said Praveen, as he approached us.

"He must have hitched a ride on the tanker," Jerry told him. "He caused the accident and killed Merhard."

Praveen went into a rage when he saw his dead friend. "You have killed the last of my men, you spawn of the devil."

"I take that as a compliment, you sniveling ass-wipe," I answered.

"Get the woman and child," he ordered Jerry.

"Wait, Praveen, we don't have time. Not here. Let's get going before the state police start asking a lot of questions."

"We don't need them any longer, you fool," Praveen told him. He rushed past Jerry and threw open the rear door of the van. "Get out!" he ordered loudly. Grabbing Suzy roughly by the arm, he pulled her out of the vehicle. "Out, now!"

He flung her to the ground. I took a step in their direction. The man behind me with the gun pointed it at my back and yelled. I froze as Suzy stood up shakily. I could see the fear and panic in her eyes.

"The boy too," ordered Praveen, brandishing the gun dangerously in my son's general direction. Just one short burst from his rapid-fire tommy gun would have been devastating. Bud got out and stood behind his mother as Suzy tried to shield him with her body. My blood ran cold.

Jerry stood rooted to the spot, his mouth open like he wanted to say something. The other man stood behind and a little to my right, with his gun drawn. He alternately looked at me and glanced behind to make sure no one was approaching.

Praveen pushed Suzy and Bud around the rear of the van to where I stood.

"Now kill them, all of them, once and for all," he commanded. When Jerry hesitated, he raised his weapon as if to do it himself.

"They'll hear the shots," observed Jerry. "Not here."

Preveen ignored him, and pointed his machinegun at Suzy and the boy.

Jerry and I both yelled out at the same time. "No!"

Jerry's yell was accompanied by a shot. The bullet from the Magnum ripped into Praveen's chest and tore out of his back, sending him flying backward in a spray of blood. His gun spewed bullets harmlessly into the pavement. At the same time, the gun of the man behind me discharged, sending a burst of lead into Jerry.

Before the gunman had time to turn the snub-nose on me, I hit him with a back kick, then another when the first one failed to have the desired affect. The second one probably fractured his pelvis. He doubled up and dropped, with the gun still in his hands.

"Run," I yelled to Suzy, who stood stock still. She seemed to be in shock. "Take Bud and run back to the police cars."

As I said this more shots rang out. The two in the tanker had finally gotten out to see what was happening. They came rushing down both sides of the vehicle with their pistols drawn, shooting as they ran. Suzy grabbed Bud and ducked behind the van as bullets ripped the ground at our feet.

I dove to the right and did a shoulder roll as lead tore up the pavement where I had stood. I landed near my recent opponent, who still clutched the gun and was just starting to sit up. I ducked behind him and reached around his body as he tried to rise. Grabbing the gun, which he held in front of him, I pressed his finger to the trigger. I used him as a shield, and spayed bullets in the direction of the men shooting at us. Their shots ripped into the ground around me. Several hit my human shield. He jerked and twitched like a puppet gone haywire as I held him in front of me. Lying flat, I continued to fire bursts of my own, which all went high. It was enough to make my opponents stop shooting and take cover behind the tanker's fat wheels.

"Now!" I yelled to Suzy and the boy, who were still crouching behind the van. "Run now!"

I continued to fire short bursts from the small machinegun. I had never shot a weapon like this before, but it practically fired itself. All I had to do was squeeze the trigger and point.

I peppered the rear of the tanker, beneath which the terrorists lay. Realizing that doing so would probably blow us all to kingdom come, I eased off the trigger. Suzy and Bud ran by me. I shot another burst from the gun, making sure to aim wide. I didn't want to hit the truck. I only wanted to keep them pinned down so they couldn't fire on my wife and kid as they ran to safety. Suddenly, both men got up and ran back to the cab of the truck. Moments later, it pulled out of the rest area and accelerated down the highway. At the same time, two state police cars sped up to us with their lights flashing.

I was still lying on the ground with the gun in my hands, bullet-riddled dead bodies all around me. The Staties screeched to a halt across the road and grabbed Suzy and Bud, who were just running past, pulling them to safety behind their cars. With revolvers and shotguns drawn, they told me to put down the weapon and put my hands over my head.

I could hear Suzy telling them that I was with them. Under the circumstances, however, these troopers weren't taking any chances. I couldn't blame them. Something ri-god-damned-diculous was going on and they had no idea what it was.

I did as I was told and threw the gun away, lying flat on the ground with my hands over my head. Moments later about four hundred pounds of man-flesh was on top of me. They roughly pulled my hands behind me and cuffed me. I was getting way too used to this.

"They're getting away," I managed to say as they dragged me to my feet. "In the tanker there. They're terrorists. They're going to bomb New York City. They've got enough explosives to blow up the Pentagon in that truck."

"Just calm down," one of them said as he peered down the highway. The truck could still be seen at the bottom of the downgrade heading up the next hill.

"Better put a call out on it, Mike," he said to the other trooper. "Look's like it might be the same kind of truck that went over the cliff back there. What happened here?" he asked, surveying the carnage.

"They shot the Chief. You've got to help him," I yelled, pointing to my fallen friend. "He tried to stop them. He saved us. They had us captive and were going to kill us."

"Get an ambulance up here," the lieutenant yelled back to one of his men who had us covered with his shotgun. "We've got a man down." Another cop came running up to help his fallen comrade.

"He's with us," yelled Suzy as she struggled with the trooper trying to restrain her.

"How is he?" I asked with concern as they bent over Jerry. "That's my best friend, Jerry LeGrande. He's the Chief of Police back in the city where this all took place. There was a big bust last night. These three got away with all the explosives in the trucks. Jerry followed them and tried to stop them."

I was already making up the story that would become the official explanation of events. It would eventually be in every newspaper and broadcast in the state, despite the authorities' attempts to suppress it.

"He drove that truck back there off the road. They had us in the van under guard. They were about to shoot us all when he stopped them. They shot him for his trouble. I got the guy who did it."

They looked around at the dead terrorists lying on the ground. "I guess he did all right."

"Is he OK?" I asked again.

"Get him out of here until we can figure out what's going on," ordered the sergeant, pointing to me.

"They're going go blow up the Trade Center buildings in New York," I warned him. "You've got to stop them."

Just then Jerry gained consciousness. I wished he hadn't. He screamed in pain and mortal terror.

"Jay!" he yelled. "Jay, I can't feel anything! Jay?"

"It's all right," I said kneeling by his side after the cops released me so I could go to him. "I'm right here. Suzy and Bud are all right. You saved them. The state police are here. It's all right, Jerry. We got them. It's all over."

"Lisa and Julie, my granddaughter, you've got to help them," he gasped.

"Where, Jerry? Where are they?" I asked, leaning close to him.

He coughed up blood. His whole body shook in agony. Blood seeped out of him through half a dozen ghastly wounds. He didn't have long.

"Jerry! Jerry, speak to me," I pleaded as he went under again. "Uncuff me," I yelled, while I tried to bend to help him. "Get these damn things off me. Get this man some help before it's too late! Isn't there anything you can do?"

The man who had been holding me looked at his boss, who slowly nodded his permission. Just then an ambulance drove up.

I bent over Jerry. He was hardly breathing, lying on his back looking up at the sky.

"Jerry, it's going to be OK. Just take it easy. Tell me where Lisa is. Where are they, Jerry?"

He was quiet for a moment. I was afraid he wasn't going to speak again. They were about to take him away when he opened his eyes again.

"Wait," I said. "Wait a minute." Bending low to the ground with my ear inches from his mouth, I heard him whisper ever so faintly, with what was to be his last breath.

"The barn. They're in the barn. You've …got … to help them."

With that he stopped breathing altogether. I stood up numb with shock as they worked on him. Granted he had been involved in the plot, helping the terrorists in ways I could only guess at. He was doing it under duress, however, against his will. He may have gone to jail for his part, but he would eventually have been exonerated because of his heroism in the end. If I left out the first part, no one would be the wiser and no one would be hurt, including Lisa and his family. That is if they survived.

While the police were preoccupied investigating the crime scene and following up the trail of the terrorists, I wandered away looking for Suzy. I wondered how I was going to help Jerry's wife and grandchild. I certainly wouldn't be much good to them detained in some interrogation room down at state police headquarters. It would be a week of Sundays before I was free again, if ever.

More police cars drove up. Before long the place was mobbed, with yet another roadblock and blue lights flashing everywhere. Forgotten for the moment, I found Suzy and Bud sitting in the back of a squad car. I hadn't seen them in days and then only under the most trying of circumstances. Suzy jumped out of the car when she saw me and ran up to me. Bud followed. We were so happy to see each other we stood hugging for a long time. Bud cried as he wrapped his arms around our legs. I picked him up and gave him the biggest bear hug of his life. It was a short if emotional reunion. I had things to do.

"Oh, Jay, it was so horrible," Suzy said when she finally found her voice. "They were going to kill us. They were going to do such terrible things."

"I know, baby. It's all right. It's all over now." I hugged her tight as she sobbed in my arms. The rain, which had stopped for a while, had started again and was coming down hard.

Even as I said these things, I knew everything wasn't all right. A woman and small child were still in danger, not to mention the ten-ton truck full of explosive chemicals heading toward New York City. The police could take care of the latter threat. I'd have to take care of the former.

"There's something I need to do, honey. Please trust me. It will be OK."

"What?" she said in alarm as I led her and Little Bud back to the nearest squad car and put them in out of the rain.

"Nothing, just stay here with the police. The less you know the better."

"Jay!" she yelled as I darted away between two state police vehicles.

No one was paying much attention to me. They were all occupied with controlling traffic and investigating a major accident and crime scene. I was the least of their worries. Jerry had died saving my wife and child. The least I could do was return the favor.

By now traffic was backed up for miles in both directions. No one was getting by.

I ran back down the highway in the direction we had come, and crossed the median strip. Someone yelled out something behind me. I ignored it and kept moving along the line of idling cars and curious drivers.

When I reached the point in the road where the truck had gone over, there was another gaggle of state police and sheriff vehicles. There were also fire trucks and a few ambulances mixed in. I spotted an empty Sheriff's car with its lights flashing. It was pointed in the right direction so I made a dash for it. For the second time in as many days, I was about to steal a police car. What more could happen? I wondered.

# Chapter 29

I sped away in the stolen police car, lights flashing. Taking a quick glance in the rearview mirror, I hoped I hadn't been noticed. No such luck. Troopers were scrambling to get into their cars and head after me. I swore to myself as I jammed my foot down on the pedal. The northern sky ahead was dark and threatening, a tower of gloom in the already gray, overcast day.

I wondered, in some detached portion of my brain, how I could keep going like this. I had forgotten the last time I had slept or eaten - that day, how long ago, at my cousin's place. I had only had a couple hours of fitful sleep and a bowl of half-eaten soup since then. Everything seemed to be going in slow motion, the sounds muffled, as if in a strange dream. Yet I knew it was deadly real. Now that I really needed them, I had all I could do to keep my eyes open.

My ribs hurt. My head throbbed. My heart pounded in my chest. Every sound made my ears ache. I fought to keep awake as a dozen cops chased me down the highway. I was sure they would radio ahead, but hoped most of the police would be back at the crime scene, behind me. I had no idea what I was going to do. I didn't even know if I'd be able to find Lisa and the kid, though I certainly knew my way around that farm by this time. Hopefully, I would have the element of surprise when I got there, if I got there. I had done all right so far, but I couldn't count on good luck forever. I just hoped there'd be enough of it left to get me through this one last mission.

I could see them gaining on me. Suddenly, a patrol car coming in the opposite direction slammed on his breaks and made a left across the median strip, just ahead of me. He tried to force me off the road, but somehow, even in my diminished condition, at ninety-five miles an hour, I was able to avoid him. Now I was pushing a hundred, my heart in my throat. I was going so fast I almost missed the Bob Moffit Road exit, which had come up on me long before I expected it.

Hardly slowing down, I swerved onto the exit going ninety in a road meant for twenty-five. The car fishtailed and almost skidded off the highway. The police cars did the same, one flying off into a ditch.

Sideswiping several slower vehicles, I ran the lights at the end of the side road, where it crossed the main highway into town, almost causing another near collision. Traffic going to the shopping malls and stores was snarled and stalled. People were beeping their horns.

The police cars were a little further behind me now. They had been surprised by my sudden exit and caught in the traffic jam left in my wake. I sped down an auxiliary road toward the rear of the shopping mall and the Bob Moffit Road, where the McKenna farm was located.

After a few sharp turns and several stoplights, which I ran, I was almost in the clear. I could no longer see any police cars behind me. Just ahead to the right were the four silos of the McKenna farm.

I ditched the car along the side of the road. I left it running with the lights on a short distance from the farm, and dashed across a field toward the barn. I was pretty sure the cops who were chasing me knew nothing about the farm and its connection with what happened down the highway. It would take them some time to trace me there. I prayed that would give me enough time to do what I had to do. Once the police caught up with me, it would be all over.

I approached the barn along the same dirt track I had come that day with Bud. As I did, a series of mighty lightning strikes lit up the late afternoon sky. This was followed a split second later by peals of thunder that shook the ground. The sound reverberated through the nearby mountains like cannon blasts across the valley.

I stayed out of sight, and moved behind the hedge that ran between the driveway and the house. I kept low to the ground as I went. Ducking behind a bush at the end of the drive, I surveyed the area. It was coming down in buckets now. The hiss of the rain drowned out all sounds but the booming thunder. It erupted every few seconds now, preceded by ever more violent streaks of lightening.

There was a Jeep Cherokee parked in front of the barn. No one seemed to be about. Other than the vehicle, the place appeared deserted. I crawled around the house, checking the windows in each room. It was empty, although I couldn't see into the upstairs rooms. I was drenched and cold, dressed only in a cotton t-shirt and shorts. In spite of the exertion, I shivered as I crouched in the rain. Only my misery and the heat of my anger kept me going.

As I thought about what to do, someone dressed in camouflaged fatigues ran out of the barn and threw some things into the back of the Jeep. He then ran back inside. It looked like he was in a hurry to leave.

Soon the man came out again accompanied by another bearded person dressed the same. They were both talking rapidly back and forth, as if arguing about something. I snuck closer, but still could not make out what they were saying. It appeared to be in another language.

227

One kept looking at his watch and gesticulating. Whatever they were talking about made me suspect that Jerry's wife and grandchild were in the barn. There was only one way to find out.

As I watched, one of the men ran back inside. The other got in the Jeep Cherokee and started it up. It was now or never. I left my hiding place and walked up to the driver's door, approaching the vehicle from the rear. The driver saw me before I reached the door, and threw it open to jump out. He reached for a gun, which he had on the seat beside him. I nailed him with a thrust kick to his ribs. It knocked him into the door. I followed up with a quick left-right combination to each side of his head. He went down on his ass and forgot all about the gun. Just then the other man came running out of the barn. His face registered surprise and agitation when he saw me.

He immediately went for the gun holstered under his arm. At the same time, I reached across the seat for the small snubbed-nosed machinegun still lying on the Jeep's passenger side. I brought it up, pointed it out the open side window, and fired. I was an expert by now. Bullets sprayed all over the place as I tried to control the gun. One hit the terrorist square in the chest as he fire back. He went down with the pistol in his hand. Luckily, his shot went wide.

At this point, the man I had knocked down, who had only been stunned, got to his feet. Pulling me by the legs, he yanked me out of the vehicle and slammed me to the ground. As he went to drop his elbow on me, I twisted to the side and out of the way. Just evading the blow, I gave him an elbow of my own. Swinging my body on top of his, I put him in a choke hold, squeezing his neck in the crook of my arm.

As he tried to rise, I jammed a knee between his legs, and then another. I had dropped the machine gun when he pulled me out of the Jeep. Letting go of the choke hold, I slammed the edge of my hand into the back of his neck. Then I jumped up to retrieve the gun.

Dragging my opponent to his feet, I shoved the barrel into his mouth, cracking a few teeth in the process.

"Where is LeGrande's wife and the little girl?" I demanded.

He shook his head as if he didn't know. I bore down on him and told him I'd blow his head off if he didn't tell me. He had three seconds.

He pointed to the barn with wide, terrified eyes.

"In there," he croaked through the barrel of the gun. "Let me go. Let me go."

"Where in the barn?" I asked. "You'd better tell me and quick. You're a dead man if I have to search for them."

"In the silo," he told me. "Now let me go. It's going to blow."

"What's going to blow?" I asked.

Instead of answering me he swiped the gun away and ran. I let him go and approached the barn.

As I ran in, that small part of my brain still capable of rational thought wondered what he had meant. What was going to blow, the barn? That thought grew more urgent as I entered the building.

I called Lisa's name. There was no response. There was no sound at all except the hissing of the rain on the barn roof. I made my way to the silo. Sticking my head through the hatchway of the main tower, I called her name again.

"Lisa, Lisa, are you in here? It's Jay. Jay Lawless. Jerry sent me. I've come to help you. Are you here? Lisa, can you hear me?"

The interior was filled with fine dust particles that floated in the air. Right above the hatchway was a bare bulb that appeared to be shortening out. Sparks leaped from it in a wide arc. I tried to turn it off, but I wasn't tall enough to reach it and could not find a switch. The smell of kerosene or gasoline permeated the air. Lisa and Jerry's grandchild were not there. The bastard had lied to me. I should have taken him with me, but it was too late to worry about that now.

As if the hair on the back of my neck understood the situation better than my frazzled brain, it stood up and sent a shiver through my spinal cord. It woke me to impending danger, spurring me on to one final exertion.

I sprinted through the rest of the barn, to the back of the building, calling Lisa's name and peering hurriedly into the stalls. When I reached the rear, where the wide doors stood open, I ran out. I was about to head for the hills, when I had a last minute thought. Going to the shed, I peered inside. There, sitting in chairs, tied up like I had been, with their mouths gagged, were Lisa and a little girl about four years old.

"Lisa!" I yelled. I was glad I had found them, but I feared time would run out before I could extricate them. "We've got to get out of here. It's going to blow."

I worked on the ropes, which were knotted tight. It seemed to take forever. I finally got them off using the tip of a sickle I found nearby. Picking up the little girl and yelling for Lisa to follow, I half led, half pulled her out of the shed at the rear of the barn.

Not stopping, I pushed her along in front of me to the edge of the field.

"Run for your life. The barn's going to blow up," I yelled.

As I said this, there was a tremendous explosion. It sucked the air in behind us, then blew us forward with unbelievable force. I felt myself being tugged back before being literally blown off my feet into a ditch that ran across the field right in front of us.

I don't remember much after that, except being thrown to the ground and tumbling down an embankment. Piles of burning debris showered down around us. The sound was deafening. I curled into a ball with the little girl beneath me, sheltering her as best I could.

The rain pelted down on me. Somehow it felt good, like something normal and familiar amidst a nightmare world where nothing seemed real. It wasn't so much that I was knocked unconscious by the explosion, as much as that I just wanted go to sleep. I had done about all I could do, gone about as far as I could go. Now it was time to rest.

# Chapter 30

So here I am, writing this story from the bed of a hospital room. The authorities are in a hurry to cover it up. There are some that don't believe me and a few who still suspect I'm involved in the terrorist plot, if not the murders around town.

With most of the people involved either dead or under federal custody, there's not much to collaborate my version of what happened. The Feds, as usual, are being tight lipped. The apprehension of a tanker truck near the World Trade Center in New York City filled with highly explosive chemical fertilizer never got into the news. However, the state police did confirm the crash of a similar truck in the Adirondacks that closed Route 87 for four hours.

My version of the story, the one I told the police, makes Jerry LeGrande out to be the hero of the day. According to my testimony, he was the one who stopped the terrorist plot and saved me and my family. It took some doing to persuade Suzy to go along. She couldn't deny, however, that Jerry had tried to protect them once they had been kidnapped.

Be that as it may, he was a key conspirator, and would have let them blow up the entire state to save his wife and grandchild. Although I didn't want to hurt Lisa and his family, who were blameless in all this, and deprive her of his police pension, I didn't want the truth to go untold either. Even if it may never see the light of day, at least not for some time, I'm writing everything down for posterity.

With Jerry gone, the murders have never been fully explained, at least not to the satisfaction of the authorities. The body of the murderer, the crazy freak with the Bowie knife, which I had last seen impaled on the harvester at the back of the barn, has mysteriously disappeared. The police, who recovered it, say embarrassedly that it has been misplaced. I wonder.

I'm not sure how much longer I'll be able to stay in this town. My name has now been connected with yet another series of grisly murders, as well as a vague plot by Mid Eastern terrorists to kill farmers and steal their chemical fertilizer to make a bomb. If I thought people looked at me funny before, they really give me the queer eye now. It's as if my association with this whole affair has made me a thing of curiosity, if not a social pariah. What I thought was going to help make my name and reputation, help me establish my business, has had just the opposite effect. Whatever reputation I may have had is ruined, along with my business. Even the karate school and Suzy's agencies are doing badly as a result of my involvement in this whole sordid mess.

At least my dad is OK. He received a nasty head wound, but recovered after two weeks in the hospital. They didn't have to operate, but we were worried for the longest time that he had suffered some sort of permanent brain damage. It took him forever to get back on his feet again, and his speech is still somewhat affected. However, the doctors say he'll be as good as new given time.

I wish the prognosis on my marriage was better. Things are kind of uncertain as far as that's concerned. Suzy still hasn't forgiven me for leaving her and Bud that day, when I went to help Jerry's wife and grandchild. Nor can she forgive me for getting her and Bud involved in the first place. If I had only listened to her none of this would have happened.

I can't say I blame her. She's right. I'm not sure if being involved with me is such a good idea for either of them. What kind of future would they have with a full-time, four-carrot, tin-plated, bona fide loser? Even when I win I lose. It's just not fair. But then who said life was fair.

As hard as it is for me to think about what happened, I've forced myself to recount these harrowing events so that the truth will be known someday. But it's not easy, even though it's all still vivid in my memory. If I let myself believe that it really happened, that I actually went through these events, I'd probably lose my mind and never be able to sleep again. I need my sleep right now.

I'm still living down by the beach. Like I said, it may be time to think about moving on and leaving the 'burgh' once and for all. But one thing at a time. First I need to recover, relax with a good book, do some form, and let things work themselves out. In the meantime, I've got a story to tell.

# Epilogue

Ibn al-Jathrine had just returned from his audience with the great one, the one who guided all their actions from the greatest to the smallest. They had discussed his most recent assignment, the task he had been chosen by Allah to perform. His handpicked team of zealots had failed despite their faith and dedication, despite the huge funds and massive support they had been given. The next group would not be so unfortunate. The next plan would be better.

He made his way between the high-walled dwellings that hemmed in the narrow alleyway, itself hemmed in by the dusty hills surrounding the small mountain village. As he walked toward his mosque, al-Jathrine contemplated his most recent instructions. They were breathtaking in their scope and daring. If only such a thing could be done. Then everything would be changed forever!

He reached the rear entrance to his place of worship, through a hallway and rooms only he, with his immense prestige and learning, was allowed to go. There, a lecture room had been set up for just this purpose, for just this day. Today he was to speak to the newest batch of volunteers, fighters for the great jihad. Today he was going to send another group of martyrs on their mission of destruction.

He entered the room and surveyed the eight students seated in a circle awaiting him. The men in the room were all young, between twenty and thirty-three, of various levels of education, from various countries around the Mid East and North Africa. They had all been chosen for their zeal and devotion. Some were from good families like himself, the cream of his culture. Others were low-born and uncouth, but all sanctified by their blind, steadfast adherence to their faith. All of them were soldiers of Allah.

He looked into their eyes, one by one, as if to gauge the depths of their belief, the extent of their courage. They would need both and more if they were to survive and carry out their purpose. Finally, he spoke.

"How many of you here would like to learn to fly?"

## The End?

# About the Author

Joe was born in upstate, New York, where he grew up and went to school. He holds a Bachlor's Degree in music composition from Berklee College of Music, and a Master's Degree in Computer Science from Boston University. Joe lives in Hudson, Massachusetts with his wife Kathy. Until his retirement a few years ago, he programmed computers for a living. Joe studied Chinese Kenpo karate in Acton MA, obtaining his black belt in 1977. He took over the school (Acton Academy of Self-Defense) when his instructor left for the west coast. Joe ran the school for several years, obtaining the rank of nidan in the process. He has won first place in kata and second place in sparring in local tournaments. Joe also studied aikido and thi-chi over the years. Although he no longer goes to the dojo, he still does all his forms (fifteen of them) and continues to teach from time to time. As Joe used to tell his students, "Martial Arts are a way of life."

# ALSO BY JOSEPH BEBO

*Lake, Land, and Liberty*

*Family Legends – The Charbonneau Letter*

*Lamp of the Gods*

*Bach Again*

*In the Back of the Van*

*Stricken: Quantum of Revenge*

*The Shivering*

*My Terrible Mistress*

*The Shot*

*Altered Realities*

*Alex – A Lesson in Courage*

*Waiting to Take Off*

*Almost Dangerous (Book 1 of the Lawless Chronicles)*